PANIC

AN ALEXANDER GREGORY THRILLER

LJ ROSS

ISBN: 978-1-912310-55-5

First published in July 2024 by Dark Skies Publishing

Author photo by Gareth Iwan Jones

Cover layout and typesetting by
Riverside Publishing Solutions Ltd

Cover design copyright © LJ Ross

Printed and bound by CPI Goup (UK) Limited

FSC
www.fsc.org
MIX
Paper | Supporting
responsible forestry
FSC® C171272

BOOKS BY LJ ROSS

THE ALEXANDER GREGORY THRILLERS:

1. *Impostor*
2. *Hysteria*
3. *Bedlam*
4. *Mania*
5. *Panic*

THE DCI RYAN MYSTERIES:

1. *Holy Island*
2. *Sycamore Gap*
3. *Heavenfield*
4. *Angel*
5. *High Force*
6. *Cragside*
7. *Dark Skies*
8. *Seven Bridges*
9. *The Hermitage*
10. *Longstone*
11. *The Infirmary (Prequel)*
12. *The Moor*
13. *Penshaw*
14. *Borderlands*
15. *Ryan's Christmas*
16. *The Shrine*
17. *Cuthbert's Way*
18. *The Rock*
19. *Bamburgh*
20. *Lady's Well*
21. *Death Rocks*

THE SUMMER SUSPENSE MYSTERIES:

1. *The Cove*
2. *The Creek*
3. *The Bay*

"Into the hands of every individual is given a marvellous power for good or evil—the silent, unconscious, unseen influence of his life. This is simply the constant radiation of what man really is, not what he pretends to be."

—William George Jordan

PROLOGUE

Four years ago

HM Prison Frankland, Durham

"Shut your mouth, Carl, or I'll shut it for you."

Carl Deere had been whispering to himself again, but fell silent and stared through the slats of the upper bunk while his cellmate puffed on one of the rollies he kept in a private stash. Gavin "Gaz" Compton was a man with a big street rep—not merely because he'd been convicted of murdering at least fifteen people, discounting those the police would never know about, but because he was a career criminal hired by gangs around the country to enforce their laws.

A man like that had no fear, no remorse, and no limits.

Imprisonment hadn't impacted Gav's life too much, all things considered. He already knew many of the men incarcerated behind the walls of Frankland prison, if not socially then by reputation. After a few well-placed shivs, Compton had secured his title as the prison's undisputed and unofficial governor within the space of a week. No money or contraband changed hands without Gav taking his cut, and he had most of the screws in his pocket— all except a frustrating few who refused to be corrupted, but he was working to leverage that. Even the most stalwart prison officer could change their mind when a child's life was at stake.

When Carl shuffled into their cell that first time, he'd looked like a quiet, mild-mannered man with well-cut "office" hair, pasty white skin, and dark, *dark* eyes heavily shadowed following endless nights without sleep. He'd walked as though in a trance, clutching his bedding and towel tightly to his chest, for all the world as if he was surprised to be there.

"You can drop the act," Gav had told him, straight off the bat. "Everyone acts the innocent when they come in here, but you don't need to bother with me, son. I know all about you— we all do. You're even more messed up than half the blokes in 'ere, and that's sayin' somethin'."

All humour drained away then, and was replaced with a hard, shark-like stare.

"Let's get a few ground rules straight, shall we?" He'd flexed his thick biceps. "C'mon then," he said, and rapped a fist against his chest. "Let's see what you've got, princess."

Carl had continued to stare at him and, if he hadn't already known what the man was capable of, Gav might have thought he was scared.

"C'mon, little fish," he said again, and rose from his chair. "Most blokes in 'ere want to plant a knife in me, so I tell them, 'You get one free swing, if you've got the mettle for it—after that, we'll both know where we stand.'"

Carl glanced over his shoulder, back through the little Perspex window of their cell, but the corridor outside was empty.

Gav grinned, displaying a mouthful of decaying teeth. "Nobody there? Funny that." He chuckled. "Let's get this over with, then we'll talk terms."

Terms? Carl thought, and fought a rising wave of panic.

"I—I don't—"

Gav caught him then, quick as a snake, one arm angled around his throat in a punishing grip that robbed him of breath while the other grabbed a fistful of his hair, pulled his head back, and smashed it hard against the wall.

"Welcome to Big School, son."

When he came around, Carl found that a couple of other inmates had joined Gav in their cell, and the three now sat together chatting and laughing like old friends while small packages were exchanged with sleight of hand.

"Welcome back," Gav said, jovially. "We were startin' to wonder."

Carl dragged himself up.

"You're the Soho Killer, ain't yer?" another man said, and his voice was pure East London. "Better watch your arses, lads!"

They all laughed.

"He only likes 'em young an' good lookin'," Gav said. "Which rules you out, Ellis."

They laughed again, while Carl dabbed the blood from his forehead.

"Thought they'd've banged 'im up in Southmoor," Ellis carried on, blowing a long stream of marijuana smoke in his direction. "Looks like a crazy bastard, even without knowin' what 'e did."

"Always the quiet ones you gotta watch," Gav told them, playing the concerned father. "Seen blokes like 'im before, 'aven't we? They come in, all nervy and shy, actin' like they've got no fight in 'em. They're the ones who'll murder you while you sleep, and enjoy it, n'all. Wouldn't you, nancy boy?"

Carl raised eyes that were black with hate, and Gav felt something he hadn't experienced in a long, long time.

It might have been fear.

"See?" He forced a laugh. "He knows the score, don't you, mate?"

Carl looked between the three men and understood something very important in that moment: the only thing that was sure to keep him alive inside Frankland was their belief that he was everything the press had made him out to be. So long as these men thought that Carl Deere was a cold-blooded killer—worse still, a *frenzied* one who took pleasure from the act—they would leave him alone.

And so, he'd let them believe it. There was only one problem, of course.

He hadn't killed anyone.

Not yet.

CHAPTER 1

Present Day

Heathrow Airport

Doctor Alexander Gregory strode through the airport terminal, bold green eyes seeking out the arrivals board. He was tall, with wavy, chestnut-brown hair and a physique that had once been slim but was now beginning to show the benefits of a monthly gym membership. He was dressed casually in jeans and a light jumper, and carried an air of purpose.

When he passed a florist's concession, his footsteps slowed.

Would it be too much?

"Flowers are never too much," he muttered.

A couple of minutes later, he was beginning to regret his own advice, for a quandary presented itself: namely, *which* flowers to choose?

Lilies? They reminded him of funerals.

Daisies? Too frivolous for the lady in question.

Pansies, peonies..? *Too bridal.*

He was about to abort the mission entirely when his gaze fell upon an array of roses, in all shades of pink and red.

"Two dozen of the Grand Prix, please," he found himself saying, and brushed a fingertip over the velvet petals of the largest variety on display, which came in a shade of deep, scarlet red.

"For your wife?" the florist asked, being possessed of a romantic heart. "Lucky lady."

Gregory didn't contradict her, which was something he would have to think about later, and merely gave a bland smile before dropping some notes into her waiting palm.

Outside, he looked down at the bouquet he held in his hands and realised something that was both unsettling and pitiable, in equal measure…

It was the first bouquet of flowers he'd ever purchased.

"First time for everything," he told himself, and continued towards the arrivals hall shortly before passengers bound from JFK were due to emerge.

Gregory was seldom surprised, nor susceptible to nerves. As a psychiatrist working from Southmoor Hospital for the best part of a decade, he'd dealt with the most disturbed minds their country had created and for whom prison wasn't deemed safe. The work had desensitized him to many of the mundane stressors that life tended to dole out but, as he stationed himself by the arrivals doors, he caught himself fidgeting from one foot to the other, and checking the time on his watch every few seconds as though he could speed up the process by willpower alone.

Eventually, the security doors opened, and passengers began to trail out, dragging suitcases and a general air of exhaustion behind them. He turned away from an idle inspection of a couple dressed in shell suits and flip-flops to face a pair of large brown eyes set inside the perfectly oval face of a very lovely woman.

"Naomi," he said, and released the air he'd been holding tightly in his chest.

They looked at one another and Alex, who was usually a proficient reader of minds, wondered what was passing through hers. The first time

Doctor Naomi Palmer had seen him, he'd been working undercover inside the exclusive Buchanan Institute in the Catskill Mountains. The man she'd met, and believed to have been her patient, had been playing a part; although, whilst he'd only pretended to be 'Michael Jones', there'd been little difference between him and the real Alexander Gregory except for a name. There'd been demons to vanquish for Michael before Alexander could return to ordinary life, and the process of slaying them had been achieved in no small part thanks to the woman who stood before him now. There'd been something between them from their very first meeting, and there were no longer any professional barriers to pursuing whatever that 'something' was.

"I brought you some flowers," he blurted out, and handed over the bouquet before he lost his nerve.

Naomi smiled. "They're beautiful," she said, and trailed her fingers over the petals, as he had done.

Gregory was not a poetic man, so he didn't tell her that their velvety softness reminded him of her skin, nor that he ached to run his fingers over it. Instead, he reached out to grasp the handle of her suitcase.

"Car park's this way."

Once they were safely inside his car, Gregory turned to look at her again. "I need to talk to you," he said.

Naomi was caught up in her own maelstrom of emotion. "Sounds serious," she said, hoping to keep things light. "Can we talk on the road? I suppose it'll take a couple of hours to drive to Cambridge from here?"

They would be staying with Gregory's good friend and undisputed doyen of the psychological world, Professor Bill Douglas, whose academic base was at Hawking College, Cambridge.

"That's why I need to speak to you," he said, and turned away from her face, which was distracting.

"In your last e-mail, you mentioned you'd had some trouble—" she prompted. "That's one way of putting it." He laughed, and ran an agitated hand through his hair. "You remember I told you about Carl Deere?"

She nodded, thinking back to the long, intimate telephone conversations they'd enjoyed over the past couple of months. "He was the man the police incarcerated for the murders of a number of male sex workers in the Soho district of London, several years ago," she recalled. "The investigative team called on you and Professor Douglas to provide a profile about the type of killer they were looking for, to help narrow the pool of suspects. They found someone—Carl Deere—who fit the profile, and set a trap for him. Unfortunately, they were mistaken. The jury convicted an innocent man and, meanwhile, several other murders were committed while the real killer walked free."

"Thomas Andersson," Gregory muttered. "Yes, that's the long and short of it."

"I thought Andersson was in prison now?"

"He is," Gregory said, and hoped that was still true. "Andersson isn't the one I'm worried about."

She frowned. "Have there been more murders? A copycat, perhaps?"

He wondered where to begin. "About a month ago, I was consulting on a case concerning a well-known film and theatre star—you might have heard of Nigel Villiers?"

Naomi's eyes widened because even she, ensconced in the rural Catskills for most of the year, had heard of their generation's equivalent to Lawrence Olivier.

"Anyway," he continued. "During the course of that investigation, a senior member of police personnel, Detective Chief Superintendent Simon Campbell, was found murdered. Campbell was intimately connected to the Andersson-Deere debacle, having been the Senior Investigating Officer at the time. But the police team wanted to believe his death was linked to the Villiers investigation—it's the easiest explanation."

"You thought otherwise?"

Gregory nodded. "The style of execution was entirely different—it was just that, an *execution*. It didn't match the established MO of the killer we were looking for in the Villiers case. For one thing, Campbell was found in the nude, propped on his downstairs toilet covered in his own blood, with a copy of Shakespeare's *Othello* stuffed down his gullet. By contrast, Villiers' killer was fastidious about not getting his hands dirty, and much preferred to kill from a distance."

"Nonetheless, leaving the copy of *Othello* is theatrical," she said. "I can see why the investigating team might have thought it was connected."

"It's the one thing that bears any resemblance," he conceded. "But what really nails it for me is that, later, when we uncovered the perpetrator in the Villiers investigation, they were clear about having no knowledge about Campbell's murder."

"Killers do sometimes lie," she pointed out.

He smiled at that. "It's not unheard of," he agreed. "But, everything else…it just didn't add up. Campbell was directly responsible for making a false accusation against Carl Deere. He gunned for him, because he wanted the collar and the prestige he thought would follow if he brought in the country's most wanted criminal to book. The only reason Campbell wasn't tainted by the failure in his own judgment was because he had Bill and me to blame, instead. We made very handy scapegoats, at the time."

"I had no idea the police had done that to you," she said, and reached out to touch his hand. "It wasn't your fault, Alex. They should never have gone outside the parameters of the profile, or tried to make the facts fit the crime."

Gregory looked down at her hand and felt a ripple run through his entire body. Silently, he linked his fingers through hers, so they were joined.

"It's in the past," he said quietly. "Unfortunately, I don't think Carl agrees with me."

"You're not thinking he's responsible for Campbell's murder?" Naomi thought of an innocent man who'd become what the world already believed him to be, and grieved.

"That's *exactly* what I'm thinking," he said. "I'm even more convinced after the judge who sent him down—a man by the name of Quentin Whittaker—was found dead at his home in London last month."

"Do you have any proof of Carl's involvement?"

Gregory gave a small shake of his head. "None," he said. "I managed to convince DCI Hope to provide some protection for Bill, because I can't be there all the time and I don't just *believe* this to be the case, Naomi, I *know* that he's in danger from Carl Deere. I feel it, in my gut."

His other hand strayed to his stomach, to punctuate the point.

"But you have no proof, Alex."

Naomi was a logical woman, which was one of the reasons he admired her so much.

"It's true, the investigating team found no identifiable DNA, but they did find trace samples at both scenes," he said.

"In that case, surely they can just check the samples against Carl's DNA record?"

But Gregory shook his head. "It isn't as simple as that. When Carl was released and given millions of pounds in compensation from the Ministry of Justice, his criminal DNA record was erased as part of the deal. The idea is to return a wronged person to the same situation they would have been in, prior to the miscarriage of justice. Carl Deere's DNA wasn't on the system before his arrest, so it was removed from the database after he was released."

Naomi was a quick study. "You're telling me that any DNA the police found at Campbell and Whittaker's crime scenes is being classified as 'anonymous' because they can't find a match, but that's only because the identity has been erased and you believe it belongs to Carl Deere? Isn't there any way of recalling his record, so you can check?"

"I'm not sure," Gregory answered, honestly. "It would represent a major data breach, and the evidence would probably be inadmissible. I need to speak to the police team again, but their patience is wearing thin. I managed to convince them Douglas was at risk, enough to have him protected for a while, but nothing has happened since Whittaker's murder—not even a break-in—and I know it won't be long before that support is withdrawn."

Naomi ran her eyes over his face. "You haven't mentioned something else," she said. "If you're right about all this, and about Carl Deere being intent on avenging himself against those he perceives to have wronged him, then it isn't only Professor Douglas who should be concerned for his safety—is it?"

Gregory looked at their joined hands. "No, it isn't," he said softly. "I'm in danger, and so is any other person connected with the case and potentially with me, or Bill. I need to ask you something."

"What?"

"Go home," he said, simply. "Turn around and catch the next flight home. Carl Deere is dangerous and highly organised. He may be watching us even now."

She jerked in fright, as he'd intended.

"I need you to understand how serious this is," he said. "I tried to tell you before, but you insisted on coming over. The selfish part of me was glad, if only to be able to see you again and hold your hand like this, but it's too dangerous for you to stay."

"I have my book tour," she argued, tugging her hand away. "I can't just cancel at the drop of a hat; the tour was arranged by my publishers—"

"Carl Deere doesn't care about any of that," Gregory interjected softly. "He cares about completing his mission. If there's collateral damage, he'll chalk it up as regrettable but necessary action. He considers himself a soldier at war."

Naomi understood his desire to protect, but she refused to live in fear.

"I'll be travelling to different events in and around London," she said, after a moment or two had passed. "If this man does have a list of people to kill, as you seem to think, then I'm probably not on it so there's no reason for him to seek me out. I'll hardly be at Bill's house in Cambridge, and whenever I am, we'll be all together so there'll be strength in numbers."

"I can't risk it," he said firmly. "I can't risk *you*."

Naomi shook her head, as torn as he was. "I understand the danger," she said. "You've told me clearly what's at stake. I want to stay, Alex."

Gregory closed his eyes briefly and, when he reopened them, they were a blazing, emerald green.

"I can't change your mind?"

She shook her head and, foolishly, his heart leaped.

"I've missed you," he admitted.

"I've missed you too, Alex."

Across the tarmac, Carl Deere watched them from the interior of his hire car and thought exactly what Gregory imagined he would.

The lady should have stayed away.

CHAPTER 2

DCI Ava Hope heaved a sigh and glanced at the clock on the conference room wall.

Come on, she thought. Let's get this over with. "They're late."

This insightful observation came from her sergeant, a man by the name of Ben Carter, who was seated in the chair beside her munching his way through a packet of cheese and onion crisps. She watched him tip the last of the crumbs into his mouth, scrunch the foil packet in one large hand and lob it towards the bin a few metres away—whereupon the foil promptly sprang forth again and became a limp, cheese-infused parachute that hung on the air, before floating to the carpet-tiled floor having scarcely made it halfway to its destination.

Hope rolled her eyes, but there was no time to scold him for being the slob that he was, before the brass entered the room.

They came to their feet.

"Hope, Carter," the Chief Constable said, nodding to them both. "Have a seat."

"Thank you, sir."

She eyed the packet meaningfully and Carter bent down to reach for it, finding it centimetres out of his grasp.

"For the love of God," she muttered, and rose to stomp past him and retrieve it herself.

Chief Constable Porter, who was a good-humoured man as far as it went, hid a smile while he waited for her to regain her seat.

"Ready, now?"

She nodded, and gave Carter a long look.

"Good. You both know Detective Chief Superintendent Irene Crossman," Porter said, turning towards the woman seated on his right, who was the department's most recent promotion since Campbell's untimely death.

Hope and Carter nodded, like a pair of bobbing heads.

"Now, this meeting has been called to discuss the present status of 'Operation Shakespeare'—

though, whether it should have been assigned to a task force at all is, frankly, debatable."

Hope had been preparing for this moment for a month, so it came as no surprise. If anything, she was surprised they'd been able to get away with it for so long.

"Perhaps you could talk us through it?"

She ran her tongue over her lips, and dived in. "Certainly, sir. I'll begin with the murder of the late DCS Campbell. Initially, we treated his death as being linked to the Villiers case, but, upon closer inspection of the killer's MO, I felt it warranted further investigation," she said. "Furthermore, after conducting numerous interviews with Villiers' killer, who denies any involvement in DCS Campbell's death, I took the decision to leave his case open, for the present."

"You say the styles were different," their new DCS chimed in. "I see from the file that, in the Villiers case, hemlock was the poison of choice, correct?"

Hope nodded, and Crossman barrelled on.

"Whilst hemlock wasn't used on DCS Campbell, a copy of Shakespeare's *Othello* was left as a calling card. Although the methodologies are slightly different, there remains a strong theatrical link, wouldn't you agree?"

Hope opened her mouth to respond, before realising the question had been rhetorical.

"Wouldn't you *also* agree that Villiers' killer would hardly wish to confess to more than they had to, at the point of arrest?"

"That's certainly true, ma'am, but DNA belonging to Villiers' killer isn't a match for the trace samples we found at Campbell's crime scene—"

"That doesn't mean he wasn't there, and it doesn't rule out the possibility of an accomplice."

Hope maintained a professional tone. "That's true," she was forced to admit. "However, taking into account the link between Campbell and the recent murder of His Honour Judge Quentin Whittaker QC, I think we need to remain open to the possibility that a third party was responsible for their murders."

"There was a strong link between Campbell and the Villiers case," Porter remarked. "DCS Campbell was friends with the late— and, I may say, *great* Nigel Villiers—from their university days, was he not?"

Hope was starting to feel the dull, throbbing pain of one who was banging her head against the proverbial brick wall. "Yes, they were friends, sir. However, Campbell and Whittaker also share a link—"

"Well, of course, they do," Crossman put in. "They've both been responsible for bringing any number of high-profile criminals to justice."

Hope linked her fingers on top of the table, and tried again. "One such criminal is Carl Deere," she said, and could have bitten off her own tongue, for she knew instantly the mistake she had made.

Chief Constable Porter leaned forward. "DCI Hope, as you are *well* aware, Carl Deere suffered a terrible miscarriage of justice and, as such, should never be referred to as a 'criminal' by any member of this department."

"I apologise, sir," she said. "I meant to say that Mr Deere's case was linked to both DCS Campbell, who was the Senior Investigating Officer at the time, and Judge Whittaker, who presided over the case when it went to trial at the Old Bailey, four years ago."

"Let me see if I have this straight," Crossman said, in a nasal tone that grated on Ava's last nerve. "Are you asking us to consider the possibility that an innocent man has now, over four years since his ordeal, taken it upon himself to seek revenge against those who wronged him?"

Hope nodded. "I don't think we should rule it out," she said.

Crossman and Porter exchanged a look, and then folded their arms across their chests with impressive synchronicity.

"Whilst I concede it's an outside possibility that some third-party vigilante might have murdered both of these men, or indeed that their deaths may be gang-related, asking me to believe that Carl Deere is our prime suspect is a bridge too far," Porter said, with a firm shake of his head. "You have *no* evidence whatsoever to connect the man to either murder, for a start. You have supposition and bias, neither of which this department stands for."

He paused meaningfully, then leaned forward to drive his next point home.

"As for the role of criminal profiling in solving either case, I might as well tell you I've reached the end of my rope as far as *that's* concerned," he said. "Funding is hereby withdrawn and, for the present, I'm ordering the closure of Operation Shakespeare. The deaths of Campbell and Whittaker are to be treated as separate cases, until such time as fresh evidence presents itself to demonstrate a link between them. Am I understood?"

Hope thought of Gregory and Douglas, and of the absolute conviction she'd heard in the former's voice when he'd begged her to protect his friend.

She'd done what she could.

"Perfectly, sir."

CHAPTER 3

When Alex and Naomi arrived at Bill Douglas' smart townhouse in Cambridge, they were met with a stream of exotic swear words emanating from the direction of the kitchen.

"You'd make a sailor blush," Gregory joked, entering into the room to find Douglas staring despondently at a collapsed cheese souffle. "I brought a visitor."

Douglas possessed what some might have called a 'stately' bearing, being a tall man in his early-sixties with a thickening waist—due, in no small part, to him having recently discovered *The Great British Bake Off*—and a shock of grey hair that generally propped up his bifocals.

"Ah! There she is!" Douglas was also possessed of an easy, graceful manner with people from all walks of life, which contributed greatly to his general popularity around campus and far beyond. It could easily have been otherwise; he'd enjoyed a long and distinguished career that showed no signs of abating, and was revered in professional and academic circles around the globe. It was that reputation which had helped him and Gregory to weather the media fall-out following the Deere case, but it could have helped a lesser man develop insufferable conceit. The opposite was true: ever modest, Douglas knew his own worth but never demanded that others should know it, too.

Gregory watched him enfold Naomi Palmer in a bear-like embrace. "Found her wandering around the airport," he said, and smiled as she caught his eye over Douglas' shoulder.

"Thank you so much for asking me to stay," she said, drawing away again. "I know the timing isn't ideal."

"Not at all, not at all." Douglas brushed that off, and hoped neither of them would notice the strain around his eyes, or the slightly forced nature of his smile. "Alex is a worrier, whereas I'm a pragmatist. We can't live our lives wondering 'what if'. We can only act sensibly, wherever possible, and avoid taking unnecessary risks."

Naomi nodded.

"It looks like you need some water for those beautiful flowers," Douglas said, and glanced towards his friend, who looked happier than he'd seen him in years.

"I could use a shower, too," she admitted.

"Well, I didn't like to say."

Gregory watched his oldest friend, a man akin to a father, together with the woman who'd lingered in his memory for more than a year. He heard their laughter and, for once in his life, felt as though he was a part of something he dared not call a 'family'.

The prospect was too sweet to bear.

"That was delicious, Bill." Gregory sat back in his chair, feeling stuffed.

"One tries," Douglas said, in an arch tone. "Y'know, I keep thinking I should give up mind-hunting and publish my own cookery book. Far more pleasant occupation."

Naomi smiled. "If I could cook like you, I'd have written one myself—rather than some dreary tome about abnormal psychology."

"Ah, yes, the book tour!" Douglas exclaimed. "Where's the first calling point?"

"A bookshop in London tomorrow," she said, taking a sip of wine. "Just a short talk and a signing, although I don't know anyone who'd turn out to have a book signed by me."

"I know at least two," Gregory said quietly, and their eyes caught again.

Douglas heard the admiration in his friend's voice, and was overjoyed. It gave him hope that perhaps, one day, there would be someone with whom he could share private smiles and unspoken promises.

"I thought there'd be a Mrs Douglas," Naomi said, as though she'd read his mind.

Bill was suddenly awkward. He'd spent too many years denying his true self, and it was time to face ordinary questions without shame or denial. That didn't make it easy, no matter how genial the company.

"Actually, I haven't been lucky enough to meet the right *fellow*," he said, taking off his glasses to polish them idly against his jumper. "All the good ones are taken, you know."

If Naomi was surprised, her face betrayed none of it.

"Well, that can't be true," she said, without missing a beat. "You're still single, for a start."

Douglas let out a hoot of laughter. "Bless you for that," he said, and leaned across to pat her hand. "I haven't told Alex this, yet, but I was thinking of joining one of those dating sites—if I can pluck up the courage."

Gregory smiled broadly. "Well, now," he said, and flexed his fingers. "I'm nothing, if not good at writing profiles."

"God, help me," Douglas said.

They all laughed, and then Douglas yawned hugely.

"Day's catching up with me, I'm afraid," he said. "I'll leave you bright young things to it. I'm glad to have you with us, Naomi. Alex? Don't forget to turn out the lights, will you?"

He'd be checking all the locks, too, Gregory thought, and bade his friend goodnight.

Once they were alone, with the soft strains of some old song playing, Alex and Naomi began to clear the dishes away. They moved easily around one another, as though it was a dance they'd done a thousand times before, and eventually he caught her hand in his and swung her into his arms for the real thing, moving her slowly around the floor in time to the music.

"Do you remember the last time we danced, in the ballroom at the Buchanan?" he asked.

"How could I forget? You were high on psychedelics, for one thing."

"I remember seeing stars, Naomi, but it had nothing to do with being drugged."

Their feet came to a standstill.

"What about now?" she asked quietly.

Very gently, he cradled her head in his hands, tipping it back slightly so he could look into her eyes.

"I've got the strangest feeling I'll see stars whenever you're around, Doctor Palmer."

He kissed her deeply, then smiled against her lips.

"Either that, or you dropped something into my drink, earlier."

She made a small sound of outrage. "I thought Englishmen were supposed to be charming?"

"I'm not most Englishmen."

"Ain't that the truth," she muttered, and drew him back to her for another kiss. "Luckily for you, I have a soft spot for the abnormal."

CHAPTER 4

Four years earlier

HM Prison Frankland, Durham

"Wakey, wakey!"

Carl awoke to the sound of a truncheon clanging against the door of his cell, and wondered what time it was. It seemed only five minutes ago that he'd finally drifted off into a disturbed sleep, and a quick glance towards the tiny window told him that the sun had not yet risen to signify the start of another miserable day. A further inspection of his surroundings told him that Gav was missing from the upper bunk, which sent a frisson of panic running down his spine. He might have been detestable, but they'd come to an understanding.

The cell door burst open then, to reveal one of the senior prison officers; an enormously fat man by the name of Andy Irwin, known more colloquially to the men of Frankland as 'Jabba'. He was joined by one of the junior prison officers, whose eyes remained firmly turned away.

"Must be 'ard for a man like you, bein' locked in 'ere," Irwin began, as he strolled around the cell, touching this and that with the edge of his truncheon. "Not bein' free to go about killin' blokes like me, eh? Bet you've 'ad a few wet dreams about it, 'aven't yer?"

Carl's stomach turned and, if he'd had the courage, he might have remarked that Irwin didn't meet the physical type of victim he'd been accused of killing. They'd been young men with fresh faces and slim bodies, not the sack of flesh and bone that stood before him.

"Where's Gav?"

Irwin laughed, his chest heaving up and down with the effort. "Gav, who?" he asked, innocently. "Only one name residin' in this cell, accordin' to my records."

Carl's breath began to hitch in and out as he sensed a trap. "What do you want?"

"Well, you might be a murderin' bastard, but I do appreciate a man who comes to the point," Irwin said, and took the seat opposite the bottom bunk where Carl was perched. "Now, you won't mind me askin', but 'ave you armed yourself?"

He didn't mean self-harm, Carl knew. He was asking whether he'd fashioned himself a shiv, or something of that kind.

"I'm not armed," he muttered, but wished that he was. The thought took him by surprise.

"Daft bugger, aren't yer?" Irwin asked. "No offence, lad, but a man in my position has to be sure."

He raised his truncheon and dealt a hard blow to Carl's stomach to immobilise him, then crooked a finger towards his silent underling, who stepped inside the cell and began patting him down to check for weapons.

"He's clean," the officer said, and stepped back out again.

"All right," Irwin said, folding his arms across his belly. "Let's you and me talk a bit o' business. Gav tells me you've come to terms. Well, not with me, you 'aven't. I 'ear you were some sort've computer money bloke, in your civvie life. I could use a man like you."

Carl finally stopped coughing and caught his breath.

"I'm sure y' can appreciate, some of us've come into a bit o' money since workin' for His Majesty," Irwin continued, pausing briefly to belch in Carl's general direction. "Problem is, I can't let the taxman know about it, can I?" He shrugged. "I need you to find a way to clean that money, and I know a few others who'd pay a tidy little commission for a service like that."

Carl raised his head, drew in a shaking breath, and looked him dead in the eye. "I'm not bent," he snarled.

Irwin laughed. "You've got a good sense o' humour, I'll give you that."

He heaved himself up, and tugged his trousers back over his sagging arse. "Have a think about it," he advised.

"I've told you before, I'm *not guilty*!" Carl almost shouted.

Irwin turned to him with a kind of pity in his piggish, bloodshot eyes. "You will be," he said, and left it at that.

Present Day

Near Durham

Carl drove through the quiet streets of a cul-de-sac in County Durham, bringing the car to a stop a few doors down from a semi-detached house built sometime in the nineties. Several porcelain gnomes and other garden paraphernalia adorned the front lawn, and an automatic hose sprayed a fan of water in a wide arc, successfully missing the grass and shrubbery and instead hitting the edge of a fancy Mercedes SUV parked on the driveway.

Carl happened to know those vehicles retailed for six figures and, on a prison officer's salary, Andy Irwin shouldn't have been able to afford it, even on credit. However, Irwin had plenty of lucrative side hustles, and had obviously grown complacent since Carl had last seen him, otherwise he wouldn't have indulged in such a flashy display of wealth in an area where a top-of-the-range luxury vehicle stood out.

"Getting sloppy," he whispered to the empty car, and raised his field glasses to gain a better view of the windows.

One large bay at the front of the house, probably a couple at the back, too.

Single garage door to the side, main door central to the house.

Two upstairs windows at the front, probably two at the back.

Couple of security lights and cameras situated above the front door and garage, probably some at the back of the house, too.

"Piece of cake," he muttered.

It wasn't so much the house itself that concerned him. It was the possibility of being observed by some snoopy, over-zealous neighbour, thereby causing him to miss his own metaphorical window of opportunity while Irwin's wife and children were away from home. Unfortunately, the children's holidays were coming up, when they'd be at home much of the time, so he needed to act swiftly or be forced to wait for weeks until they were away during the daytime at school again.

He didn't *want* to wait any longer.

He'd waited long enough to bring Andy Irwin his comeuppance. Sadly, that pleasure would have to wait a little while longer, until the moment was ripe.

Besides, he had other places to be, other people to see.

CHAPTER 5

The following morning dawned brightly, with shards of pale amber light bathing the rooftops and spires of Cambridge in a warm, ethereal glow. Much of the city centre was devoted to university buildings, botanical gardens and cobbled streets, which brimmed with pedestrians and bicycles laden with students hurrying to their first tutorial of the day. Naomi dodged them as she walked alongside Gregory and Douglas, who was making his way towards Hawking College and the students who awaited him there.

"Cambridge is exactly as I imagined it would be," she said.

"Is that good or bad?" Gregory asked.

"Definitely good," she replied, admiring the Gothic skyline towering overhead.

Naomi was herself an alumnus of Harvard and New York universities, so was hardly a stranger to Ivy League institutions of learning, but she was forced to admit Cambridge held a certain gravitas that came from having such a long and distinguished history and a quaintness that was hard to replicate elsewhere.

They stopped briefly to pick up some take-away coffees, served in eco-friendly craft cups printed with a slogan terribly *à la mode*, and made their way towards an impressive stone entranceway, with bells, arches and a finely manicured quadrangle.

"Well, this is where I leave you both," Douglas said, and gave them a cheerful toast with his coffee cup. "See you this evening."

Discreetly, Gregory surveyed the crowds passing to-and-fro, his sharp green eyes searching each face for one he might recognise.

"I—ah—I was thinking of showing Naomi around the grounds a bit," he lied. "I might pop into the office, too."

Thanks to Douglas' immense popularity, they'd secured a small room in one of the dustier towers of the college, which they'd transformed into their fledgling profiling unit—

with a standing membership of two. However, both men knew there was nothing to work on at present, having taken the decision not to accept any new commissions until the matter of Carl Deere was settled one way or another.

Douglas tipped down his glasses and favoured Gregory with a stern look.

"I don't need babysitting," he told him clearly. "There'll be people in my office for back-to-back tutorial sessions throughout the morning, and I have a faculty meeting this afternoon. I won't be alone, Alex."

When Gregory didn't respond, he heaved a sigh that was part remorse, part impatience. "Try not to think of it," he told him, and gave his friend's arm a reassuring pat. "I promise, I won't speak to any strangers."

With that, he winked at Naomi and headed off, whistling beneath his breath.

"He thinks I'm over-reacting," Gregory said, when Douglas was out of earshot. "Perhaps I am."

Naomi looked at him, then towards the professor's retreating back.

"I doubt it," she said. "People sometimes make mistakes, and you're as human as the rest of us, but I couldn't accuse you of being a man prone to over-reactions. If anything, you hold yourself tightly in check."

He turned to her. "Do you think I should be more spontaneous?" he asked. "Unbutton my collar—that sort of thing?"

The mood shifted with his own mercurial spirit, and her body responded with a flood of sudden heat that took her by surprise and made her question whether she, too, held herself too tightly in check.

"I could help you with the buttons," she offered, with a shy smile.

There was a short, crackling silence before he replied.

"What are you doing, right now?"

"Not a thing," she said.

Naomi would later realise it was then, in that moment, with the sun burnishing his hair a rich, golden-brown, that she truly began to fall.

"There's a picnic basket back at the house," he said, conversationally. "We could go punting on the river and bring it with us. The boat might run beneath the low-hanging branches of a weeping willow and stay there for a while, shaded from the rest of the world."

Naomi's eyes slid back to his. "I like the sound of that," she said.

He held out his hand. "Shall we?"

Naomi watched the play of morning light over his face, saw the crinkles at the corners of his eyes that revealed themselves when he was happy, and realised she was happy, too.

"Will you be wearing a striped jersey and a straw boater?" she asked him.

Gregory surprised her again by leaning forward to whisper in her ear.

"I'll wear whatever you like, Doctor Palmer."

While Alex and Naomi made their way back to Douglas' townhouse, the man himself greeted his first tutorial group of the day, which happened to be one of his favourites. Unlike the usual crowd of undergraduates, his Friday morning session belonged to a small group of mature students who were completing a Masters' degree part-time by distance learning, and were required to attend only a limited number of face-to-face sessions, usually a couple of months apart.

"Good morning, everyone," he began, settling himself into a comfortable leather desk chair. "Make yourselves at home."

The assortment of men and women of varying ages and backgrounds took their seats on one of the large sofas or individual armchairs spread around his office. Douglas occupied one of the largest rooms in the building near the clocktower, thus commanding views of the quadrangle and far beyond. It was exactly as one might have expected, being panelled in weathered oak partly obscured by a set of enormous bookcases that were stuffed with books of all description. A general air of mustiness mingled with the scent of good, strong coffee and, above all else, it carried Douglas' warmth, which wrapped itself around whoever entered his domain.

He smiled at them while he reminded himself of their names and faces, and then a small frown crossed his forehead.

"Are we one short?"

Just then, they heard footsteps in the stairwell outside his door, and, with a peremptory knock, it opened to reveal an attractive man of around forty, with a mop of dark, curly hair, and glasses very similar to Douglas' own jaunty purple spectacles. To his embarrassment, his was the face Douglas remembered the most, and had instantly missed from the group.

"Sorry I'm late," he said, betraying an accent that was vaguely continental and spoke of international schooling. "My flight from Paris landed later than expected."

Douglas found himself wondering what had taken him to Paris.

None of your business, he reminded himself.

"Right, well, we're all very glad you could make it, Jacob," he said. "Let's make a start."

The small band of students were an able bunch—admittedly, some more so than others, which was to be expected. Douglas considered it part of his job not only to impart his wisdom about the machinations of the human mind, but to teach them how to think and express those thoughts in a way that others would understand. It was a life skill, he supposed, but it was one he was still learning himself.

"That's all for today, folks," he said, with genuine regret. "I look forward to receiving your essays on the topic of neuroplasticity following childhood trauma and its relationship with recidivism; I'm sure you'll have some very interesting things to say about the correlation, if any, between the two. We aren't scheduled to see one another again until"—he paused to check his diary—"hm, yes, another eight weeks' time. Still, that affords plenty of opportunity to read around the subjects we'll be covering, and I'm always available to discuss any queries or concerns in our online meetings. Have a lovely weekend."

Most of the group lingered to pick his brain about this or that, and he found himself laughing easily with them. One thing that could be said of an older student was that they were often more comfortable with themselves, having lived a little more of life than the average eighteen-year-old; though, of course, there were exceptions to every rule.

"Professor?"

Douglas turned to find Jacob standing patiently in front of him, leather satchel clutched beneath one arm.

"I was hoping to ask you some questions about your work in profiling?"

Douglas felt his heart rate quicken, and admonished himself for being all kinds of old fool over a man who must have been twenty years his junior.

"Ah, well, it would've been a pleasure, but I have my next tutorial group to think of—"

"Perhaps later, over a coffee?" Jacob smiled.

"Well. Ah. Well," Douglas said, parroting himself.

There was nothing wrong with sharing a coffee and discussion with a student. It happened all the time, and remained purely professional.

Were his intentions strictly professional, in this case?

"I'm rather busy today," he said, apologetically. "Perhaps another time."

Jacob was crestfallen, but mostly hid the emotion behind a friendly smile. "Of course, Professor." He gave an embarrassed laugh. "As you say, perhaps another time." He turned, and the action dislodged the various papers and books he clutched in his satchel, which had a faulty catch.

"Sorry," he muttered, and fell to his knees to begin scooping up the detritus that spilled onto the floor.

Douglas crouched down to help him, and saw reams of notes on all manner of subjects as well as a book written by a man he admired very much from the FBI's former Behavioural Science

Unit. More than that, the author was now his friend, for they'd known one another for many years.

He didn't bother to mention the last part, in case it would inhibit conversation.

"Did you enjoy this book?" he asked.

Jacob considered the question, and then nodded.

"It was written more like a memoir than a textbook," he observed. "The concepts were put across far more easily because of that format, in my opinion."

In Douglas' opinion, too.

"You know," he said, "I *do* have an hour or so, after my next tutorial finishes at eleven. If you still wanted to go over some of the things we discussed, or talk about the role of profiling in police work, I suppose I could spare some time, after all?"

Jacob's face broke into a smile. "Thanks," he said. "That would be wonderful, Professor."

"Call me Bill."

CHAPTER 6

"Tell me about your profile."

Gregory opened his eyes, blinked against the dappled sunlight filtering through the leaves of the low-hanging branches overhead, and looked across to where Naomi lay sprawled beside him on the picnic blanket they'd laid out on the riverbank.

"I like to think of it as noble, with a strong jawline—"

She jabbed him playfully, not bothering to open her eyes. "I meant the original profile you created for the Metropolitan Police, back when they were investigating Andersson's murders," she said. "I'm interested to know why the police thought Carl Deere could have been the one, and why *you* think he might be the one now."

Gregory crossed his ankles, and exhaled a long breath before speaking. "That's a question I've asked myself, many times," he said. "When the investigating team, led by the late DCS Campbell—who was a detective chief inspector, back then—began to say they had a man within their pool of suspects who was in the area at the time of the murders and seemed to fit the bill, I looked long and hard at the information they gave me and compared it with the profile I'd written."

"And?" she prompted softly. "*Did* he fit the bill?"

Gregory looked across at her. "In many ways, yes," he said truthfully. "I was outspoken about the methodologies the police employed, because their idea of entrapment was deeply flawed, but I couldn't argue with the fact that the information they had about his background and character fit neatly with the profile I'd created. Just because it happened to be the case that he *didn't* kill those men doesn't mean Deere isn't in possession of the requisite psychological indicators that have provided a fertile breeding ground for the type of killer you and I have met in our clinical experience."

Naomi nodded. "On the other hand, it's also true that a person's history or childhood trauma doesn't mean they'll grow up to be killers. Being *capable* of something and actually *doing* something are two different things."

"I couldn't agree more," he said, and gave a short laugh. "I'm a prime example of that."

She turned to look at him. "You mean... because of your mother?"

Before her suicide, Gregory's mother had been diagnosed with what was commonly known as 'Munchausen's Syndrome by Proxy' or 'Factitious Disorder by Proxy'. It was a condition she'd suffered from so severely throughout his childhood it had led to the deaths of his two siblings, and had almost killed him, too. That might have been trauma enough for any young mind to cope with but, factoring in his father's abandonment and his mother's total lack of insight or remorse, Gregory could easily have grown into a man riddled with misplaced anger. Instead, and with the well-timed guidance of a few good friends like Bill, he'd taken a different path and become a healer, in his own way.

"There's a saying about parents being the ones who mess you up," he remarked. "I could write a book on that topic alone, if I wasn't liable to bore myself silly during the process. However, it's true

that my experiences might have made me"—
he paused, wondering how honest he should
be—"*averse* to forming longstanding romantic
attachments with women. I recognise that's a
by-product of latent anger I harboured towards
my mother. I've found it hard to trust women in
general."

He glanced across at her, then away again.

"At least, in the past," he added, softly. "People
have the capacity to change, especially when they
meet a person worth changing for."

Naomi smiled, and reached across to touch his
cheek. "Alex, if you're trying to tell me you're a bit
troubled, I already got that memo," she drawled.
"You might as well have 'COMPLICATED'
tattooed on your forehead."

He laughed. "Well, that's a blow to my ego," he
said. "Here I was thinking I'd done a pretty good
job of hiding all my skeletons."

"I can practically hear them rattling," she said.
"But we all carry some baggage. We could trade
syndromes and debate nuances from dusk till
dawn but, the fact is, we choose to get up in the
morning and see the world as a place of hope.
That's what counts."

It really was as simple as that, he thought.

"I thought you said you weren't much of a speaker," he said, turning onto his side and propping his head on his hand so he could look at her properly. "Carry on like that, and this tour of yours will be a breeze."

"You're too kind," she said, and accepted a daisy he offered her. "More flowers?"

"I'm on a roll," he said, with a self-deprecating shrug. "I want to thank you, Naomi."

"For what?"

"For taking my mind off the imminent threat of death, for one thing," he said, with a certain dark humour. "And, for reminding me that the past doesn't need to define the future. That's something Carl Deere's forgotten, I think…or perhaps I'm mistaken. Perhaps he's been looking for an excuse to let his demons roam free. He might've been wronged by the system, but he was already on a bad path when they brought him in. There's a reason he was singled out as a suspect, and it wasn't just because he suffered a traumatic childhood with an abusive father, or that he was cruel to animals as a kid. He was cruel to his sexual partners, too, although none of them made a formal report at the time because they were too ashamed. He might not have been a killer, but Carl Deere was a deeply unpleasant person with a penchant for sexual sadism."

A shadow passed over his face, as Gregory thought back to the witness statements he'd read.

"To answer your original question, my profile set out the character of a perpetrator with strong sadistic tendencies. I told the police they'd be looking for a man with means and life experience enough to instil trust in his younger victims, all of whom were men in their late teens or early twenties," he said, with a note of sadness. "I gauged the killer to be in his mid-thirties to late forties—possibly early-thirties but that was less likely. I said he wouldn't identify openly as homosexual, certainly not to friends or family, because he kept his intimate life entirely separate from other parts of his life. I thought it unlikely the killer would be heterosexual because, frankly, the physical evidence suggested degrees of intimacy that would have made it unlikely, even if the killings had been homosexual hate crimes or execution murders. I said the perp would likely have a juvenile record of aggression, possibly one or two minor pops on his record for assault or something of that nature, as well as indecent exposure."

"Did Carl have a record?"

He nodded. "Deere had a caution for exposing himself to a man on a tube train, late at night," he said. "He also had a sealed juvenile record, which included several counts of animal cruelty and countless social service interventions during his early teens. According to the report from his child psychologist, Deere's aggression seemed to flow from feelings of sexual rejection, particularly from other boys he'd liked, or had previously been friends with. He took people by surprise, because he was otherwise well mannered and very quiet."

"He loves men, but also hates them?" she asked.

"I think so," Gregory said. "He hated his father with a fiery passion, after years of systematic trauma which ultimately led to him being removed from the family home and put into the system. He doesn't think too much of women, either, because he associates them with his mother, whom he perceived as being weak for allowing his father to act the way he did."

He shook his head, recognising a parallel there. "It all adds up on paper but when you look at the facts, Carl's partners weren't exclusively younger, as Thomas Andersson's were," he said. "It's a crucial difference, because it goes to motive. In Carl's case, the men with whom he was most cruel tended to be *older*, and, if I were to hazard a guess, I'd say they probably reminded him on some level of his father, whom he'd have liked to punish. For Andersson, it was all about controlling younger men, for very different reasons."

She digested the information, thinking of personality types and past cases, before asking another question. "Overall, you're saying that, although he wasn't the perpetrator of Andersson's crimes, he still has the capacity for that level of violence?"

"Oh, yes," he said simply. "I'd guess Carl Deere planned to kill his father in a hundred different ways. Unfortunately, he was robbed of the opportunity by the hand of Fate, because his father died of pancreatic cancer while he was away in prison."

"How do you know?" she asked.

"Because he was the first person I looked into, when I made my list."

She sat upright, no longer able to enjoy the sunshine nor the birdsong.

"What list, Alex?"

"His hit-list," Gregory said. "The people I believe Carl wants to eliminate, before he considers his mission complete. I've compiled a list of the those I think would qualify, if I step into his mind. Carl Deere Senior would have been somewhere near the top, if he hadn't already died from natural causes, although it's possible Carl would have chosen to kill his father last of all, if he'd had the choice."

Naomi agreed.

"If Carl's a sadist, he'd have wanted to savour the experience," she said, and Gregory nodded.

"I think he'd have saved the 'best' till last, but that doesn't mean his father wasn't still number one in his mind."

"Who'd be number two?"

"Evidently, that was DCS Campbell, with Judge Whittaker falling into third," Gregory said, and thought of the fact they were both men of a certain age.

Naomi opened her mouth, and then shut it again.

"I know what you're thinking," he murmured.

She said nothing, and didn't need to. The fear in her eyes spoke volumes.

"If you're wondering who's likely to be fourth on Carl's list of preferred kills, it's probably Bill or me," he said, without inflection. "That's if Carl had his way, which he doesn't entirely; not so long as we remain vigilant. There are others on his list who may be sitting there, like ducks, oblivious to the danger and therefore easier to kill, so he could bump them up the list. If the police won't warn them, then I must. I've been gathering the information I need to reach out to the people I believe are in danger, and put them on their guard."

"Won't the police help?"

"That remains to be seen," he said, and a muscle clenched in his jaw as he tried to keep his frustration in check.

They fell silent for long minutes while they sat there, side by side on the soft grass, until Naomi interrupted the reverie with a confession, of sorts.

"I quit my job at the Buchanan today," she said quietly. "I sent them an e-mail with a letter of resignation attached."

He turned to her in surprise. "Why?"

She smiled as a couple of swans glided by, far more serene than she felt at that moment.

"I decided it was time to stop hiding myself away in the mountains and start living. I thought you might be just the person to help me with that, Alex."

He reached out a hand to hold hers. "I'm not a safe bet, Naomi. I'm—" His lips twisted. "I'm still chasing my own demons. Not as many as before, but enough to keep me awake at night."

"Yeah, well, so long as you don't leave the toilet seat up, it's a decent start."

He grinned and then leaned closer, taking in the angles and shadows of her face. "Enter freely, and of your own will," he said.

In answer, she moved swiftly, rolling over so that he lay beneath her. "I'll take my chances," she said, and the last thing he saw was her face framed by the branches of a weeping willow, before he allowed himself to be swept away into fantasy once more.

CHAPTER 7

While Doctors Gregory and Palmer enjoyed a brief respite from talk of psychology and psychopaths, Douglas indulged himself in a stimulating discussion of both.

"I think we could probably debate the efficacy of the term 'psychopath' until the cows come home," he said, polishing off the last of his coffee. "The fact of the matter is this—what we know of the mind and of human behaviour is evolving all the time."

Jacob nodded, and crossed one leg over the other in an elegant motion that drew the eye.

"What about offender profiling, the other string to your bow?" he asked. "Would you say that's an evolving discipline, too?"

"Certainly," Douglas said, pushing his glasses a little higher on the bridge of his nose. "Profiles are informed by real-life cases. Ask any murder detective and they'll tell you the same thing; it's an uncomfortable and sad truth, but, the more examples we have of serious crimes, the more we have to learn from and try to use as predictors of future criminal behaviour, which informs the profiles we create."

Jacob chewed thoughtfully on the last crumbs of a chocolate brownie, and licked the residue from his lips.

"Hardly what you'd call an exact science," he said, after a long moment. "Have there been times when you've doubted yourself?"

Douglas leaned back in his chair and considered how best to answer. It was his policy always to be honest, especially to his students, but the man seated opposite him had a quiet manner that was certain to draw the truth from him in any event.

"Of course," he said. "It would be reckless of me to become complacent, in any of the professional spheres in which I work. Any good clinician, as with any good profiler, must be constantly learning."

Jacob cocked his head to one side. "I read about the Deere case, four years ago..."

Douglas smiled, but it held no mirth. "It was a sensational case," he agreed. "And it was widely reported."

When Jacob continued to look at him, Douglas raised his hands in a mute gesture of frustration. "I can guess the question you want to ask me," he said. "The answer is *no*. I don't feel either myself or Doctor Gregory made a mistake in the profiling work the Metropolitan Police commissioned from us. I *do* think there were mistakes in how that profile was applied."

"How so?" Jacob asked, and waggled his notepad to seek Douglas' consent for him to take some notes. "I thought for a while about becoming a profiler, but the professional risks seem high—especially when you consider the aftermath of Deere's arrest."

"There's an element of risk in all that we do," Douglas reminded him. "You cross the street at your own risk. You drive a car at your own risk… and yes, you produce psychological profiles on serious offenders to help a police investigation *at your own risk*. We take these risks with the intention of producing positive outcomes, and there have been many over the years—in fact, the times our profiles have helped police teams to narrow their search and eventually find killers, rapists and other serious offenders vastly outweigh the rare times when they haven't. The Deere case might have been a minority example of when our profile was misused, but it was significant enough to outweigh a hundred other positive cases."

Jacob nodded. "Is there anything you would have done differently?" he asked. "Hindsight being a wonderful thing, of course."

They both smiled.

"I don't know that I could have done much to stop those in charge from continuing down the path they'd chosen," Douglas said, with a frown as he remembered past events. "I would, perhaps, have acted more swiftly in speaking out against the methodologies that were employed to ensnare Carl Deere, but both Alex and I were vocal in our objections."

He thought of the young man who'd been used as bait, and sighed.

"Much of what we do is dependent on trust," he continued. "As profilers, we depend on our profiles being used properly and ethically, within the boundaries of their competency and with integrity. As clinicians, when we sit with a patient, we depend on them being truthful in their interactions—in the absence of any objective facts we may have at our disposal. It's hard to help anyone if they choose not to tell us the truth about the things that are troubling them."

"Perhaps they don't want you to know the 'real' version of themselves," Jacob said.

"Very often," Douglas agreed. "It may be part of their disorder."

"How can you tell?" Jacob asked. "Some people are very proficient liars."

Douglas merely smiled. "Experience," he said simply.

Presently, talk changed to other things. They spoke of music and art, of complex neurological ailments, until Douglas expressed his regrets that it was time for him to return to the college.

"It's been a very interesting discussion, Jacob."

"Thank you for your time," the other man said, and then, with a certain shy hesitation, decided to go out on a limb. "I wonder…ah, perhaps, the next time, we could chat over some dinner or a few drinks?"

Douglas was taken aback, before his heart began to beat wildly in his chest.

"That would be…"

Impossible. Inadvisable.

"Lovely," he said.

Jacob smiled, the corners of his eyes crinkling in a manner Douglas found charming.

"Until then," he said. "I'll look forward to it, Bill."

"Impressive—if that's the right word to describe an entire wall dedicated to murder."

Alex had, with his friend's permission, taken the liberty of commandeering the entire length of a bedroom wall in the room where he'd been staying at Douglas' townhouse. Now, rather than featuring a series of modern art prints against an attractive, painted backdrop, the space was covered in photographs, cuttings and post-it notes charting Gregory's personal investigation into the current whereabouts and motivations of Carl Deere. After a lazy morning and early afternoon spent on the riverbank, he and Naomi stood in front of it now, with the latter wearing an expression that conveyed both professional curiosity and personal concern.

"I hope Bill doesn't mind you defacing his property like this," she said.

Alex shrugged. "I've promised to pay for any re-decoration, once it's all over," he assured her.

Gregory thought of his friend in the North, a murder detective who swore by old-fashioned methods wherever possible. "I have it on good authority that nothing beats a large-scale visual."

Naomi nodded, and moved to the centre of the bedroom wall, where a single face formed the apex of an enormous web.

"Is this him?" she asked.

Gregory moved to stand behind her. "Yes, that's Carl Deere," he said, staring into the dark eyes of a slim man in his late thirties, with pale skin that bore the look of one who'd been deprived of nutrition or sun...perhaps, both. "At least, it was what he looked like a few years ago, following his arrest."

"He isn't memorable," she said. "You might see somebody who looks vaguely like him on every street corner."

"Yes, I know," he murmured. *It was a worry.*

"More than four years have passed," she mused. "Do you have a more recent photograph?"

"Sadly not," he replied. "Without the help of the police, it's very difficult to run any proper checks against driving license records or a current address; it also doesn't help that, as part of the State making amends following his wrongful conviction, they agreed to give Deere a new identity."

"And you don't know his new name—without the help of your contacts in the Met?" she surmised.

Gregory shook his head. "They're very unlikely to help," he said. "It's a sealed record, available only to those with clearance. Without official approval, they wouldn't even consider recalling that record, let alone telling me anything it contained."

"I thought a task force had been set up?" she asked. "That's why Douglas has been protected, so far, isn't it?"

"Yes, but there was no unmarked car parked on the other side of the road when we left this morning," he said. "No bland-looking officer following at a safe distance as we made our way to the college, either. They've withdrawn protection, which means it's very likely they've shut down the task force that was set up a month ago. I expect a phone call from DCI Hope at any moment to tell me so herself."

"Does Douglas know?"

"I don't think he noticed their absence earlier," Gregory said, and hoped it was true of his wily friend. "I don't want to worry him but, unless I can convince the police to re-open the investigation, things will need to change around here. I'm going to walk back into town to meet Bill at the end of the day, for a start."

Naomi stepped forward and took his hand.

"We'll walk together," she assured him. "You don't have to do this alone, Alex."

Aside from Douglas, they were words he'd rarely heard from anybody else in his life.

"Thank you," he said.

"No need to run out and get me any more flowers," she teased. "But the next time you do happen to pass a florist, you should know I'm partial to sunflowers. They always cheer me up."

"I'll keep it in mind."

CHAPTER 8

DCI Hope could have made a phone call and washed her hands of the whole thing with minimal fuss. She could have told Gregory she'd done her best but it was out of her hands now, and that would've been pretty much that. She wasn't a miracle worker, and her colleagues at the Met needed evidence to continue a risky, high profile investigation into a man who'd already been falsely accused once in his lifetime. She could have regurgitated the words used by her senior officers or given Gregory some platitude or other along the lines of, 'keeping in touch if new evidence came to light'. Distancing herself from criminal profiles and profilers would be advisable, given what the Chief Constable and DCS Crossman had told her, only the day before.

But that would have been cowardly, and a coward was one thing Ava Hope had never been.

So, instead of making a phone call, she found herself stepping off a train onto the platform at Cambridge as the sun began to set, already wishing she'd gone home to her cat, an omelette and a hot bath. At least the walk from the station was scenic, and afforded the opportunity to clear her mind and think about what she would say when she saw Alex Gregory and Bill Douglas again.

Particularly, Doctor Gregory.

Alex.

It was astonishing how some people had the ability to wheedle their way beneath any psychological defence, disarming unsuspecting individuals such as herself with little more than a pair of pretty green eyes and a smile. During the short time they'd spent together, she thought there'd been something between them...some *frisson* that could be explored further, if either of them wished to. Then again, instinct warned her it was very possible that a man like Alex Gregory could give many women the impression of intimacy; people of all sexes and genders, come to that. He had a quality about him that was approachable and attractive, and made the object of his focus feel *heard* and *seen*.

She paused to look up at the sky, which was a melting pot of deep pinks and blues, before continuing toward Douglas' home address. Inevitably, her thoughts crept back to his friend and profiling partner, and she wondered...

What? her mind whispered. What do you wonder?

"Nothing," she muttered, drawing a curious glance from a passing student. "We're incompatible. There's no reason to imagine anything between us; he only ever held my hand, and that could have been in friendly support at a difficult moment, nothing more."

Liar, her mind whispered, but she ignored it and kept her head down, concentrating on the paving stones beneath her feet.

Soon enough, Ava reached a smart, double-fronted townhouse. She raised a hand to press the bell, and a smile was already hovering on her lips when the front door swung open. However, rather than finding Gregory or Douglas standing on the threshold, she was faced with a very beautiful woman of around her own age. Before she could formulate the words to ask who the vision was, it smiled at her.

"You must be from the police," the woman said, in a soft, North American accent that was probably East Coast, if she was to hazard a guess. "DCI Hope?"

Ava looked down at her clothing, but there was no name badge on display. "Is it that obvious?"

"Maybe not to everyone," Naomi said, and took a step forward with her hand outstretched. "I'm Doctor Naomi Palmer, a friend of Alex and Bill's."

Hope took the hand and found it soft yet firm at the same time, which was a balance she often sought but failed to achieve.

"We're just about to sit down to dinner—"

"Who is it, Naomi?"

Gregory appeared, dressed casually in jeans and a linen shirt rolled up at the sleeves, a tea towel spattered with tomato sauce slung over one shoulder. Framed in the doorway, he and the beautiful Doctor Palmer wouldn't have looked out of place on the pages of a glossy spread for *Ideal Home* magazine.

"DCI Hope," he said, and, whilst his pitch was faultless, she judged from his expression that

Gregory was under no illusions about the reason she'd come. "I wondered when we'd be hearing from you. Please, come in."

She would rather have left them, then and there.

"Thank you," she forced herself to say. "I won't stay long."

———————

Though his vision might have been somewhat myopic, there were many things Bill Douglas could still see with absolute clarity, and the look of dismay on young Ava Hope's face was one of them. He admired her professionalism, and the smooth mask she wore to protect herself, but he'd been a psychologist for too long not to recognise that which she sought to hide.

L'amour, he thought, sadly.

There was nothing so painful as attraction unrequited. He glanced at his friend and knew that Alex was, most likely, entirely unaware. As with so many of their kind, where he possessed a brilliant knack for understanding the minds and lives of others, he was yet to develop a similar proficiency when it came to his own.

"Ava, my dear, I hope you'll join us for dinner," he said. "There's more than enough for everyone here, in the vat of pasta Alex seems to have made."

"Never was any good at gauging quantities," Gregory threw back over his shoulder. "Besides, I'm hungry."

Ava glanced at the woman standing beside her, then away again.

"That's very kind of you, Professor Douglas, but I should be getting back soon."

"Nonsense," he admonished. "After coming all this way to see us, I won't hear of you being sent home without so much as a morsel at the end of a long day."

He gave her one of his most persuasive smiles.

"Well…" Ava wavered, because her mouth was indeed watering, and the prospect of a carton sandwich from the newsagents beside the train station wasn't much to get excited about. "If it isn't too much trouble…all right, then."

Douglas nodded, and sloshed a generous amount of Montepulciano into a wine glass before she had time to refuse it.

"It'll help," he murmured. "I find a glass of something fruity works wonders when one is faced with three doctors in a confined space."

Hope looked up into his eyes, saw the understanding reflected there, and nodded.

"Thank you," she said, and took a healthy glug before facing the woman who'd taken the seat to her right. "So, ah, how do you know these two reprobates?"

Naomi smiled, and her eyes slid towards Alex, who was plating up the food.

"I was Alex's psychiatrist, while he was an in-patient at the Buchanan Hospital," she said, and watched Ava's mouth fall open.

"He was—what?"

Gregory laughed, and set steaming bowls in front of them. "It isn't *quite* how it sounds," he said. "I was working undercover for the FBI, at the time."

"That's what they all say," Naomi chimed in, with a meaningful wriggle of her eyebrows for Ava's benefit. "He gave an extremely convincing display of mental illness."

Hope found herself laughing. "I can't imagine he was easy to deal with," she said.

"You've got that right," Naomi grinned. "If he wasn't breaking and entering, he was riling up the other patients or wandering around stoned."

Ava took another drink. "Sounds like you had your hands full," she said lightly. "What brings you over to the UK, Doctor Palmer?"

"Naomi," the other corrected, while twirling a long strand of spaghetti around her fork. "Officially, I'm here for a book tour but, unofficially, I'm thinking of staying a while longer."

Gregory looked up with a smile, and Ava watched a message pass between them. Feeling voyeuristic, she looked away sharply and found herself caught by Douglas' gentle gaze.

"Why don't you tell us what's brought you to Cambridge?" he asked, and Gregory redirected his attention to hear the response. "Has there been any news on Carl Deere's whereabouts?"

Ava set down her fork, and dabbed her lips with a napkin.

"No, I'm afraid that isn't why I'm here, Professor," she said. "I'm sorry to tell you that Operation Shakespeare has been shut down, with immediate effect."

There was a heavy silence, and Hope took the opportunity to push back from the table.

"Thank you for the meal—"

"Now, now," Douglas said, and patted her hand. "There's no need to run off. You caught us off guard, that's all."

Gregory, for one, did not seem surprised. "What was the reasoning?" he asked, calmly. "Lack of DNA evidence?"

"Partly," she answered. "Factor in *extreme* sensitivity associated with Carl Deere, and you've got a recipe for disaster as far as the brass are concerned. They want nothing to do with it."

"So, if not Deere, who do they think killed Judge Whittaker?" Gregory asked. "The fairies?"

Douglas pursed his lips, while Hope levelled a hard stare in his direction.

"I can do without the sarcasm," she said. "I understand you're frustrated and, as far as it goes, so am I. I went to bat for you, Alex."

Naomi heard more than professional frustration in the other woman's voice, and was sorry for it.

"This isn't about *me*," he shot back. "It's about—"

He bit off the rest of his sentence, but Douglas was no fool.

"You think I'm next," he said quietly.

Gregory scrubbed his hands through his hair, then rose from the table to clear his plate.

"I don't know who's next," he admitted. "Nobody knows that, except Deere."

"You could be wrong," Hope threw at him. "What then?"

Gregory spun back around.

"Then I'll be bloody glad!" he snarled, and the sound came as a surprise to all of them, including himself. "I'll be *glad* if I'm wrong, because it means that nobody else will die. There won't be any more corpses turning up with anonymous DNA trace samples we can't identify. There won't be any more families to console, and we won't have to live with this awful, creeping sense of impending doom."

There was a short, humming silence in the wake of his outburst, and then Naomi stepped quietly into the breach.

"We know you care about our safety, Alex," she said. "But DCI Hope has done all she can. I think you owe her an apology."

Ava wanted to hate the woman for her beauty, her grace, her intelligence, but that simple act of female solidarity melted any kernels of envy that might otherwise have been burrowing into her heart.

For his part, Gregory agreed. "I apologise unreservedly," he said, with all sincerity. "I allowed all of...*this,* to get the better of me, and I forgot myself. I'm sorry."

Hope nodded, and picked up her fork again. "Forget it."

"Is there really no way of recalling Deere's DNA record?" Naomi asked, after a couple of seconds had passed.

Ava shook her head. "It's been erased," she said. "The process of extracting the original file through a bit of nifty computer hacking would be entirely illegal. We can't make the comparison between the samples we have and Deere's DNA record because, to all intents and purposes, it no longer exists."

"What about the man himself?" Douglas asked. "Does Deere still exist?"

Hope had done her own share of digging, and had come to much the same conclusion Gregory had. However, that information was confidential, and ought not to be shared outside official personnel.

She fought a brief battle with herself, and lost. "There's no record of Carl Deere anywhere on mainstream systems," she found herself telling them. "As for his new identity—"

"Which is?" Gregory asked.

"Don't push it," she growled, and then heaved a sigh. "It hardly matters, anyway. It doesn't seem that his new identity has been used at all, at least not for the past two years. Before then, we've got an address on file for a 'Euan Squires', as well as a driving license and a passport record under that name, but the passport has never been used and no vehicle has ever been registered. He hasn't paid any tax or National Insurance under that identity, and that's because there's no record of him being employed."

"What does all this mean?" Naomi asked her. "Has he managed to get his hands on a fake identity that he's now using, rather than his real name or the new one he was given by the state? How can he possibly live without a regular income?"

Hope gave up on any pretence of professionalism, and stuck her neck out, again.

"I can only assume he's surviving under an alias, or several aliases, and that he's squirreled his money away somewhere," she said. "I went to the old rental address for Euan Squires, and nobody had ever heard of him. The landlord never met him, and he told me that, after six months of pre-paid rent, the tenancy lapsed. He swore the place was never inhabited during that time. As for employment…well, Deere was given over five million in compensation from the Ministry of Justice, so he doesn't have any immediate need to work, especially if he invested his money wisely."

"He's gone to ground," Gregory said, and leaned back against the kitchen counter. "Why would an innocent man do that, especially given a new identity and a nice pay-out from the MOJ?"

"He could have been traumatised," Hope said, reasonably. "It's possible he wanted to disappear because of the degree of public abuse he'd received. In any event, he doesn't want to be found."

"What about bank accounts?" Douglas put in. "Where did the millions go?"

Hope shovelled another spoonful of cooling pasta into her mouth, partly to give herself time to respond, and partly because it was too good not to.

"I'd need a warrant to request bank records," she said, after a thoughtful chew. "And, for the aforementioned reasons, I don't have the legal grounds nor the official approval."

"What would you need in order to get the warrant, or the approval?" Naomi found herself asking.

Hope gave a funny little laugh, which turned into a grimace.

"A body," she said bluntly. "One with a clear connection to Carl Deere…or, perhaps we should say, to Euan Squires."

"Do you have a recent picture of him—Carl, as Euan?" Gregory asked.

Hope shook her head. "Other than the image on his new passport photo? No, I don't have anything else on file. As I keep trying to tell you, we've spent four years trying to distance ourselves from the Deere affair," she explained. "As soon as he was gifted a new identity, the Met sent the newly christened Euan Squires on his merry way and hoped he'd go off quietly into the sunset, giving no further interviews and preferably keeping himself to himself. My seniors are delighted that he seems to have done just that, and the last thing they want to do is risk opening up that old can of worms."

She cleared her throat, having come to the most awkward part.

"On which note, I've been asked to convey a message. With the closure of Operation Shakespeare, the department will no longer be needing the services of an offender profiling unit at the present time," she said. "We thank you—both of you—for all your help, but we've come to the end of the road. I'm sorry, Alex—Bill, Naomi—but there was nothing more I could say or do."

Frustration leaked from every pore of his body, but Gregory reminded himself it did no good to burn bridges. This was a marathon, not a sprint, regardless of the chief constable's current mood.

"Thank you for everything," he said. "We're here, should you need us in the future."

Bill nodded his agreement, and whisked her plate away so that he could replace it with a bowlful of baklava he'd picked up from the market on the way home.

"Try one of these," he urged her. "They're delicious."

"Oh, well…" Hope popped one in her mouth, and, as the honey hit her taste buds, she swore the old fox was weaving some sort of spell through a clever use of pasta and pastries. "Sweet baby Jesus…that's good."

Bill laughed, and patted his stomach. "Explains a lot," he admitted. "Is there any way of getting our hands on that passport picture of Euan Squires?"

Oh, he was a smooth one, Hope thought, but it was impossible to dislike him for it.

"I'm sorry, I can't," she said, for to access sealed records would have been a step beyond which she could never return, and she'd worked too long and too hard to build a professional reputation to see it thrown to the winds.

She stood up, and tucked her chair neatly beneath the table.

"Thank you again for the food," she said. "Now, I really must get back to London. I have things to do."

Nobody tried to stop her, having correctly surmised that the action would have been futile and, after a polite farewell to Alex and Naomi, Bill walked her to the door.

"Take care of yourself," he said, pulling it open for her. "Don't burn the candle at both ends."

Hope turned as if to step outside onto the pavement and then, at the last moment, turned back.

"Alex and Naomi," she said, in a voice low enough not to be overheard. "Are they— together?"

Douglas gave a lopsided smile. "Alex met Naomi before, when we were in America," he said simply. "He never forgot her, and it seems the feeling was mutual. Let's be happy for them, and hope to find something similar for ourselves, hm?"

Ava forced a smile to her lips. "Of course," she said. "I was curious—that's all."

When she stepped out into the chilly night air and made her way across the road with quick, agile footsteps, Douglas remained standing in the doorway.

"Safe travels," he murmured.

CHAPTER 9

One week later

"Are you sure about this?"

Gregory shrugged into an overcoat despite blue skies overhead, with an eye for the weather further north. "Yes," he answered Naomi, who was perched on the end of his bed. "The senior policeman and judge who sent Deere down are both dead. Aside from myself and Douglas, there are jurors and other police staff, journalists, paparazzi, even his mother, but it's hard to know who features on his 'most hated' list. If I speak to some of the prison staff and his former cellmate during his time at Frankland Prison, it might give us a steer."

"Perhaps they're on the list, too," Naomi remarked.

"It depends how they treated him while he was inside," he said, considering the prospect. "Frankland isn't known for being the most salubrious environment, nor the most enlightened. It can't have been easy for him."

He moved to stand in front of Naomi, taking her hands as she rose from the bed to meet him.

"Please, be—"

"*Careful*, I know," she said, with a smile. "I need to be in London this evening for a book event, but Bill says he's arranged to have dinner with a friend, so he won't be alone. By the time he's finished, I'll most likely be on my way back."

He didn't like it, but there was nothing else to be done. "Which friend is he meeting?"

Naomi shrugged. "Somebody from the college, I think he said."

Gregory nodded, and wondered idly which of Bill's colleagues would be chewing his ear off over steak and chips. So long as Bill wouldn't be alone, he could only be grateful to whichever crusty academic would be keeping him company that night.

"And you?" he asked. "Is somebody meeting you in London, as we discussed?"

Naomi touched his cheek, trying to ease the anxiety writ large on his face. "We're getting the train in together, and when you change at King's Cross to head north, I'll be meeting someone from the publishing house," she said. "I hammed it up a bit to my agent about being a stranger in a foreign land, so they're sending a chaperone to make sure I find my way to the bookshop. You can travel with an easy mind, because neither Bill nor I will be alone, which is more than can be said for *me*, knowing you'll be without a friend on the journey—or inside Frankland."

He tugged her against him for a brief hug. "You don't need to worry about me," he said, and kissed the top of her head. "I'm like a cat with nine lives."

"How many are left?"

He smiled, and then glanced at his watch. "C'mon," he said. "Time to go."

It had taken a week for official approval to come through but, eventually, Alex had been granted a meeting with Andrew Irwin, one of the senior prison officers at Frankland Prison, as well as an audience with Gavin Compton, Deere's former cellmate. The three-hour train journey north to Durham was straightforward but, with every passing mile, Gregory felt the distance lengthening between himself and those he loved. As the fields and villages of England whipped by in a flurry, and flat plains gave way to undulating hillsides, he thought of all the times he'd travelled the same route but never with the same sense of urgency. Out there, in one of the many cities, towns or villages that peppered England's green and pleasant land, was a man who'd lost his humanity and, perhaps, his mind. There was no way of knowing where Carl Deere was, and therefore no way to dissuade him from his present course.

No way to help him, either.

With these troubling thoughts circling, the city of Durham materialised through a gloom of mist and drizzle, its cathedral rising tall and majestic like a beacon against the landscape. As Gregory reached for his coat, a shard of sunlight broke through the steely grey clouds and, for a moment, it was magical.

Stepping off the train, he began making his way towards the exit, lost in thought as he considered the best approach to take when he was faced with the notorious murderer that was Gavin Compton.

"Watch your step," a man said, as Gregory passed by and almost tripped on an uneven paving stone.

"Thanks, I—"

Gregory turned to thank the good Samaritan, and saw a striking man of around his own age who'd been lounging against the wall, one hand tucked into the pocket of an all-weather jacket.

"Thought you'd be able to sneak up here without telling your mates, eh?"

Gregory's face broke into a grin. "Ryan."

"The very same," the other man said, and held out a hand to him. "It's good to see you, Alex."

Gregory took the hand that was offered and then tugged his friend forward for a hug. "How d'you know I'd be here?"

"It's the sleuth in me," Ryan said, and it was no joke; he was one of the country's foremost murder detectives, whose patch happened to be Northumbria. "I had a few choice words with Gav Compton earlier today. I always like to see who's planning on visiting him and, imagine my surprise when I spotted your name on the roster. I put a call through to Bill Douglas, who was very helpful in letting me know which train you were on."

Gregory held up his hands. "It's a fair cop."

Ryan nodded towards his car, which was parked on double-yellows nearby, demonstrating precisely the kind of wanton disregard for traffic laws that Gregory could only admire.

"C'mon, I'll give you a lift, and you can tell me what you're doing in my neck of the woods—and why you didn't offer to buy me a beer while you're at it."

"It's a long story," Gregory warned him.

"I'm all ears."

"Are you sure about this?"

It was the second time somebody had asked him that, but Gregory's answer didn't waver.

"Yes, I'm sure."

Ryan didn't press him further. He knew Alex to be a pragmatic, well-reasoned man so, if he was worried about a killer roaming undetected, protected by his former innocence, then they all had cause to worry.

"How can I help?" he asked. "It's not my jurisdiction, but I still have some old friends from my days at the Met."

Gregory was tempted, but shook his head. "I don't want to ruffle any more feathers," he said. "This is an exploratory trip, where I hope to gather more information about the real Carl Deere. I want *insight*, so I can take my findings to DCI Hope and ask her—beg her, if I have to—to re-open the task force."

Ryan nodded, manoeuvring his car out of the city centre towards the outskirts.

"Why are you coming to see Compton?"

"He was Deere's former cell-mate while he was inside," Gregory explained. "I want him to tell me what he knows about the man."

"Do you want company?" Ryan asked.

Gregory smiled again. "Thanks, but it'll probably be easier if I do this alone," he said. "Compton doesn't know me, so I can use that to my advantage. He *does* know you, so if we turn up together it'll put him on his guard."

Ryan acknowledged the truth in that. "Why are you doing this, Alex? Why not leave it to the police?"

"Aside from self-preservation? Because prevention is always better than cure," Gregory murmured. "You're the sword, Ryan, but I'm the shield. I want to protect Carl Deere from himself, as well as from others."

They approached a stark, gated entryway leading into the grounds of Frankland Prison.

"I'll tell you a secret, but keep it under your hat," Ryan said, when he'd brought the car to a stop in the prison car park a few minutes later. "I'm a shield, too, Alex. I try to shield innocent people from the mindless and bloody actions of a minority few, and I hate wielding the metaphorical sword, even when I have no choice. I hope you're wrong about Carl Deere, I really do, because I'd hate to think the system was to blame for what he might have become."

Gregory leaned back against the headrest. "The system might have been the catalyst, but I think the embers were already burning long before he was banged up," he said. "Blame nature or nurture, as you wish, but I can't stand by and let this man carry on."

Ryan understood that kind of duty, and the responsibility it brought. "Stay for dinner?" he asked suddenly. "Anna would love to see you, I'm sure."

Gregory's face softened as he thought of Ryan's wife, and their baby.

"Another time," he said, with regret. "I need to get back to Bill and Naomi."

Ryan's ears pricked up. "Naomi?" he asked. "This wouldn't be the lovely Doctor Naomi Palmer you told me about last year, would it?"

Gregory inclined his head.

"*Well*," Ryan said, and the word was rich with meaning. "Bring her to meet your friends in the north, next time, so we can share embarrassing stories, including the time my sergeant dragged you up to sing a duet of Dolly Parton's 'Jolene' at the karaoke bar."

"I will," Gregory promised, smiling at the memory. "As soon as this episode is behind us, I want to introduce Naomi to all my friends."

Ryan smiled broadly. Being alone was no bad thing, but being *lonely* was something else, and, just lately, he'd begun to worry that Alex had tipped over into the latter rather than the former. Perhaps, with Naomi's help, he would no longer be either.

"Right, well, bugger off," he said, cheerfully. "I've got work to do, and part of that involves preventing Frank from eating his own body weight in beef pasties before the day is out. I left him alone at the Pie Van, and it's almost lunchtime."

He referred to his sergeant, Frank Phillips, whose love of meat and pastry was the stuff of legend.

"I'd put your blues and twos on for that kind of emergency," Gregory quipped, as he unfolded himself from the car. "Thanks for the lift—and the chat."

Before he moved off, Ryan lowered the window to impart one last message.

"I'm happy for you," he said, seriously. "Some people search a lifetime and never find the right person. If you've found yours, hold on tight."

Don't mess it up, was the unspoken advice.

Gregory nodded, and tapped the bonnet of the car. "Go on, and save Frank from himself."

He waved Ryan off, then turned to face the austere frontage of Frankland Prison. Here, there were no Elven arches nor Gothic towers, no trailing ivy or cobbled streets. Function triumphed over form, and the Category A prison was little more than a heap of weathered brick fashioned into two storeys of blocky architecture, its high walls lined with an electric fence and any number of CCTV cameras surrounding the perimeter.

Easy to get in, but not so easy to get out.

"Here goes," he muttered.

CHAPTER 10

"Compton! Visitor!"

Gaz Compton made his way from his cell with unhurried movements, his already sizeable bulk having benefited from four more years of steroid use, such that his muscles bulged beneath the prison clothes he wore, and his neck shone with an oily layer of acne.

"Two days, Jay," he muttered, as he passed the cell of a man who'd fallen behind in his payments. A little reminder was usually all that was needed to enforce 'Gav's Law', but there were exceptions; young men after his crown, who refused to pay their debts and liked to spread ideas about it being time for new leadership...

Gav soon took care of idle tittle-tattle.

It was awfully hard to gossip, when you no longer had a tongue.

He was curious about meeting the doctor who'd come all the way from London. There'd been plenty of students over the years who'd come to stare at him like an attraction at the circus, or journalists looking to write his story and paint him as a victim of a broken society. They'd used big, fancy words to describe his upbringing, slagged off his mum a bit, and talked about various neuroses and diagnoses they wanted to pin on him to explain why, somehow, he wasn't to blame for plunging in the knife or pulling the trigger.

It was all bollocks.

So, his dad roughed him up a bit, back in the old days. So what? That was par for the course, on the street where he grew up. All right, he *might* have taken it a bit too far, when he'd thrown his mother out of a second storey window. He remembered being angry about that, at the time, but, as his dad had explained, she'd had it coming.

They all did.

If this quack wanted to sit and talk about his dreams or his misspent youth, he could play up the trauma of a lost soul for the bloke's benefit. A bit of sympathy never went amiss, did it? It was easy enough to find some head doctor who believed they could *help* you and *change* you, so you could become what society wanted you to be.

The fact was, Gav enjoyed violence, and always had.

Was there a name for that?

"Half an hour, Compton."

He eyed the screw to his right, who lowered his eyes deferentially.

"If—if you go a bit over…it doesn't matter too much."

Gav grunted, and stepped into one of the private visitation rooms, usually reserved for meetings with a solicitor. Inside, he saw a tall man standing on the other side of a four-seater table screwed to the floor, his dark hair slicked with a light dusting of rain. Once the preliminaries were over, and the prison officer had stationed himself on a stool in the corner, the man invited him to sit.

"Mr Compton? Please, have a seat. I'm Doctor Alex Gregory."

He held out a chair and, after a second's pause, Gav took it.

"Thanks for agreeing to meet me," Gregory continued, pulling back the chair opposite to settle himself.

"Not much else to do round here, son," Gav said, with a slow smile. "Question is, who are you, and what do you want from me?"

Straight to the point, Gregory thought, and it was no bad thing. Neither of them had time to spare, albeit only one of them had the freedom to put it to good use.

"I'm here to talk to you about Carl Deere."

Gav's face betrayed no emotion or reaction, whatsoever. "Oh? Why's that, then?"

"I understand you were his former cellmate?"

Gav nodded. "That's no secret. Been a while since he was given the Golden Ticket, though."

He referred, of course, to the reversal of Deere's conviction and his subsequent release.

"Heard he's done all right for 'imself," Gav continued. "I could tell you about a few wrongful deaths I'm innocent of, but I've never been 'anded a few million quid to say 'sorry' for it."

Gregory merely smiled. "I'm sure you've met all kinds of people."

"Could say the same o' you," Gavin shot back, and took a slurp of sugary tea from the cardboard cup Gregory had remembered to bring. "Seems your name crops up all over the place, the more I ask around."

It should have been no surprise to learn that Compton had done his homework, but knowing that he'd been thoroughly researched and dissected was enough to elicit a small shudder of disquiet along Gregory's spine.

"All good things, I hope."

Compton grinned, flashing gold-capped teeth.

"What're you cookin' up, Doc? Workin' on your next book, and lookin' for a few juicy titbits about Carl, is that it? Because there's a price for everythin', and mine just went up."

Now, Gregory was the one to smile. "Yes, I—"

"On the other hand," Compton continued, lazily. "Could be that you're feelin' a bit nervous, now that old bastard, Whittaker, was found dead the other week, and Campbell before 'im." He chuckled, linking his thick fingers on the tabletop. "We read the news in 'ere, too," he said.

"That's precisely why I'm here," Gregory said, and decided to try a bit of flattery. "I'm not completely unaware of the reputation you command, Mr Compton, and I certainly believe nothing happens inside these walls without you knowing or finding out about it."

Compton said nothing but, to demonstrate the point, turned to the officer on his right shoulder and asked for a cigarette, despite the room being a designated 'no smoking' area.

He lit up the proffered tab.

"So, if I'm catchin' your drift, you think Carl's tried his hand at a bit of murder," Compton said, after the first couple of puffs. "You reckon he's getting' a bit of his own back. Is that it?"

"You tell me," Gregory said, leaning forward. "Most people seem to think Carl Deere wouldn't be capable of murder."

Something flickered in Compton's eyes, possibly disbelief, and Gregory caught it.

"How was Carl, as a cell mate?"

Gav lifted a shoulder. "Been so long, I can hardly remember."

Gregory looked at him, into the scarred face of a man who'd killed for money, for fun and out of sheer boredom, and knew he'd never tell him what he needed to know. No amount of cajolery or coercion—even contraband, if he'd been minded even to offer it—would sway Gavin Compton.

Unless…

Perhaps there was one thing that could persuade him to talk; something he couldn't arrange for himself, not like drugs, knives or cigarettes.

"The Kray Brothers had a real *legacy*, didn't they?" Gregory remarked, taking Compton by surprise. "All the big names of that era are icons now, aren't they? Plenty have had movies made about them, or television shows."

Compton gestured with his cigarette. "So?"

"Wouldn't you like to have that kind of fame?" Gregory said. "Wouldn't you like to have people write books about you? To be so feared, revered, and *fascinating* that they'll talk about you and write about you—even make films about you, for years to come?"

Of course he'd thought about it. Gav had seen *Peaky Blinders*, just like everyone else.

"Doesn't matter to me," he lied. "Everyone who knows me knows what I'm about."

"Yes, but think of all the people who *don't* know," Gregory purred. "Your story will never reach them, until, eventually, you'll be forgotten and some new kid on the block will obliterate your memory."

That hit a nerve.

"Who's gonna tell my story, then?" Compton demanded. "*You*?"

"Maybe."

Compton laughed. "Who'd read it?" he scoffed, but Gav was interested…oh, yes, he was interested.

"There's a huge market for true crime," Gregory said, and that was true. "It so happens I was thinking of writing up a collection of my case histories, including my experiences with some of the country's most notorious criminals. It would be a shame for your name not to be included in that list, don't you think?"

He paused to let that sink in.

"Of course, if you feel worried about repercussions—"

"Nothing worries me."

The denial was flat, and unequivocal.

"So," Gav continued, stabbing out his cigarette in the palm of his hand without a flinch, before tucking it into the breast pocket of his shirt to save for later. "You want me to tell you about Deere, and, in exchange, you'll write about me in your book. Is that the measure of it?"

Gregory nodded, and Compton took his time thinking about it.

"VINDICTA SERVIVIT FRIGUS," he said.

Gregory blinked. "Sorry—?"

"You 'eard me," Compton said. "I said, *vindicta servivit frigus*. It's what Carl wrote on the wall in our cell, and what he used to repeat again and again, like a broken bloody record. No idea what it means...some gibberish or other. He was always blabberin' and mumblin'."

Gregory's schoolboy Latin was long out of date, but he thought he could take an educated guess at the meaning.

Revenge served cold.

CHAPTER 11

Romola Harris wasn't proud of the work she did.

Back in her university days, when she'd been a dewy-eyed English graduate with dreams of becoming the big investigative reporter of her generation, she'd foregone nights out at the Student's Union to write and lay out the student magazine, having been appointed editor during her final year. She'd turned down theatre trips to follow up leads and scoffed at the very idea of romantic dinner dates, in order to speak to confidential sources about the *real* reason the English departmental budget had fallen for the seventh year in a row.

Romola had a nose for a story, and nosiness had taken her all the way to *The Daily Scoop,* where she'd been offered her first graduate opportunity as a crime correspondent. That was back in the days when there'd been a residual interest in things like 'truth' and 'facts', as opposed to the more recent shift towards soundbites and easy, celebrity gossip that wasn't too taxing on the brain. She'd never intended to stay at *The Scoop* for more than a year, having set her sights on bigger and better things.

That had been sixteen years ago.

With bills and a mortgage to pay, her ideals had flown merrily out of the window. Still, from time to time, the echo of her former self returned, often while she scrolled through a batch of salacious paparazzi images or typed up her latest fluff piece about who was cheating on who, and with whom. 'Old Romola' would whisper about an interesting case at The Old Bailey or remind her of the research from criminal justice academics whose findings were unequivocally at odds with political policy. Sometimes, when she followed the whisper, it led to a sensational story.

Such had been the case with Carl Deere, and her fine nose for scandal meant she was the first to break the story about his arrest. Her editor had been delighted, sales of *The Scoop* had sky-rocketed and she'd taken home a tidy bonus, thank you very much.

It hardly mattered that Deere turned out to be the wrong collar; the damage had been done—and she'd already spent the bonus.

"Romola? Post for you."

A stack of letters was dumped unceremoniously on her desk and, bored with the opinion piece she was writing about the latest celebrity divorce, she began sifting through them.

Her eye focused on one in particular, which she opened:

Dear Ms Harris,

I hope this letter finds you well—or as well as can be expected for one who lives off the proceeds of human misery.

I wonder if you remember me? Probably not. Today's news becomes tomorrow's fish and chip wrapping, does it not?

Allow me to refresh your memory.

My name is Carl Deere. I was born in Canning Town, London, and spent my working life as a computer analyst for a private equity house, before I was lured, trapped and falsely imprisoned for the murders of several male sex workers.

Is this ringing any bells for you?

Perhaps your own headlines might be a useful reminder:

SOHO SADIST CAGED
STREETS SAFE AGAIN AS
KILLER PUT IN SLAMMER
SICK PSYCHO FINALLY BEHIND BARS

There were many others, but the above were my personal favourites, betraying as they did the extent of your moral bankruptcy.

There are many things I could say and many things I could do. Instead, I have decided to give you a reprieve, of sorts, in order to redeem yourself. This is your ONLY chance, Romola. Don't waste it.

I have a scoop for you, which you won't want to miss.

CD

There was no further message, nor instruction, but enclosed within the envelope were printed copies of the articles she'd written, in chronological order of their publication, as well as recent reports following the deaths of DCS Simon Campbell and Judge Quentin Whittaker. The first letter of each man's surname had been circled in red, and Romola began to wonder about the significance; no killer had been found in either case, she knew, and statements from the detectives in charge of those investigations had tailed off, lately.

Was Carl Deere suggesting that Thomas Andersson had been responsible for their deaths, as he had been for the other crimes?

No, she answered her own question. Andersson was incarcerated, and, while he might have cause to resent Campbell, it had been another judge who'd handled his trial, not Whittaker.

Whereas…

It *had* been Whittaker who'd put Carl Deere behind bars, if she remembered correctly.

What did he mean when he said he had a 'scoop'?

Did Carl Deere know who murdered Simon Campbell and Quentin Whittaker? Perhaps he'd made some connections whilst he'd been in prison, and heard some whispers on the grapevine…

All thoughts of celebrity divorce now forgotten, Romola began to hunt for her old notes, her nose following the unmistakable scent of a juicy story.

———

Gregory drummed his fingers against the edge of an uncomfortable faux leather chair in the waiting room at Frankland Prison. After a brief but interesting discussion with Gavin Compton, he'd spent the past two and a half hours confined in the unventilated space, with its shabby beige walls and stained carpet tile floors, and he was starting to lose patience.

He was on the cusp of leaving, when the outer door opened to reveal an enormously fat man in uniform.

"Doctor Gregory, is it?"

There was no apology for being left to wait, only the smug air of a man who knew he was the one with all the power. *Psychopath?* Gregory wondered, and mentally recalled the checklist.

"Mr Irwin," he said, reading his name badge. "Thank you for agreeing to meet me."

This time, he chose not to offer his hand, surmising correctly that Irwin wasn't a stickler for personal hygiene.

"Where d'you want to talk?" Irwin demanded. "Here or in a meeting room?"

"Wherever you're most comfortable."

Since nobody else was around, Irwin shrugged his shoulders and wheezed across the room, whereupon he slumped into one of the sagging chairs.

"Can I get you something?" Gregory offered. "A drink?"

Irwin shook his head, and began picking something from his teeth. "Just had lunch."

Gregory sat down again. "In that case, let's get down to it," he said. "I'm here to discuss a former inmate, Carl Deere."

Irwin continued to pick his teeth, but his eyes sharpened. "What about 'im?"

"I understand you were responsible for his welfare, during his time here," Gregory said. "Is that correct?"

Irwin shrugged again. "Suppose so," he said.

"I was hoping you could tell me about his character, your impressions of him…that sort of thing."

Irwin tugged his shirt back over his belly. "Look, mate, I don't care about their characters," he said. "I come in, I do my job, I go home again. That's it.

I don't stop to wonder whether this one's innocent or that one's guilty, because I'd be chasin' my tail."

"Of course," Gregory said. "All the same, how would you describe Carl, thinking back to the man you knew?"

Irwin called to mind Carl Deere, and the words he could have used to describe him.

Skinny.

Runt.

Whizz-kid.

Sadist.

"He kept his nose clean," he said, blithely. "Did as he was told and didn't get into any trouble while he was here…that's about it. Why d'you ask?"

Gregory didn't answer directly. "Mr Deere certainly has plenty of cause to feel resentful about how the system treated him," he said. "I can't imagine prison life would have been a walk in the park."

"What d'you mean?" Irwin snapped. "He never made a single complaint while he was inside. There's nobody who'd say he came to any harm while he was in here."

Gregory watched the other man's eyes shift this way and that, saw the sweat bead on his upper lip, and wondered just how much Deere had really endured.

"*If* somebody of Carl's temperament and personality felt they'd been wronged or mistreated, there's a chance they'd turn their sights on the source of that mistreatment and take revenge in some form or another, wouldn't you agree?"

"What're you gettin' at?" Irwin blurted out. "Deere's long gone, and good riddance. What's all this talk of revenge and mistreatment?"

"Call it a hunch," Gregory said. "Nice watch, by the way." He nodded at the Omega adorning the other man's wrist.

"It was a present," Irwin told him. *To himself,* he could have added.

"You must have some very kind friends," Gregory said lightly. "Look, Mr Irwin, cards on the table: I think Deere has changed. Two men were murdered recently, both of whom were intimately connected with Deere's imprisonment. I believe he was responsible for the deaths."

Irwin laughed, but it was all bluster. "Sorry to hear it, but all it means is that I might be seeing Carl in here again, soon enough."

"Unless he finds you before the law catches up with him," Gregory averred.

The mirth died on Irwin's face. "Come again?"

"You heard me," Gregory said. "I'm here to warn you. I think Carl is seeking out everyone who wronged him during that time in his life. I don't know how things really were in here, and I'll never know. Only you and he know the true answer to that. But, from one human being to another, I'm here to tell you that he's on a mission to punish. I'm here rather than the police, because they won't act without evidence and they don't have enough of that, yet. So, you need to be vigilant—we all do."

Irwin frowned, and then his forehead cleared. "I remember who you are, now," he said, pointing a stubby finger in Gregory's direction. "You're the bloke who wrote that profile about him."

"Not about *him*," Gregory corrected. "About Andersson, as it turned out."

Irwin's lip curled, and he folded his arms across his chest. "I think you've lost your marbles, Doc— but, even if you're right about this cock 'n' bull story, I think you should be lookin' a bit closer to home. I'm not the one who stitched him up, that was down to you and your police mates."

Gregory could have argued, but it would have been a waste of breath. "If nothing happened in here, as you say, then there's nothing to worry about," he said, rising from the table and reaching for his coat. "On the other hand, if you can think of any reason Carl Deere might feel vengeful towards you then it's time to take precautions, because he's out there and he's on a vendetta."

Irwin thought of the times he'd humiliated, ridiculed and abused Carl Deere. "I sleep well enough," he declared.

"Good for you," Gregory said. He moved towards the door, while the other man remained lost in thought. "One last question, if it isn't too much trouble."

Irwin was distracted. "Eh? What now? The Ghost of Christmas Future comin' to haunt me, or somethin'?"

Gregory's lips twisted into a tight smile. "Does *vindicta servivit frigus* mean anything to you?"

Irwin's face screwed up in confusion, then fell back into folds. "Sounds like gobbledygook, to me."

Gregory nodded, and reached for the door handle.

"Just a minute—"

Gregory waited.

"I might've seen somethin' like that written on the wall beside Carl's old bunk," he admitted. "Thought it was some old nonsense, just like half the stuff these buggers write. What does it mean?"

Gregory put it into terms he could understand. "It means, 'Watch your back'."

With the words still hanging on the air, he slipped quietly from the room and made swiftly for the security gates and freedom beyond.

CHAPTER 12

"I hope you don't mind having an early dinner? I need to catch a train later this evening."

Bill and Jacob were seated at one of the bistro tables inside an intimate little French restaurant, not far from Hawking College. It was almost empty since it wasn't yet five o'clock, and the other diners consisted entirely of couples.

"Not at all," Bill said, and kept his eyes trained on the wine list. "Do you have a preference?"

"White, although I'm planning on having the boeuf bourguignon, so I suppose I should opt for red," Jacob replied, and tore off a bit of bread from the basket to nibble on.

They ordered and, once they were alone again, he gave a self-conscious laugh. "I—ah—I never really thought we'd end up here…like this."

Bill took a sip of his wine, then set the glass down again. "That makes two of us," he said. "I don't have private dinners with students, as a rule."

"I'm a mature student," Jacob reminded him. "After the course ends, I won't be your student at all."

The proclamation left all manner of things unsaid.

"What would we be, if not student and professor?"

Jacob's eyes twinkled in the light of the candle that flickered between them. "Friends, I hope…at least, to begin with."

Bill stared at him for so long, he thought he'd made an error of judgment.

"Perhaps, I'm mistaken? I thought there might have been something more than a penchant for rigorous academic debate between us."

Bill laughed at that. "You're not mistaken," he admitted. "I can certainly be your friend. As for anything else…let's see how things go, shall we?"

Jacob reached a hand across the table to brush his fingers. "Thank you," he murmured. "It's been difficult to find someone I can relate to, on every level."

"I'm sure that's not true."

Jacob gave a self-deprecating laugh. "I find that, when I tell people I'd like to be an offender profiler, or perhaps a forensic psychologist, they run a mile in the other direction."

Bill chuckled. "People worry you're going to psychoanalyse their every move," he said. "They worry about being judged."

"Judgment," Jacob said, and let the word roll around his tongue. "Yes, we're all guilty of that, aren't we?"

They paused to thank the waitress who delivered their meals and, after the first couple of bites, picked up their conversation.

"I wonder how many people I've judged, subconsciously or otherwise," Jacob mused. "It must be an occupational hazard, when you have clinical training running alongside ordinary social conditioning."

"It's something to be aware of," Bill agreed. "We may be members of the psychological profession, but we're human beings, first. We're susceptible to the same flaws and foibles as the people we try to help."

"How did you find it, working with violent offenders?"

"At Southmoor Hospital?" Bill cast his mind back. "It's been a few years since I spent any considerable time there, so Alex would be the best person to ask about that, nowadays. I think we'd both agree it was rewarding work, for the most part, because we accept from the outset that neither one of us is anybody's 'saviour'. We do our best to ease invisible pain of the mind, and hopefully prevent re-offending. Ours is a dual purpose."

"Do offenders *want* to be helped?"

Bill looked up from his food and nodded. "*Always*," he said. "Beneath the bravado and belligerence, there is always a soul crying out for help. The mind isn't so very different from the soul, as it happens—in fact, they could be one and the same thing. I haven't met a single violent offender who didn't want to know why they were the way they were, despite what they might say in their first therapy session. At the very least, people like you and me can help those in torment to understand their own actions and behaviours and begin to regulate them. Understanding can be the first step towards change."

"But not always," Jacob was bound to say. "Perhaps there are some who don't accept they're at fault."

"No," Bill agreed. "Occasionally, there are those who are beyond help."

"How do you know?" Jacob asked, while his food grew cold. "How do you know when to stop trying and just accept the person for who and what they are?"

"Well, that brings us around to the topic of the essay I set your class regarding the link between neuroplasticity and reoffending," Bill replied, with a smile. "Studies have shown that, when children are severely traumatised, the neural connectors in their brain are often damaged or stunted, which can lead to problems later in life. However, the brain has a remarkable capacity for replenishment and regrowth, given the right conditions. If we provide those conditions, as a society, I don't see any reason why a person couldn't change from whatever form they'd taken, over the course of time."

Jacob propped his chin on his hands. "You really do believe the best of people, don't you, Bill?"

"It's part of my job," came the reply. "Some of the offenders you speak of have been abandoned or terribly hurt by those who're supposed to love and protect them. They were given no model for 'right' and 'wrong' behaviour and, if they were, it was usually an exemplary model of how *not* to behave. By the time they come to me, society has already rejected them, and they've rejected themselves, too. I must believe they're better than even *they* believe themselves to be, if we're to make any progress at all."

Jacob nodded slowly and then reached for his glass, which he raised in a toast.

"To you, Professor," he said. "May you always look for the best in people."

"May they always look for the best in *themselves*," Douglas added, and watched Jacob knock back a mouthful of wine.

"Cheers."

"Detective Inspector Ian O' Shea, meet your new boss, DCI Ava Hope."

Hope looked up from her position at the bar at their local boozer, where she'd been nursing a generous glass of gin and tonic.

"Welcome to the team," she said, and gestured to the motley crew of people who were crowded around one of the larger tables at the pub, attempting to wind down after a busy week fighting crime in one of the largest and busiest capital cities in the world.

"Thanks," O'Shea said, and nodded at Carter's suggestion that he get a round in for all of them. "I just got off the train, actually."

"Oh? Where've you come from?"

"Birmingham."

"You don't have much of an accent."

"Born and raised in London, to Irish parents," he said, sliding onto the stool beside her. "I was in the Vice Squad down here for a while."

"Why'd you leave?"

O'Shea thanked Carter for the pint, and took a healthy swig before answering.

"A girl," he said. "She moved home to Birmingham, and I followed her like a puppy."

He huffed out a laugh, presumably at his younger self.

Hope raised a glass to that, in mock salute. "Sounds like you're a wise sort of guy," she said, turning on her stool to face him properly.

She was taken aback to find herself looking into the laughing eyes of a blond-haired, buff-bodied demi-god.

Well, that was unexpected.

Deciding it must've been far, *far* too long since she'd enjoyed any male company, Ava spun away again, delivering a stern internal lecture to herself about professionalism and the various ills of workplace relationships.

"What about you? What's your story?"

Hope sucked in a long breath, which ended on a bit of a laugh.

Her story?

Where should she begin?

"Born in London, stayed in London, went through Police Training College and by a mixture of grit, tenacity and hard work, I find myself commanding a team of ballsy, cheese-and-onion-crisp-eating layabouts," she replied, deadpan.

"I said 'sorry' about the crisps!" Carter called back over his shoulder, having overheard that portion of the conversation.

"Slob!" she threw back, and reached for a handful of peanuts, choosing not to question their origin in order to appease her rumbling stomach. "So, with all this glamour, are you after my job, newbie?"

O' Shea laughed, and took another swig of his pint.

"Not yet," he replied, and she had to respect his honesty. "Maybe in a year or so?"

"What makes you think you'd get it?"

He angled his body and favoured her with his most dashing smile. "Because, for one thing, I only eat ready salted," he said. "Less offensive, by far."

Her lips twitched. "And for another?"

"It would only be in the circumstances of you having been promoted first," he said. "Looking back on your meteoric rise through the ranks, it doesn't seem like you're stopping at DCI."

"Maybe I like the hours," she argued.

"Nobody likes the hours," he retorted. "But we do them because we want to get somewhere."

"Get somewhere? What about public service and balancing the scales of justice?"

"You and I both know, 'justice' isn't doled out evenly," he said. "It's an imperfect system, and sometimes people slip through." He shrugged one muscular shoulder, getting on a roll. "Take the case of Jack Denby," he said. "Miserable bastard spent his life taking money from poor pensioners to line his own pockets, through pyramid schemes and God knows what else, and the Financial Conduct Authority can't put together a strong enough case to pin him down for fraud. Slimy git was probably feeling pretty chuffed with himself. Fast forward six months, and he winds up dead on the banks of the Thames."

Hope knew the case, although it had been investigated by another of the teams that made up the Homicide and Major Crime Command Unit.

"Did they ever find out who was responsible?" she asked, but already knew the answer.

O'Shea shook his head. "Nah, and they probably never will," he said, not sounding particularly cut up about it. "Look, the bloke was a cretin—we all know it, and *he* probably knew it, too. Most likely, he got into some bad business with one of the gangs and they put a hit out on him. It was a professional job, no DNA evidence, no mess. The point is, 'justice' caught up with him in the end, didn't it?"

"I suppose it did."

"Exactly," he said, downing the last of his drink. "And, just between you, me and the gatepost? I can't say I feel all that sorry for him. Do you?"

Hope chose not to reply, but she did turn around in her seat to look at him again. "Another one?" she asked.

"You've twisted my arm."

CHAPTER 13

Andy Irwin was not required to work the number of late shifts that would ordinarily have been expected of him; such was the privilege of rank and position within the parallel hierarchy at Frankland Prison. However, for the sake of appearances, he put in a token late shift on the last Friday of every month. It happened to coincide with collection day, which was a nice bonus and allowed him to go about the business of receiving monies owing to him without having to worry about any prying eyes.

It happened to be the last Friday of the month, so it was after nine o'clock by the time Irwin left Frankland and began his journey home through the darkened streets of County Durham, a wad of dirty cash burning a hole in the breast pocket of his jacket. Lately, he'd been wondering whether it was time to upgrade the modest house he'd lived in for more than twenty years to something bigger, better and more befitting his new station in life. The investments he'd made had borne plenty of fruit, and the ongoing income stream from some of the bigger fish in the prison was more than enough to sustain a nice five-bedroom affair in an upmarket little corner of the county, maybe even with a cinema room and a wine cellar.

Not that he drank wine, of course, but that was beside the point.

The problem, as always, was finding novel ways to clean up his money, so that any prudent mortgage lender wouldn't worry themselves too much about where it had come from. To that end, he'd scooped up a little nail bar and a souvenir shop down in Hartlepool—both of which did *amazingly* well, considering there was hardly any footfall in either. He supposed he had Carl Deere to thank for the financial advice, if he'd been a man in the habit of thanking anyone for anything.

Thoughts of Deere reminded him of the conversation with that doctor earlier in the day, and his mood took a turn for the worse.

"Meddlin' bugger," he growled, and flew over a mini roundabout to the accompaniment of angry toots from other road users.

It made him feel better to exert a bit of power.

Carl Deere.

In the privacy of his own company, he could admit to feeling a certain degree of unease. It had been four years since Deere had departed Frankland, never to darken his door again. In fact, he'd been the man to open the gate for him, and hand him his first tenner for a taxi ride to the station. He'd have done anything to put distance between the two of them, *anything* never to see Deere's face ever again.

Hello, Officer Irwin.

Carl's voice replayed in his mind, and, despite his best efforts to shove it away, the past came rushing back.

Who's in charge now, Andy?

To his shame, tears began to fall down Irwin's puffy face and, spotting the comforting yellow sign, he steered his car into a nearby McDonalds' car park, where he cut off the engine and turned on the radio as he willed the memories to recede.

Lift so much as a finger to me again, Andy, and everyone in this prison will know what happened here, today. I'll tell them all about how much you enjoyed it, too.

Do you understand me?

Irwin looked up, staring through the windshield into the night, watching but not really seeing the people walking in and out of the fast-food restaurant for their late-night fix of hamburger and fries.

Would Carl come for him, as the doctor seemed to think he would?

He was a free man, able to go wherever he wanted. Why would Deere come back to Frankland to seek him out? After what happened between them, he'd never touched Carl again, either by word or by deed—he hadn't dared. He'd left him well alone, except for necessary interactions and their weekly financial summit, in which Carl had continued to lend his expertise in growing his nest egg, alongside Compton's and others, while siphoning off a healthy percentage for himself. In those days, when he'd thought the system had left him inside to rot without a bean, Carl had been compelled to find an alternative means of income and he'd more than succeeded in the pursuit.

Before the shift in their power dynamic, things had been far more one-sided. Andy remembered every blow he'd delivered, every casual smack and foul-mouthed insult designed to keep the man at heel. It wasn't personal; he'd dished out the same treatment to more inmates than he could count, but the fact that his efforts had ultimately failed with Carl was neither here nor there—if the man wanted to avenge himself for any of it then he could, and nobody would stop him. That much was painfully clear: nobody within the police was looking at Carl for the murders of Whittaker and Campbell, otherwise it would have been one of the flat-foots to pay him a visit today, not Doctor Alexander Gregory.

Unless, of course, there was nothing to worry about, and it was all a storm in a teacup.

Yes, that's what it was.

Irwin scrubbed his hands over his face, wiped the sweat from his brow with a grimy shirtsleeve, and laughed at himself for allowing that fancy London doctor to mess with his mind. The idea that Carl Deere could have become a *killer* was…

"Ridiculous," he muttered, but his voice sounded hollow even to his own ears, for he'd seen what Deere was capable of. He hadn't killed anyone during his time at Frankland, but Carl had done other things…things that scarred the mind and left a person weak with fear.

Carl Deere could kill, and maybe even enjoy himself doing it.

He'd seen it in his eyes.

The music on the radio changed, and Bruce Springsteen began to croon about having been born in the USA. Listening to it, Irwin wondered whether it might be time for him and his family to make a more permanent change.

Running away? his mind whispered.

If he was, there was no shame in it.

Engrossed in the fantasy of starting a new life, Andy didn't hear the soft click of the backseat door opening and closing.

"Hello, Officer Irwin."

Andy thought his mind was playing tricks, that thoughts of Carl Deere had conjured him into being. But he saw the whites of the man's eyes in the rear-view mirror and found there was no time to speak nor cry out, no time to thrust open the car door and make a run for it before a garotte whipped around the heavy skin at his neck. Pulling the wire tight, Deere braced both knees against the back of the driver's chair and held on, breathing hard with the effort of slicing through Irwin's trachea while he writhed and choked, fighting against the constriction that cut through the layers of skin like a hot knife through butter.

Eventually, Irwin stopped jerking and his body slumped, chin propped against his chest while blood and other matter leaked down the front of his shirt. Once his heart rate had returned to normal, Deere gave a deep sigh of contentment and retrieved the wire, waiting patiently for a crowd of teenagers to pass by the car, praising Irwin's foresight in having forked out for tinted windows.

"Night, night, princess," he said, and laughed to himself before slipping back into the shadows.

CHAPTER 14

"It roughly means, 'revenge served cold'."

Gregory supplied the translation for Naomi, who stood in front of the murder wall in his bedroom. He'd scribbled additional notes on the paintwork soon after returning from Durham, including the Latin phrase, which he'd written in block capitals beneath the central image of Carl Deere.

"I suppose it makes his intentions known," she said. "He isn't trying to hide them."

"Deere hides his physical self in order to complete his mission," Gregory qualified. "Aside from that, I agree with you: he isn't ashamed of what he's doing and it seems to be a necessary part of the whole enterprise that people should understand exactly *why* he's doing it."

"Did Compton tell you anything else?" she asked. "Anything useful?"

"Not especially," Gregory admitted. "Gavin Compton enjoys the sound of his own voice and wants to create a legacy for himself, so it was easy enough to come to an agreement with him in exchange for information. I didn't specify exactly what my conclusions would be about his life's work, if and when I ever do write him into a book and, in any case, I declined to specify a time frame for its glorious release."

"Sneaky," Naomi said, with approval. "And, take it from one who's just suffered the ignominy of a poorly-attended book signing, writing down your life's work ain't all it's cracked up to be."

Gregory chuckled. "Should've written a spicy romance," he remarked. "They'd be queueing in the aisles to meet the woman behind Sylvester McManly's 'pulsating bratwurst'."

Naomi grinned. "Sylvester McManly?" she queried. "Is that your alter ego?"

"I'll leave that for you to decide," he said.

They looked at one another, then Naomi folded her arms.

"Coming back to Mr Compton, do you think he knows more than he's saying, or has that well run dry?"

Gregory rubbed the back of his neck, kneading the knots which had formed sometime during the past eight to twelve hours. "My feeling is that he could tell me more, once he's drawn things out a bit and come to trust me. Unfortunately, time is a commodity that's in short supply at the moment."

"Yes, killers don't tend to work to the same schedules as everyone else, and they usually have the advantage—Carl Deere certainly has," Naomi said. "What do we do now?"

Gregory gave in to fatigue and lay down on the bed, feeling his bones cry out in relief.

"I can try Compton again in a couple of days," he said. "The prison officer—Andy Irwin—is my immediate concern. Either man could be on Deere's list, but only one of them is an easy target and it would take more than Deere's level of clout to put out a hit on Gavin Compton."

"Even if Carl has the money and influence to pay for someone to execute Gavin Compton, he wouldn't have the pleasure of driving the knife home himself," Naomi remarked, having assumed correctly that Deere derived great relief from the act of killing and would rather not sub-contract the task to a prison thug.

"I think you're right," Gregory said. "If he was responsible for Whittaker and Campbell's murders, then we can safely assume Carl isn't shy about getting his hands dirty. Both men died spectacularly badly, in a manner that was both execution-style and frenzied, which is quite a feat for Deere to accomplish."

"Yeah, but he wouldn't be the first," she said, thinking back to some of the patients she'd spoken to over the years. "The internal narrative execution killers employ, the one they must believe in order to continue their plans and keep any finer feelings at bay, tells them that murder is a fair punishment. However, their true reason for killing leaks out during the act. I wouldn't be surprised if Deere actively enjoys it now, which might have come as a surprise to him."

Gregory nodded. "If past cases have taught me anything it's that, without intervention, a killer's behaviour tends to escalate," he said. "Deere was a sadist before, but perhaps he didn't acknowledge that to himself. He might have passed previous incidents off as being 'consensual', and therefore nothing to worry about. The truth is that, judging from their own individual and unbiased accounts, Deere coerced his partners into performing acts to which they didn't fully consent, leading to mental and, in some cases, physical trauma. As for his current endeavours, murder is a disproportionate response to false imprisonment, and the plain truth is that Carl's developed a taste for it."

"What's the next degree of escalation for him?" she wondered aloud.

"I wouldn't be surprised if future killings betray even more aggression, as he sheds the guise of 'execution and punishment' and comes to terms with his own enjoyment," Gregory said, staring into the man's dark eyes, which looked back at him, unblinking, from the picture on the wall. "My only hope is that he'll make a mistake somewhere, which allows us to find him more quickly."

Before he could seek out the next person on his list, he added silently.

"Another feature of his narrative would be 'recognition'," Naomi pointed out. "If Deere wants people to know *why* these victims are being punished, surely the best thing would be to make sure that information was brought into the public eye."

Gregory agreed. "I have a list of one or two journalists who could be in danger themselves, considering some of the coverage and opinions aired about him at the time of his arrest and trial. I agree that Carl would want his perceived successes to be documented and broadcast, but that would conflict with his hatred of the press. I can't decide whether he'd seek any of them out, so I plan to get in touch with a few of them, just to be on the safe side."

"What about the police team?" she asked. "There must be others who were involved in the original case, aside from Simon Campbell."

Gregory nodded. "Yes, I have a few names that stand out—"

"DCI Hope, for instance?"

He shook his head. "No, I don't think Ava was involved in that case."

Naomi decided to face the elephant in the room, head on. "Perhaps Carl might see her as a target, given your closeness."

"We are on good terms, generally," he mused, and Naomi rolled her eyes towards a higher power, if there was one.

"*Alex.*"

He looked up at her tone, noted the elevated right eyebrow and watchful look in her eye, and the penny finally dropped. "Ah, you think—" He cleared a sudden constriction in his throat. "You think we were…an item?"

An item? she thought. Was this the turn of the last century?

"It had occurred to me, yes," she drawled.

"Perhaps I've been too unguarded," he thought aloud. "At one time, yes, there was an attraction. But—"

"But?" she prompted him, when nothing else seemed to be forthcoming.

Gregory looked at her. "There was the memory of you," he said, with simple honesty. "Whenever I've met someone, who may have been lovely in every respect, I've found myself comparing them with you, Naomi. I haven't met anyone else I could imagine more than just…"

He made a turning motion with his hand.

"*Sex* isn't a dirty word, Alex," she said. "I don't expect you to have been sitting by the fireside all these months, pining away for me. You're a healthy man, and you're not a monk. In the interests of full disclosure, I haven't exactly been a nun this past year, either."

Gregory was surprised by the swift and vicious stab of jealousy that rocketed through his system. "In any case, there's nothing between DCI Hope and myself other than a shared professional interest in removing killers from the streets."

"I think Ava might disagree."

His heart sank at the thought of having been the cause of any pain. "She didn't say anything… how could I have missed it?"

DCI Hope was proficient at concealing her thoughts, Naomi decided, but, even so, they were there to be seen for anyone who cared to look. It was quite a contrast to find that Alex, given all his skills at reading the minds of others and healing them so far as he was able, was so blind to the emotions of those closest to him—especially himself.

"I could be way off base," she conceded. "On the other hand, sometimes we don't see the things we don't *want* to see."

He nodded, and told himself to be more careful in future. "Regardless of whether it's the case or not, what matters is what Carl Deere, or Euan Squires, or whatever he happens to be calling himself, *believes* to be the case," he said.

"Therefore, if he's garnered the impression that DCI Hope is close to anyone who was involved in his incarceration, then she has to be added to the endangered list—as do you."

Naomi shivered, and rubbed her hands over her arms. "I don't know how you sleep in this room," she said suddenly. "It's too macabre, with all of this stuff on the wall."

"I don't, really," he admitted.

"In that case, why don't you come and sleep in my room, instead?"

He sat up with such indecent haste that she laughed.

"Is that a 'yes, please'?"

He rose to his feet and closed the distance between them.

"Yes, please," he said softly, and held out his hand.

Sixty miles south, another couple lay naked, side by side in the semi-darkness.

"Well," O'Shea said.

"Well," Hope agreed.

Ian turned to look at her profile, and wondered if it would be greedy to expect a second round.

"They told me you were standoffish," he said, deciding not to repeat some of the less complimentary adjectives that had been levelled at the woman sprawled beside him.

Ava closed her eyes, wondering what madness had possessed her. "Look," she said. "I don't make a habit of this, and nor should you. If I find that you've been running your mouth to all and sundry, so help me, I'll kill you."

The grin he gave her was devilish. "What would be the method?" he asked, walking his fingers towards her.

She slapped his fingers away, but could feel herself weakening again. "I mean it," she said, turning to look at him. "I won't have our working relationship affected by anything that might have—"

"*Might* have happened?" he queried. "I'd say things *definitely* happened, wouldn't you?"

"Whatever," she said, between gritted teeth. "Don't think that this changes how things will be on Monday morning."

"Understood, boss." To his credit, he said the word without any undertone. "All joking aside, I understand; really, I do," he said, shuffling into a seated position so that she was treated to a close-up view of his abs, which only served to irritate her further. "Look, there was a connection, and we acted on it. There's nothing wrong with that."

"Right," she said, shuffling upward herself, though far less smoothly as she tried to keep the bedsheet over herself. "Exactly."

"I've seen you naked, remember?" he said, watching her fiddle with the cotton covering. "It was a beautiful view."

For a second, she was no longer a murder detective but simply a woman. "I—thanks. I don't need you to say things like that," she muttered.

"I don't need to," he agreed. "But I say it because it's true."

She stole another glance in his direction. "I—it's been a while since I was with anyone like this," she admitted. "Probably, too long. I've forgotten the etiquette."

"Are you telling me you've experienced a drought, recently?" he replied, and the mischief resurfaced. "In that case, it seems only fair that we remedy it."

He reached out to brush the hair from her eyes.

"What do you say, chief inspector?"

"I've never met a more *arrogant*, self-assured—" she began, but then reconsidered her position. "Fine. Twenty minutes, then I'm kicking you out of my house."

"You're a hard woman," he declared.

A moment later, her mouth was caught up in a kiss and, however briefly, she was able forget the horrors she'd seen that week and all the weeks before.

CHAPTER 15

The next day

Bad news travelled fast.

Alex and Naomi awakened to the persistent drone of his mobile phone, which bleated out a tinny version of an old Tears for Fears song about the virtues of shouting to let it all out.

Gregory fumbled for his phone, recognised the caller and didn't bother with any pleasantries.

"Mmfh?"

"Alex? It's Ryan."

"Jesus, it's—what the hell is the time?"

Alex peered through the gloom and thought he read 'five-fifteen' on the clock.

"Too late for someone you and I both know," Ryan said. "Our mutual acquaintance, Officer Irwin, was found dead in his car during the early hours. I asked a mate in Durham CID to let me know if they caught anything interesting over the next couple of weeks and he called me straight away. I've just been down to take a look and, I can tell you, it ain't pretty."

Alex sat bolt upright, and Naomi watched him with sombre eyes.

"How did he die?"

"Asphyxiation," Ryan said. "Wire garotte to the throat. He was found slumped in his car in a puddle of his own blood. It would have taken extreme force and a steady pair of hands to finish off a man of that size."

Alex frowned, thinking of Carl Deere. Years ago, he'd been a man of average height and build, verging on slim. A man like that would have struggled to overpower someone of Andy Irwin's bulk, but it was very possible Carl had acquired some prison muscle during his time at Frankland; in fact, with the means at his disposal, he could have changed almost anything about his appearance, which only made their task all the harder.

"I'll speak to the Met again—" he began to say.

"Durham CID are already making noises about this being a local job," Ryan warned him.

"I told them about your concerns but, the fact is, Irwin was in bed with all the wrong people. If you launder money for convicted murderers and gang members, you have to expect they won't take kindly if you cream a bit off the top."

"It complicates things," Alex agreed.

At the other end of the line, Ryan looked back over his shoulder to where a forensics tent billowed in the early morning wind.

"Look, I've got to go, but I wanted to give you the heads-up," he said. "The offer still stands, Alex. If you need me, I'm here."

Alex opened his mouth to decline, then looked across at the woman lying beside him and thought better of it.

"I'll call you," he said instead. "I need some time to think."

"Think fast," Ryan advised him, and rang off.

There was an undeniable spring in DCI Hope's step as she covered the short distance from the tube station to the main entrance of The Yard, but she was damned if she'd put it down to anything so demeaning as having spent the night with Ian O'Shea.

Certainly not.

Her mood was far more likely to have been improved by the sight of the sun shining on the Thames, bouncing off the skyscrapers lining either side of it so that an otherwise grey city was elevated to something quite special.

One look at her sergeant's face was enough to bring her back down to Earth with a *thud*.

"Good night, was it?" Carter enquired, while stirring instant cappuccino into a mug featuring the slogan, 'KEEP CALM, I'M A POLICE OFFICER'.

He didn't bother to hide a smirk.

"Better than yours," she shot back. "What was it? Kebab and a box set?"

DS Carter made a face because, of course, she was right. "No need to rub it in," he grumbled, and then sidled over to her desk. "*Well*?"

"Well, what?"

"Aww, don't be like that."

"Carter, I haven't the foggiest idea what you're rambling on about."

He slurped his coffee, and eyed her over the rim. "You were seen leaving the pub together, guv. Might as well own it."

Hope gave a long sigh, which caught in her throat as Ian spotted her across the open-plan office space and flashed one of his bright white smiles.

She looked away, sharply.

"I'll own your *badge*, if you don't stop gossiping and get back to work," she hissed. "Who else knows?"

Carter took pity on her. "I don't think anybody else noticed, to be honest."

Ava searched his face and found him sincere. "Thanks," she said. "The last thing I need is to be undermined any more around here."

Carter made a sound of sympathy. "Seems a nice enough bloke," he remarked. "You could do a lot worse."

"Thanks, Dad."

He grinned, and drank more of his coffee. "I'm in favour of anything that puts a smile on your face and gets you off my arse," he said. "Especially when I tell you who's waiting to see you."

Hope rolled her eyes. "You didn't think to mention that first?"

Carter shrugged. "Priorities," he said. "Anyway, Doctor Gregory's wearing a hole in the carpet over in Meeting Room 2C. Apparently, there's been another one."

"Another what?"

"Murder," he said. "What else?"

She expelled a long sigh. "Got any more of those cappuccino sachets?"

Carter nodded. "You want a Jammy Dodger as well?"

Hope spared a fleeting thought for her waistline, then threw caution to the wind. "Just give me the packet."

CHAPTER 16

Gregory stationed himself beside one of the windows, where he could watch the people of London scurry about their daily lives. As always, he wondered how many of them had been adulterous to their spouse or unkind to their children; he wondered how many had stolen, lied or cheated to move up the professional ladder, and how many had been violent or had the capacity to be.

All of them, he decided, and caught his own reflection staring back at him in the glass.

"Alex?"

He turned to see DCI Hope hovering in the doorway, one hand balancing two coffee cups while the other clutched a notepad and a packet of Jammy Dodgers.

"Dextrous," he remarked.

"I thought you might need a coffee," she said, and nudged the door shut with her hip.

"I always need a coffee," he replied. "Thanks."

While he took a fortifying gulp, she searched the lines of his face and chose not to think about the shadows beneath his eyes, or wonder what—or *who*—had been keeping him awake at night.

"Why are you here?" she asked. "I've already told you, the task force has been shut down. The Chief Constable isn't interested in using a profiling service. If he finds out you've been in the office, questions will be asked."

"I'm here because there's been another murder," he said. "It's connected to Carl Deere, just like the others."

"Who?" she asked.

"Andrew Irwin, formerly a senior prison officer at Frankland, which is where—"

"Carl Deere spent his time inside. Yes, I remember."

He watched her take a long, deliberate swig of coffee.

"Well, he was strangled sometime late last night. His body was discovered in a McDonalds car park in the early hours."

Hope hadn't picked it up on the internal bulletin, but that was probably because she'd muted the daily notifications, there being too many murders, rapes and other violent crimes to deal with in London without needing to worry about those as far afield as Durham. That being said, nothing had been reported in the mainstream news either, which begged an obvious question.

"How do you know about this?"

"Friends in helpful places," he replied. "Incidentally, I went to speak with Irwin yesterday before he died."

Her eyebrows raised a fraction. "Quite a coincidence," she muttered, and reached for the packet of biscuits. "I take it you went up to Frankland on a fishing expedition."

"I hoped to warn some of the people on Carl's list," he explained, and might have added that it was a job the police should be doing themselves.

Hope bit into a biscuit and then offered him the packet, which he refused.

"Oh, for God's sake, Alex...have a biscuit."

Now, it was his turn to raise an eyebrow. "Is this a new interrogation technique?" he asked. "Administer sugar and caffeine, so the suspect is kept permanently on edge?"

"You're not a suspect," she said, and then gave in to curiosity. "So? What did you learn from Irwin before he died?"

"He was frightened," Gregory replied. "He'd heard about Campbell's death—Whittaker's, too—and had already made the connection back to Carl. So had Compton."

"Compton?" She frowned, then her brow cleared. "*Gavin* Compton, you mean?"

"Compton was Carl's cellmate for most of the time he was at Frankland. He and Irwin probably knew him as well as anyone."

"And you thought one of them might be able to tell you his whereabouts?" She snorted.

"No," he said quietly. "I'm not that naïve. I don't imagine they were friends, or that Carl would have trusted either one of them with that kind of information. But I thought I'd be able to warn them of the very real danger they were in, and, in return, they might be able to paint a picture for me of the man they'd known."

"Why? Why do you *care* what kind of man Carl was?"

"It's the only way to find him," Gregory replied. "Carl Deere is nothing more than a spectre, a ghost from the past. Whoever and whatever he is now is a chameleon; he could *look* like anyone, *live* anywhere and go by whichever name he likes."

And it was terrifying, he might have added.

"But it's all superficial," he did say. "Carl may not exist anymore on paper, but his character remains the same and that's what we need to look for. You can run from many things, but you can't outrun your own mind."

She stared at him for a long moment while she processed that last devastating statement, then cleared her throat. "You think he's gone mad, then?"

He thought of all the ways he could reply to a sweeping question like that; all the politically correct answers according to the sensibilities of the day and, he need not add, his own life's work to rehabilitate those society had deemed unfit.

Mad.

It was a word laden with meaning, but he decided to keep things simple.

"I believe the accepted definition of 'madness' refers to a person suffering from a serious mental illness," he replied. "I don't believe that Deere falls into that category, because having a desire for revenge is not a serious mental illness."

"What is it, then?"

Gregory thought of all the times he'd sat in a stifling consultation room with his mother, listening to her self-justifications and warped narratives, all the while knowing the truth of her crimes and the very real effect they'd had on him, her last surviving victim. It would have been so easy to kill her while she slept behind the high walls of Southmoor Hospital; so easy to leave a string of rosary beads as a weapon, so that she could end her suffering as well as his own, and pass it off as mercy.

No, he thought. Revenge was not psychosis, although obsession and compulsion could lead a person there, and they looked awfully similar to the untrained eye.

"Revenge is self-indulgence," he snapped. "We all feel wronged, in large and small ways, throughout our lives; a feeling of injustice doesn't give us carte blanche to run around murdering and maiming people."

"You don't think Deere has any right to seek payback?" Hope shot back. "More often than not, people don't get the justice they deserve—I know that, better than most, because—" She sucked in a frustrated breath. "I see it, every day. *Every day*, Alex. I do my best for the victims, but I can't bring back the dead, or wash away the crime that's broken them, irretrievably. I can't blame some of the survivors for taking matters into their own hands—can you?"

Gregory was surprised by the question, coming as it did from a guardian of the state.

"I didn't think you'd have so much sympathy for individual vendettas," he said. "I hear vigilante violence is frowned upon by the Met."

She turned away, and thought about snaffling another biscuit to take away the bad taste in her mouth.

"So it is," she said. "Thank you for the reminder."

Gregory's eyes ran over her face in that infuriating way again, cataloguing the non-verbal behaviour she was trying to hide, seeking to peel back the layers of her skin to see what festered beneath.

She ignored it, and met his gaze with a cool one of her own.

"So, what did Irwin and Compton have to say about Deere?" she asked him.

Watching her, Gregory saw the disquiet and the restlessness, so clearly, but it was not his place to interrogate the secrets of her heart, nor wonder who and what had hurt her so greatly that she would set her duty aside to avenge it.

Instead, he told her of the Latin phrase Carl Deere had repeated during his time at Frankland Prison, and explained its meaning.

"*Revenge served cold,*" she repeated softly. "I'll admit it doesn't sound good for Carl, but I don't understand why he would mount a vendetta against Irwin, specifically. Why him and not any of the other prison officers?"

"Every execution poses some degree of risk and Carl is an organised killer," Gregory replied. "He wouldn't want to waste time, energy, or the possibility of exposure killing someone who wasn't worth the effort. My best guess is that Irwin treated him particularly badly. He wasn't the kind of man to be troubled by scruples and, having met him briefly before his untimely demise, I can confirm he didn't bowl me over with his decency—nor his personal hygiene, I might add."

"You think he was dirty?" she asked him.

Gregory nodded. "Literally and figuratively. The only difference between someone like Andy Irwin and Gav Compton is that one is notionally free, while the other isn't. I'm told—"

"You're told an awful lot," she muttered.

"I'm easy to talk to," he countered, with a smile.

Hope thought of all the patients he'd spoken to during the course of his clinical career, including all the people who'd killed, and began to pace the room to escape the uncomfortable feeling that, even if she chose *not* to confide in him the darkest secrets of her soul, he'd probably see them lurking behind her eyes anyway.

It was unnerving.

"Does this...*oracle* of yours happen to know whether there was any identifiable DNA found at Irwin's crime scene?"

"Too early to say," he replied. "But, if there is, and it matches the DNA samples found at the other crime scenes, that'll make three remarkable coincidences."

The sarcasm wasn't lost on her.

"It would add weight to your theory," she corrected him.

"Enough to re-open the task force?"

Hope turned to look through the glass panels separating the meeting room from the rest of the open-plan office space. DCS Crossman was establishing herself amongst the staff and had taken to regular, unplanned walkabouts, which could prove awkward if she were to happen across the pair of them. For the time being, there was no sign of her new boss, but it would be unwise to tempt fate.

She needed to wrap things up.

"What do the local police team have to say about Irwin's death?" she asked. "Do they have any suspects?"

Gregory told her the truth, as he knew it. "They think it's gang-related," he said. "That's because Durham CID don't really know anything about the possible connection to Carl Deere. Without an active task force, there's nothing to connect their investigation to any other active investigation, nationally. On paper, Prison Officer Andrew Irwin had no connection to Judge Whittaker or DCS Campbell, so they have no reason to look into it. But, with our help—"

"*Our*?" she queried.

He said nothing, and waited patiently for her to step into the middle ground.

"You're asking a lot of me," she said, and pointed an accusatory finger. "It's taken *years* to get where I am today, do you know that?

This job didn't fall into my lap, I had to fight for it."

"*How* did you fight?" he asked her.

"What do you mean?"

"I want to know how you fought," he said quietly. "Did you always play it safe, Ava, or did you take risks, sometimes?"

She gave a funny half-laugh. "No, I didn't always play it safe," she admitted, and an image of Ian O'Shea popped into her mind. "I took calculated risks based on the evidence at hand."

"Doesn't investigating Carl Deere count as a calculated risk? We can save lives if we act now," he said, and took a step forward, compelling her to listen. "Do nothing, and you allow fear of reprisals to outweigh your own good judgment. I wouldn't have pegged you for a coward, DCI Hope."

She turned on him, as he'd known she would.

"*Nobody* calls me a coward," she snarled. "I'm many things, Alex, but never that."

Too late, she saw the gleam in his eye and gave a self-deprecating laugh.

"You're a cool one," she said, letting the anger drain away. "You know which buttons to press, don't you?"

"It's my job to try," he said, without remorse. "I'm a doctor, so my first duty is to preserve life. I have to use whatever means necessary, including a bit of reverse psychology when the occasion calls for it."

"What do you expect me to do?" she said, raising her hands in mute appeal. "There are no evidential links connecting any of the murders to Carl Deere, or whoever he is nowadays. I can't start a witch hunt based on supposition."

"What if it was based on instinct—what you know to be the case but can't prove, just yet?"

"Funnily enough, that isn't covered in the PACE guidelines," she said. "Instinct is unreliable—just as unreliable as a criminal profile, some might say."

If her remark was intended to hurt him, it fell short of the mark. Even if Gregory hadn't already been immune to personal attacks, he had more important things to worry about than wounded pride.

He planted his palms on the table, head bowed as he made his case.

"I hope I'm wrong but, if I'm not, Carl will move on to the next person and then the next, and he won't stop until he's sated himself.

None of us knows when that will be; he could have a finite list of people he'd like to punish, or one that just keeps growing as he becomes more powerful and more addicted to the rush."

Hope didn't argue with his logic. "You mentioned Carl's 'list', earlier," she said. "How do you know he has a list?"

Gregory raised his hands to scrub at his face, then reached inside the breast pocket of his coat to retrieve a folded piece of A4 paper. "I don't *know* he has a list, but I think it's extremely *likely* that he does. Judging from past victims— assuming they *are* his victims—any such list will contain the names of those people he blames for his incarceration and loss of reputation. First, Campbell, the man who led the operation against him, and who gave the order to set up the honey-trap to ensnare him. Then, Whittaker, the man who brought down the hammer at The Old Bailey—"

"Whittaker was a judge," she interjected. "He was only doing his job; the jury had already made their decision. He was bound by the sentencing guidelines for murder."

"Yes, but that doesn't prevent Carl viewing it as a public spectacle of betrayal," Gregory said. "Reason doesn't factor into the emotional element of his crusade."

She nodded, thinking of the psychology of one who kills for a cause, whether real or imagined.

"You speak as if he's *compelled* to kill," she said quietly. "You don't believe he's in command of himself, or that he could stop at any time?"

Gregory thought about it, then shook his head.

"The ultra-violence tells us Carl is both fearless and imaginative," he replied. "He enjoys his victims' fear, and likes to give it an opportunity to percolate, if he can. The anticipation is part of the rush. You have to factor in the physiology, too; every time Carl takes another life and feels vindicated, his brain will release a huge dose of dopamine into his bloodstream, and he'll feel like a king. That's a very intoxicating, very addictive feeling."

"He should have stuck to sugar and caffeine," she said, and Gregory managed a smile.

"It would have been better for all concerned," he agreed, and then handed her a copy of the list he'd drawn up. "Here's a list of all the people I can think of who might be of interest to Carl. It covers the names of all the police personnel I can remember having worked on the case; the prosecution legal team; jury members; journalists, prison officers and…" *Profilers,* his mind whispered. "I've kept Campbell, Whittaker and Irwin's names on there, for completeness."

Hope unfolded the paper, glanced at the list of names and her eye was immediately drawn to one in particular.

Ian O'Shea.

Beside it was written 'original investigative team'.

Confused, she thought back to her conversation with the man himself only the day before, when he'd told her he hadn't been involved in the Deere case whatsoever while he'd been stationed at The Yard.

Could there be two officers with the same name?

It seemed wildly improbable.

"You're sure about all the names on here?" she asked, as casually as she could.

Gregory nodded. "They're the men and women who played a pivotal role in Carl's incarceration. Why?"

She shook her head, fearful now for a man she barely knew, and looked back down at the list. There, written at the very end, was the name 'BILL DOUGLAS'.

"You've missed a name off the list," she said softly.

He smiled, and made a turning motion with his finger.

"Look on the other side."

She flipped over the paper and there, in stark black and white, was his own name.

Hope looked up and into his eyes, which were unreadable pools of dark green. She thought back to the crime scene at DCS Campbell's home in Kent, where he'd been brutally murdered, then of Whittaker and Irwin.

Gregory could end up the same way, and they both knew it.

"All right," she said, coming to a decision. "This the deal, Alex. I'll reach out to Durham CID and see what I can find out. If there's any possible connection between the murders, we can try to find it. I'll look into things *quietly*, which means no more turning up at The Yard unannounced. This conversation remains unofficial, but I'll check the whereabouts of the other people on this list and keep the lines of communication open. It's the best I can do."

He felt some of the weight lift from his chest.

"Deal," he said simply.

CHAPTER 17

Ian O'Shea whistled an old show tune to himself as he filled the kettle in the break room, and was enjoying a vivid daydream about a long-legged, brown-eyed beauty when the lady herself appeared before him.

"Chief inspector," he said, and smiled broadly. "Are you feeling thirsty?"

There was a ludicrous glint in his eye, and Hope wondered what kind of signal she was emitting to attract so many cocksure men in her life; from Carter's buffoonery to O'Shea's general air of arrogance, it seemed there was a surplus going around.

"No, thanks," she said, and then nodded towards the kettle in his hand. "You seem to have settled in awfully well."

"I've had a warm welcome," he replied, and had the nerve to wink at her.

She glared at him. "I told you before, Ian. I don't mix business and pleasure."

"You told me," he said, and gave his tea a quick stir before cupping the mug between his hands. "Seems you broke your own rule, last night."

She opened her mouth to deny it, but emitted a small, strangled sound of outrage instead.

"*Ian—*"

"In the first place, let's get one thing straight," he said, becoming serious. "I told you I wouldn't jeopardise your position, and I won't. Nobody can overhear us talking, so I thought it might lighten the mood to share a joke, that's all." He shrugged. "If that isn't allowed...then, okay, I understand."

"What's the second place?"

"Hm?"

"You told me the first place," she muttered. "What's the second place?"

"Oh," he said, and leaned back against the counter. "In the *second* place, I enjoy rattling your cage, chief inspector. Your eyes turn an even deeper shade of ebony when you're pissed off—as you are, now—and they're very beautiful eyes."

Tears threatened, unexpectedly.

"Hey," he said, taking a step towards her. "I'm sorry, I was only trying to be"—he made a panicked gesture with his hands—"*romantic*, I suppose. I'm not much good at it, apparently."

He looked so crestfallen, she had to smile. "I don't need romance," she lied. "I need a decent inspector on my team. Is that understood?"

He searched her face for a long moment, before nodding again.

"I understand," he said softly.

She wanted to scream. At whom, and about what, she didn't know. Thrusting that aside, she reminded herself of the reason she'd sought him out in the first place.

"Incidentally, the Deere case came up in conversation earlier," she said.

"Oh, yeah? How come?"

"After Campbell and Whittaker's deaths, there's been renewed interest," she said, and watched as he turned away to make a cursory inspection of the fridge. "One of the analysts said they recognised your name from the original file, but I thought you said you didn't work the case?"

There was only a second's pause.

"No," he said. "They must be thinking of someone else."

She glanced at the notice board with its assortment of flyers and fire evacuation plans, but saw nothing except his name printed on Gregory's list.

Carl Deere's list.

"Do you want to do something, later?" he asked. "I could throw a pizza in the oven, or we could get a takeaway?"

"Sure," she said, and gave him an easy smile. "We all have to eat."

"We certainly do—" he began, and smiled hugely.

"Don't you dare finish that sentence, O'Shea."

His smile grew even wider. "Yes, ma'am."

Gregory made his way along the Embankment, heading east in the general direction of Blackfriars station. Not far from there stood one of London's most infamous buildings: the Central Criminal Court of England and Wales, more commonly known as 'The Old Bailey'. Though it had an illustrious history, the building was unprepossessing from the outside; no different from a hundred other imposing structures erected at the turn of the twentieth century. The court took its name from the street upon which it had been built, which had once formed part of the ancient wall or 'bailey' that had fortified the City of London centuries before, such that its foundations were inexorably linked to that hallowed ground— along with all the vengeance that society had wrought in the name of justice, now so much a part of the fabric of the place that it might have been a living, breathing thing.

Gregory considered all this as he walked, not with his usual purposeful stride but with a slower gait that was less assured. He thought of the first time he'd been called upon to give evidence at The Old Bailey, in a case concerning a young woman with acute paranoid schizophrenia and a penchant for killing old men who resembled her uncle, who was long dead at the time. Gregory could remember how nervous he'd been taking the witness stand inside Court Number One, surrounded by the musty scent of old wooden panelling, suffocated beneath the weight of oppressive legal jargon. Then, he thought of Carl Deere, and of how he must have felt upon entering that same austere courtroom charged with committing multiple murders, all the while knowing himself to be innocent.

It was nightmarish.

But, as Gregory had come to realise, 'innocence' was a word to which very few people could truly lay claim.

There had been no hope for Carl back then; not against a jury of twelve who'd seen and heard the press coverage of the murders for which he stood charged. They'd read the sordid and violent details of how young, vulnerable men had come to die before taking up their civic duty, which precluded an absence of bias. They'd drawn their own conclusions as to the killer's evil character—and who could blame them? Not the victim's families, nor any 'right-thinking' person who abhorred murder. For them, as for the jurors, it became a question of putting a face to an already tarnished name. The prosecuting barrister for the Crown, acting upon evidence provided by the police team, had been eager to give them a name upon which to transplant all their fears and furies: *Carl's* name, and they'd thoroughly wiped the floor with it.

Isn't it true, Mr Deere, that you have a penchant for sexual domination?

My private life is my own—

Isn't it true, Mr Deere, that you groomed the person you'd come to know as Mark Shaunessy, with a view to eventually orchestrating a liaison in which you hoped to engage in auto-erotic sex, followed by brutal murder?

No! Of course not—

And so the line of questioning had continued. Witnesses had come forward to testify about Carl's predilections for domination and aggression; past behaviour which, though not directly relevant to the facts of the case, went to credibility, motive and character. Their information might have been sourced through entrapment, but the police were nonetheless in possession of full transcripts of recordings between Carl and their undercover operative, which included explicit conversations in which Carl had been goaded into discussion of his deepest and darkest fantasies. But fantasies were not the same as reality, as Gregory knew better than most. One might kill a hundred people in their own mind, but that didn't make them a murderer, as every writer of crime fiction could attest. All of that was moot in Carl's case, where the jury had found, beyond all reasonable doubt, that his self-confessed fantasies had slipped over into reality such as to be indistinguishable from it and, to make matters worse, he'd acted upon those fantasies and had taken life.

And, while the foreman of the jury had pronounced their collective verdict against Carl Deere, Thomas Andersson had killed again.

Suddenly, Gregory found himself weary of putting one foot in front of the other, and the muscles in his legs felt leaden inside the casing of his skin. To his tired eyes, the paving stones appeared greyer than before, dirty with the footsteps of millions who'd trodden the same path before him, grimy with wear and tear. They were as dirty as he felt, knowing that a thousand disturbing images from the past were harboured somewhere in his mind.

Perception, he thought. It coloured everything.

Gregory stood for a while; a tall, lone figure against the waterfront, until the barking of a dog roused him to turn and take stock of his surroundings. He'd come to rest at the foot of the gardens belonging to the 'Inns of Court', which were the four governing organisations for practising barristers in England and Wales. When the Order of the Knights Templar had been dissolved hundreds of years ago, their property and lands had eventually passed to the barristers who now occupied the princely buildings inside the gardens, which had been split into a series of collegiate-style offices known as 'chambers', law libraries, dining and communal spaces as well as the cloisters and Temple Church, all of which resided within a rarefied oasis of calm amid the hustle and bustle of one of the largest and most densely-populated cities in the world.

As he peered through the ornate iron railings separating the gardens from the Embankment, Gregory was reminded again of Carl Deere and of the prosecuting barrister who'd subjected him to a grilling during those long, soul-destroying days spent at The Old Bailey. He knew, as any sane or rational person would know, that Leonora Stewart QC had done nothing more than discharge her duty to the Crown, to the best of her ability. She harboured no particular bias towards Carl Deere, having brought any number of similarly brutal murder cases to trial during the course of her distinguished career, and with the detachment required of any professional she probably viewed him as the latest in a continuing stream of cases to be tried according to the laws of the land.

No more, no less.

Gregory also knew that Carl Deere was no longer interested in man-made laws, which he'd already found to be fallible. He operated according to what he told himself was a higher, 'natural' law, taking whatever necessary action he deemed appropriate to redress what he saw as a cruel and wicked imbalance caused by the actions of many, including 'tools' of the State such as Leonora Stewart.

Perhaps it was madness, after all, Gregory thought, but not without reason.

Following their discussion, he trusted that DCI Hope would be making her way through the list he'd compiled, but she was a busy woman with an already full caseload that might prevent her from acting as quickly as either of them might have liked. What was he to do in the meantime? Wander the streets of London and Cambridge beneath a cloud of fear and trepidation, waiting for Carl Deere to tick more people off his list?

Not forgetting that he would be on Carl's list, too. He was under no illusions about that.

There was one thing he could do...

He could act.

Act now.

CHAPTER 18

On Thursday afternoons, Leonora Stewart routinely hung up her wig and gown early, and made her way across town from the Inns of Court to the cosy, private nursery her three-year-old daughter attended. It was a small thing, she supposed, but a welcome relief from the crushing weight of motherly guilt to be able to collect her child halfway through the day, following which they would often feed the ducks on the waterway leading back to their comfortable home in a part of London known as 'Little Venice'. Though Mark, her husband, was a successful barrister in his own right, they both knew it was she who laid claim to being the main breadwinner in their household. It was a title she'd never sought, nor carried with any particular sense of pride except in knowing that, together, they could give their daughter the kind of education that would set her up for a successful life. In the early days, she'd experienced a flush of professional pride whenever she'd won a case, but time and experience had taught her that the 'wins' were never so cut and dried as they seemed. A person tended to be dead or injured, a family devastated, and another person incarcerated at His Majesty's pleasure.

Was that 'justice'?

Apparently.

"New case in your pigeon-hole, Miss Stewart!"

Any jurisprudential questions were forestalled by a timely interruption from her head clerk, a man by the name of Percy Kimble, whose disembodied voice intercepted her stealthy dash towards the main door. Ostensibly, his role was to manage diaries, negotiate fees and otherwise avert any legal mishaps on behalf of the gaggle of wig-toting intellectuals who inhabited the premises. More importantly, Percy had one of the most incisive legal brains in the city, despite having never acquired more than a few O-levels sometime in the late seventies. It was a foolish person who mistook the matter, by virtue of his pronounced East End accent and humble demeanour—but they soon learned.

Leonora popped her head around the clerks' room door. "I was just on my way out—"

"O' course, love. Don't want to hold you up. All the same, I *did* 'ear from the CPS—they want someone to confirm availability for this un by the end of the day," he said, and waggled a file to inveigle her.

She hesitated. "What is it?"

Percy leaned forward. "Bit o' juicy murder," he said, in a hushed whisper. "It's that geezer who snatched the young girl from Clapham Common. By all accounts, 'e 'ad 'is way, then dumped 'er body all the way dahn in Southampton. 'e 'ad a wife an' three kids waitin' for 'im at 'ome, n'all, the dirty so-and-so."

Percy tutted, and left the rest unsaid.

For her part, Leonora had always detested those who hurt children, especially now that she was a mother herself. Prosecuting the scum of humanity might not be pleasant work, but it was necessary, and she had never been one to shy away from her public duty.

"What defence is he planning to run?"

"Well, he's claimin' it's all a set up by the police," Percy said, and gave a shake of his head to indicate that it was by no means the first time either of them had heard that particular line before. "You've gotta larf, ain't yer? Accordin' to these killers, every copper in London's as bent as a nine-bob note."

Leonora's eyes flicked to the big clock on the wall.

"He's looking to plead 'not guilty'?" she said, and thought back to the recent reports of the murder, which had been damning. It was enough to whet the appetite of any prosecutor, and she wasn't hypocrite enough to claim otherwise. "Oh…hand it over, and I'll take a look after Zoe goes to bed. If the CPS want an answer any faster than that, they'll have to look elsewhere."

He handed her the file, with a smile like a Cheshire cat.

"All right, I'm off," she said, and raised her hand to give him and the other clerks a wave. "See you bright-eyed and bushy-tailed in the morning."

"Don't know how you manage to stay so cheerful," Percy said. "But it makes a change from the usual. Mind 'ow you go, love."

"Cheerio," she called back, and made for the exit.

As she opened the outer door, Leonora almost collided with a tall, dark-haired man standing on the doorstep outside.

"Sorry—" she muttered.

"My fault—" Gregory replied, and stepped aside to allow the lady to pass.

He rang the outer bell for good measure, then made his way towards the clerks' room.

"Can I 'elp you, guv?"

Gregory was faced with an enormous bear of a man, somewhere in his early to mid-sixties, but in possession of eyes so sharp they belied his advancing years.

"Yes, please. I was hoping to speak with Leonora Stewart—I'm afraid I don't have an appointment, but it's urgent."

From the corner of his eye, Percy spotted her walking past one of the large sash windows towards the gardens, where he happened to know she'd be making her way towards the Embankment to pick up the Bakerloo Line towards Warwick Avenue.

"What's it concernin'?"

Gregory hadn't rehearsed an answer to such an obvious question, so he stuck to the truth.

"Her safety," he said, and Percy's eyebrow's drew together in alarm.

"What d'you mean by that?" he growled, and began to draw back from his chair.

Gregory held up his hands, and tried again. "I'm Doctor Alex Gregory," he said, and retrieved his driver's license for proof of identity. "I'm a clinical psychiatrist and criminal profiler, and I was involved in one of Leonora's past cases—you remember Carl Deere?"

Percy grunted, and sank back into his chair, much to the other man's relief.

"Hard to forget. Feller's out of prison now, ain't 'e?"

"Yes, but his whereabouts is unknown, and, frankly, there are concerns. You'll have seen the reports of the murders of DCS Campbell and Judge Whittaker?"

"Course," Percy replied. "What's all that to do with Miss Stewart?"

She'd always be *Miss Stewart* to him.

"I believe Carl Deere has turned vigilante," Gregory said. "She might be at risk, along with other parties who were involved in his prosecution. He's out for revenge, and I believe she should be made aware of the danger."

"If that's the case, why ain't the police 'ere tellin' me all this?"

"They probably will be, in the next few days," Gregory replied. "Unlike them, I don't have an entire city to police, so I thought I'd expedite matters since I was passing. Please—can I speak with her?"

Percy Kimble had often said, especially to the young men and women who came to work for him, that it took more than commercial acumen and an encyclopaedic knowledge of the legal world to be a first-rate clerk. It required an understanding of *people*. Developing insight into their basic psychology was the one thing that kept an office full of intellectual egos happy, because, with a bit of well-placed flattery and careful management, they made sure that every barrister believed themselves to be all that they *claimed* to be, in the annual *Chambers and Partners* digest.

In the case of the man standing before him, a simple assessment told Percy that Doctor Alex Gregory wasn't looking to make any personal gain; he was there for one reason and one reason only, which was to perform a public service.

That frightened him more than the most miserly of instructing solicitors.

"You just missed her," he said, wasting no further time. "Nora does a half day on Thursdays unless she's in court. If you run, you'll catch her before she reaches the Underground— she'll be headin' for the Bakerloo line from the Embankment."

Gregory could have kicked himself for failing to recognise the woman who'd passed him in the doorway.

Reading his thoughts with ease, Percy raised a hand and tapped his wiry grey hair.

"Changed her colour," he explained. "She had it all lightened up, just in the past fortnight. That's probably why you didn't recognise her."

Gregory nodded, and turned to leave.

"I'll try 'er mobile!" Percy called after him, seconds before the outer door slammed shut again.

In the relative hush that followed his departure, he put a hand to his stomach, feeling deeply unsettled. He was worried now, as he thought of the woman he'd known for almost twenty years, whom he'd nurtured and watched blossom into an assured, intelligent lawyer. She was a rare flower, that one, with a rare heart, and if anyone were to hurt her—

Percy's gnarled fingers trembled as he keyed in her number, and the distended knuckles on his arthritic hands turned white as he gripped the receiver and listened to it ringing out.

No answer.

"C'mon girl," he muttered. "Pick up, love. Pick up."

He tried the number six or seven times, then covered his eyes with the same shaking hand.

He hoped there was nothing to worry about, but he'd seen the doctor's face and read the message in his eyes. He didn't need to be any kind of expert in human behaviour to understand what was written there.

Danger.

Leonora was in danger.

He tried her number again, then again, and again.

There was still no answer, because she'd left her phone sitting on her desk upstairs, where its shrill cry echoed around the empty room.

Leonora had no idea she'd left her phone behind.

It had been a busy, emotionally-charged week dealing with everything from child murders to serious fraud, and it had taken every last ounce of her reserves to make it this far. As a small concession, she allowed herself the luxury of enjoying the walk from the Inns to the underground station at Embankment, choosing to take a short detour through the smaller garden beside the station to admire some of the winter planting. It was a place she often went to if she wasn't in court, to enjoy a quiet respite from the legal world.

She didn't see the man who followed at a discreet distance, nor hear his quiet tread on the pavement behind. She saw only the afternoon she envisaged making sugar biscuits with Zoe, perhaps watching a bit of Winnie-the-Pooh.

She smiled at the thought of it, and quickened her pace, eager to see her daughter.

The man's footsteps quickened too.

CHAPTER 19

Gregory ran through the Inns, back towards the river. He covered the ground with long-legged strides and burst out of the iron gates onto the Embankment, where he paused briefly to scan the road for any sign of Leonora. By then it was lunchtime, and the pavement crowds had swelled so there was now a sea of people wearing the same homogenous city uniform, which made it hard to distinguish one woman of average height and build from the next.

He jogged towards the tube station, eyeing the people he passed, ignoring the strange looks they gave him in return.

Then, miraculously, he caught sight of her entering the station a few hundred yards ahead of him.

"Thank God," he muttered. "*Leonora!*"

She didn't hear his call, but Carl did.

He turned to look through the crowd, eyes bright with a hint of madness, pupils dilating as they fell upon the good doctor. He stood still, waiting for a dangerous moment to allow Gregory to see him, to really *see* him. It was reckless, he knew; but he wanted the doctor to recognise him and know that he'd *lost*, and that there was nothing he could do to change the course of events that were now in motion. There was no action he could take, no apology he could offer, no amends to be made—all of that was much too late now. Rather, he needed Doctor Alexander Gregory to look into his eyes and see the hatred blazing there, and be afraid, as he had been afraid every night he'd lain his head upon a stained prison pillow.

But Gregory did not see him. Carl Deere went unnoticed, as always; just another city dweller whose face and clothing might have belonged to a thousand others.

Disappointed, *angered*, Carl turned away and followed his quarry down into the bowels of the station.

There would be time enough for Alexander Gregory to understand the meaning of fear.

Leonora couldn't say how many times she'd passed in and out of the turnstiles at Embankment tube station, but it must have been somewhere in the thousands. She placed her card on the reader, heard the familiar *bleep*, and moved towards the escalators, part of a throng heading in the same direction. If she'd stopped to look at her fellow passengers, she'd have seen tourists, lawyers like herself, grifters, security workers, students…an endless carousel of people from all walks of life. She probably wouldn't have looked twice at the man with dark hair and glasses, who was quite good-looking but so very *tired*, of life and of death. Perhaps, if she'd seen him, she'd have recognised the danger and called for help. She'd have looked for her phone and realised it was missing, then turned back to retrieve it.

But she did none of those things.

Leonora continued toward the escalators, her mind far away as she thought of one killer and how to prosecute him, while another watched her.

Gregory saw Leonora Stewart passing through the turnstiles as he flew into the station, and called out to her again. His voice was drowned out by a series of loudspeaker announcements and, by the time they were over, she'd disappeared onto the escalators beyond.

Panic rising, he fumbled for the tube pass he kept in his wallet then, throwing good manners to the wind, elbowed his way to the front of one of the queues.

"*Oi*! You wanna watch yourself, mate—"

Gregory didn't stop, but dashed across to the escalator and, when he reached the top of the mechanical beast, found it heaving with people standing still on one side while a steady stream trudged down the other. He leaned this way and that, searching the back of each head for one he recognised, jostling against the blockade to make headway.

Eventually, he caught sight of Leonora again; so close, yet impossibly far away.

"Leonora!"

"*Hey*!" the woman in front of him snapped, holding a pair of gloved hands to her ears.

With a mumbled apology, Gregory began to push through the crowd, eliciting every kind of curse.

He didn't care about any of that.

He cared about saving a life.

Carl glanced back over his shoulder to watch Gregory making his slow progress, while a breeze rushed through the tunnels to indicate a train was due.

Better hurry, or he'd miss it.

In the thrillers Leonora sometimes liked to watch, the victims always experienced a feeling of impending doom, or possessed a sixth sense to warn them of the peril they were in.

Reality turned out to be very different, if only she'd known it.

There was no 'prickle' down her spine, nor any physical awareness that Carl Deere followed her through the underground tunnels of London. The people surrounding her formed a single, solid mass of bodies that surged like a flock of birds towards the train, which arrived with a flurry of hot air and a deafening screech of brakes. Leonora moved with them, clutching her bag to her chest as she jockeyed for position, closing her mind and her nostrils to all but the desire to reach her destination.

Carl moved with her, easily within striking distance, and wondered whether she'd recognise him now that he was a 'new' man.

Probably not.

His own mother wouldn't recognise him.

A part of him wanted to rush the moment. He wanted to see the flash of shock in her eyes as the knowledge dawned, and see her panic, smell her fear, and be intoxicated by it.

But that would be foolish, and he was no fool.

Instead, he watched and waited, savouring the anticipation. He had a plan that had been laid after weeks of research and surveillance, and he would not deviate.

What was a few more minutes, after the years that had gone before?

The train doors closed and, through the grubby windows, he watched Gregory rush onto the platform, seconds too late. He muscled through the crowd and began peering through the neighbouring carriage, focused, attentive, before moving on to the next. Carl knew he should turn away, turn his back before he was seen—

Then, it happened.

Their eyes locked.

Carl saw his own surprise reflected in the doctor's eyes, inches away from his own, separated only by a sheet of toughened glass. He smiled, revelling in the exquisite feeling of power, and grasped one of the handrails to steady himself against the sheer force of it.

Then, Gregory was shouting, banging his hand against the window and the side of the train, running alongside as it began to move off again, his feet stumbling too close to the edge as he dodged people milling beside the yellow line.

Stop the train!

The train didn't stop, but gathered speed, its tail-lights staring at him like unblinking red eyes until they disappeared into the shadows of the underground.

CHAPTER 20

Gregory was frozen for seconds only, but it was a lifetime.

Then he spun around, searching blindly for a conductor or someone from the London Transport Police who might be able to stop the train or get word to its driver. He shoved his way through the crowd but found nobody in their welcoming blue and red uniform to help. Later, he would think they were probably engaged in some emergency at the other end of the platform, but there was no time to think of it, now. He had two choices, neither of which would be likely to prevent the consequences of his own abject failure: he could wait for the next train and hope to catch Leonora at her destination, intercepting Carl Deere before any attack, or he could hurry back to ground level, where there was mobile reception with the outside world, and put an urgent call through to DCI Hope. The plain truth was that he didn't know Leonora Stewart's address and, being at least five minutes ahead of him, there was little chance he would be able to catch up with her at Warwick Avenue before she disappeared onto the leafy streets of London. However, if he rang Hope, there was a chance she could dispatch a squad car to pick Leonora up before any damage could be done.

It was the only logical choice.

Aware of every wasted second, Gregory raced back towards the escalators and hit the revolving metal at a run. The stairs were almost empty since the last trainload of inbound passengers had already dispersed, so he took them two at a time, muscles screaming alongside the voice at the back of his mind which told him that, once again, he was to blame.

If only he'd rung her the day before, or even a week before.

If only he'd made it to her chambers five minutes sooner.

If only he'd recognised her in the doorway.

Fool. Fool!

Breathing hard, he emerged back into the concourse at Embankment Station and immediately grasped his mobile phone.

After a couple of rings, the call was answered.

"DCI Hope?"

"Ava—it's me. It's Alex. I—I'm at Embankment Station, I tried to see Leonora Stewart, the barrister who tried Carl Deere, you remember? I saw him, too, just now, on the train beside her—"

He was talking too fast, the words tumbling from his mouth in one stream of consciousness.

"You're not making any sense," Hope told him, but heard the note in his voice and the harsh breathing down the line. "What's happened?"

"I'm trying to tell you—I just missed Stewart as she was getting on the Bakerloo line to go home, somewhere around Warwick Avenue. I saw her through the carriage window and he was there too—"

"Who?"

"*Carl*! He's beside her, stalking her! You need to send a squad car right now, Ava, there's only minutes—"

Hope looked across the room towards the conference suite, where she was expected to deliver a briefing about another case they were working on.

"There's no chance you've made a mistake?"

"*No!*" Gregory almost shouted. "Please, for God's sake, get a car dispatched to Warwick Avenue!"

Hope waved at Carter, who was crossing the room on his way to the briefing.

"What?" he mouthed.

She held up a single finger.

"Keep the line free," she said to Gregory, and ended the call before turning back to her sergeant. "I need two cars dispatched to Warwick Avenue immediately—blues and twos. Carl Deere has been sighted, and he was right next to Leonora Stewart, the woman who helped to put him away."

"Jesus—"

"Has nothing to do with it," Hope snapped, before hurrying from the room.

Leonora exited the train at Warwick Avenue and made her way towards the exit gates, which were quiet at that time of day. Little Venice was a pretty, suburban area in the heart of the city, popular with affluent families who liked to feel a sense of removal from the centre of London. It comprised of large, stucco-fronted townhouses painted in varying shades of white or cream, peppered with the occasional sixties monstrosity which local estate agents liked to call "mid-century modern." Hers was one of the former, and commanded an especially nice location beside the water, with a garden leading all the way down to the canal. They'd recently finished building a small boathouse and planned to invest in a rowing boat one day, when Zoe was older. In the meantime, Mark had commandeered it as his 'man cave', and took himself off to watch the football occasionally and have a few beers with friends, which saved her from having to feign interest in the varying fortunes of Arsenal FC.

Her daughter's nursery school was a stone's throw from the tube station, and less than a five-minute walk from their home. Later, DCI Hope would remark that, if she'd only chosen to take a direct route through the streets where other people walked, there was a chance Leonora might have lived. But the clouds had parted to reveal blue skies overhead, and it was a fine day to stroll along the canal. So, she turned away from the safety of numbers and made her way to the narrow, moss-coated stairwell beside the station that led down to the waterside.

Carl smiled at the Fates.

He'd been sure she would take that route, considering it was the same route she'd taken every other week, too. There were no cameras along that stretch of the canal and, given the time of day, the path was likely to be quiet.

Perfect.

He followed at a steady pace and, when he reached the top of the stairwell, he looked back towards the station, where he watched two police squad cars pull up with a screech of tires. Officers spilled out, their plodding feet hurrying inside the station in search of a man they'd barely recognise and a woman they'd never see again.

Not alive, at any rate.

He blew them a kiss, and was gone.

Leonora smelled the wild garlic growing in the hedgerows lining that part of the canal, then watched the sunlight reflecting on the rippling water. It was a good life, and she was grateful to have found a partner to share it with and to have been blessed with their daughter, who'd joined them after several rounds of unsuccessful IVF treatment. She supposed it was that 'never give up' attitude that had seen her through much of the ups and downs of her legal career, so that she could begin to relax— just a little—and enjoy the fruits of many years of tenacity and hard work. There was no possible way to be all things to all people, but she tried, and, on that sunny day in autumn, she felt that all was right with the world.

Her eye fell on a pair of mallard ducks as she passed beneath one of the bridges spanning the waterway, and Leonora crouched down to watch them for a moment or two, wondering if they'd still be there when she brought Zoe along the pathway on their way home from the nursery.

She hoped so.

She straightened up, rubbed a hand over her lower back, *and*—

Strong arms grasped her from behind, banding around her ribcage like steel. A gloved hand clamped over her mouth and she struggled for breath; nostrils flaring, choking, spluttering, fighting as much as she could. Then, with a brutal kick to the back of her legs, she fell to her knees and the same hard hands took her head and forced it down so the murky water rushed into her body, filling her lungs until they burst. Those hands remained hard and unyielding, never giving an inch until her body went completely limp.

Carl let the rush claim him, crying out his pleasure, then cast furtive glances in either direction before grasping the collar of her coat. He dragged her a short way to a spot he'd found the previous day, a nice little nook set back from the canal, where a body could lie unseen until the stench began to draw attention. He spent a few moments arranging her to his satisfaction, stopping only to watch a young man walk by wearing headphones, oblivious to everything except the beat inside his head.

A few minutes later, Carl re-joined the pathway.

It had been an excellent morning's work.

CHAPTER 21

"We missed her, Alex."

Gregory snatched up his mobile phone before the second ring, but DCI Hope did not have good news to impart.

"We have Leonora's address, but nobody's home," she added, and glanced at the smart, black-painted front door to her immediate right. "There's no sign of her on the roads in this direction. Do you have any idea where else she might have gone?"

Gregory commanded himself to think.

"She has a daughter," he said, and swallowed the bile that rose to his throat. "A little girl; I'm not sure what age. She might have been collecting her from school?"

"Too early," Hope remarked, checking the time on her watch. "School pick-ups are usually between three and four. There might be a nursery, though."

They fell silent, both grieving what they knew to be the truth.

"We've been trying to get hold of her husband," Hope said. "He's also a barrister, so he's probably in court."

"What can we do?"

"I've got officers fanning out in the immediate area," she replied. "I'm going to try the husband again, and Carter's going to stay here at the house, in case she turns up."

"Ava, if you find her body—"

"Let's cross that bridge when we come to it," she interrupted him. "There's still a chance you're wrong."

Even to her own ears, the words sounded hollow.

"There's a canal," he said, after a short pause. "If I was Carl, that's where I'd go."

Hope didn't stop to ask how or why he chose to put himself into the minds of men like Carl Deere, because, at least in that regard, their work was the same.

To find a killer, sometimes you had to think like one.

"Try the next person on your list," she said. "In case I'm the one who's wrong."

Gregory thought of the names he'd identified, and one in particular jumped out as being an easy, accessible target.

Romola Harris.

He could only hope he wasn't too late.

Romola Harris exited the tube station at Warwick Avenue, and her eyes were drawn immediately to a couple of police officers standing near the entrance. She wondered idly why they were there, her journalist's nose always keen to sniff out a story, but, on that occasion, there were bigger fish to fry and so she scuttled past them and emerged into the early afternoon sunshine. It was a pretty day, but she didn't pause to enjoy it because her sole focus was on the contents of the e-mail she'd received less than twenty minutes earlier.

Dear Romola…

She shivered inside her coat, and stuck her hands inside the pockets as she scanned the vicinity to find the entrance to the canal. Her fingers brushed folded paper and she pulled out the printed e-mail to read again, to be sure she'd followed Carl's instructions correctly.

When you arrive at Warwick Avenue, head east along the canal until you reach a footbridge. A few metres beyond it, you'll see an old wooden gate…

The note began to ramble about natural justice and the penance that must be paid to balance the scales.

As if the world was that simple, she thought, with a touch of pity, before shoving the paper back inside her pocket. Across the street, she saw another cluster of police officers who spoke briefly amongst themselves before fanning out in pairs. She didn't like the coincidence, but then, it was London. They could be responding to any number of emergencies in a city that harboured millions; it was only her own suspicious mind that led her to imagine the worst. Besides, if there was a *real* emergency, they'd have closed the station, wouldn't they?

Pleased with her own reasoning, Romola followed a couple of the officers, not expecting them to peel off from the main road and begin making their way down to the canal, which was the same direction she was headed.

She hesitated at the top of the stairwell, a safe distance behind their high-vis jackets.

Was there a connection?

In his last note, Carl had spoken of giving her the opportunity to put things right, and she assumed he referred to her previous reporting of his wrongful conviction. She assumed he would be waiting for her at the allotted place in order to give an exclusive interview for the paper, and she could already see the headline—

DEERE BREAKS SILENCE AFTER HARROWING MISCARRIAGE OF JUSTICE

Or perhaps—

DEERE BREAKS SILENCE IN WORLD EXCLUSIVE

Yes, that sounded better.

However, if Carl happened to see the police presence, there was a good chance he'd be spooked and run a mile in the other direction; it didn't require any special insight to understand that he had no trust in the long arm of the law. For her part, she *needed* that scoop. There were only so many times she could regurgitate anniversary articles about past murders, or put out speculative bit-pieces about the stars of yesteryear. Deere had never given an interview after his release and, God knew, she'd tried to find him in those first few months. The man was a ghost, a pariah who'd left mainstream society behind him, and she assumed he might have forged a new life with a new name somewhere, with friends, a dog, maybe an easy nine-to-five job managing a Pizza Express.

Eager now, Romola trotted down the steps and, assuming correctly that the police officers had gone west along the pathway, walked briskly in an easterly direction, keeping a sharp eye out for the landmarks Carl had mentioned. Spotting the bridge up ahead, she scurried along the pathway towards it, not giving a second glance to a family of ducks circling the water, before moving quickly towards a patch of thick bracken entwined with an overgrown hedgerow surrounding a wooden gate. The wood was rotten and splintered with age and lack of upkeep, but that was no surprise; some owners of the waterside houses never used their garden access onto the canal, and—

Oh, God!

She almost tripped over the body, and let out a garbled sound of horror.

The woman lay on her back in a cruciform position, arms outstretched in the overgrown grass. Two small brass measuring plates hung from chains looped through the fingers of each hand, which were beginning to curl. Her smart trouser suit was sodden and caked with mud from the pathway, while her face—

Her face.

Romola's stomach heaved, and she stumbled away so that her body could expel the bile that rose swiftly to her throat.

The woman's face was horribly bloated, the skin marred by a web of broken vessels, the eyes bulging and bloodshot. The mouth gaped open, and something had been stuffed inside it.

Despite her revulsion, Romola needed to know what it was.

She steeled herself, taking several deep breaths, and then turned to look once more.

It was a white envelope, with something written on the front.

Feeling her stomach roll again, she fixed her eyes on the envelope with a kind of tunnelled vision, and crept forward to try to read the inscription. As she drew closer, the bold, black lettering became visible and she saw the name that was written there.

Romola.

Her breath lodged tightly in her chest, she froze, hovering over the body like a vulture, dimly aware that, elsewhere, the world continued to move though she could not.

There was only one person who could possibly have known she would be there, only one man who could have reason to stage a body in a grotesque parody of 'justice', yet he was the man whose innocence had been proclaimed, and was beyond reproach in the eyes of the law.

Carl Deere.

She cast wide, terrified eyes up and down the pathway, chest rising and falling rapidly as fear took a stranglehold, heart hammering inside her chest like a trapped bird.

He could be there, somewhere, watching her.

Watching both of them.

Every rustle became a footstep, the breeze no longer welcome in the afternoon sunshine but an unpleasant brush, like fingers against her skin.

But there was nobody there.

Romola opened her mouth to call for the police, who might be out of sight but within hearing distance, but the sound died in her throat. She thought of who else might be within earshot and her eyes fell on the envelope again, frittering over the woman's lifeless skin.

He'd left a message for her, in more ways than one.

Shaking badly now, she clenched her teeth and reached down to snatch it up, the movement dislodging the woman's head so that it lolled to one side. A scream rose up and, this time, could not be contained.

Romola ran, as far and as fast as she could.

CHAPTER 22

"Hello?"

"Oh, hello, this is Jill from Little Stars Nursery."

At the other end of the line, Mark Grayson experienced a small burst of irritation. He was due back in court within the next five minutes and his daughter's nursery had obviously forgotten that it was his wife Leonora's day "on call" for any minor emergencies that might arise.

"Er, *hi*," he said, in harried tones. "Look, I'm just about to head back into court—if it isn't urgent, would you mind calling my wife? She's the point of contact for today. You should have her number—"

The woman at the other end of the line made a small, awkward sound.

"Um, well, the thing is, Mister Grayson, we've already tried calling your wife and have left a few messages," she said. "It's absolutely fine if Zoe needs to stay a bit longer with us today, but I know Mrs Grayson usually likes to collect her by one o'clock on Thursdays and, since it's almost two, we were beginning to wonder."

Mark pulled a face, and thought that Leonora had probably just lost track of the time. She was usually incredibly punctual, so that would be unusual, but not outside the realms of possibility.

Just then, the usher appeared to indicate the judge was ready to hear his client's case.

"Sorry about this," he muttered. "Okay, look, I'll try her chambers and see if I can get hold of her—my wife's probably been held up, that's all. If you wouldn't mind entertaining Zoe for a bit longer, that would be a great help."

The nursery agreed, and he rang off. There was no time to place any more calls, but family duty overcame his duty to the court, and he was about to look up the number for his wife's chambers when the display on his phone signalled another incoming call.

Number withheld.

He binned the call, suspecting it to be a cold call or something of that kind, but the same number rang again.

Thoroughly impatient, now, he snatched it up.

"Look, I'm not interested—"

"Mr Grayson? This is DCI Hope, from the Metropolitan Police."

A funny, ringing sound began to thrum in his ears, and he waved away the usher who was gesticulating wildly for him to come inside the courtroom.

"I—yes, I'm Mark Grayson."

His voice sounded far away, as though he were floating.

"Mr Grayson, can I ask if you're in a private space, and whether you're able to sit down?"

He was no fool but, even if he had been, Mark would still have known that something was very badly wrong.

Working on autopilot, he forced his legs to move, and he stepped outside into the lobby area, ignoring the furious cries from the couple he was supposed to be defending from a civil liability claim.

He found an old, rickety chair and sat on it.

"I'm—I'm sitting down."

From her end, Hope took a deep breath. "I'm sorry I can't be there to tell you this in person," she began, and it was true. She knew what it was to receive the worst news from a disembodied voice on the telephone, and hated to be the person to inflict that pain upon another. "I regret to inform you that your wife has been found dead, and we are treating her death as murder. You have my deepest sympathies."

They were words she'd spoken many times before, but they never became any easier to say, nor any less sincere.

"I—I don't understand—"

Mark clutched the telephone to his ear as he struggled to compute the information.

"Leonora was in chambers this morning," he said, with a touch of hauteur. "You must have made a mistake."

But the nursery haven't seen her, his brain whispered. You know this is true.

"I'm very sorry," Ava repeated. "We don't believe there's been a mistake, but we will need you to come and make a formal identification."

He began to shake, and the file he still held beneath his arm slipped noiselessly to the floor, scattering papers at his feet.

"Leonora," he said softly. "Leo."

Hope swallowed hard, and switched the receiver from one ear to the other.

"If you tell me where you are, Mr Grayson, I can have a squad car come and collect you," she said.

"I—I need to collect Zoe," he whispered.

"Zoe?"

"Our daughter," he said brokenly. "She's…she's only three."

Hope turned away from the small crowd of forensic and police officers who were huddled nearby, so they would not see the weakness that threatened to overcome all else. Metres away, a woman lay discarded in the earth, and a child would never see her mother again.

"Give me your address," she said, when her voice was strong enough. "I'll send a car right away."

———

Gregory rang the news desk at *The Daily Scoop* and spoke with a bored-sounding intern, who told him that Romola Harris wasn't at her desk, they had no idea of her whereabouts or whether she'd be back later in the day, and that was very much *that*. They were frustratingly tight-lipped when he tried to procure a home address, and favoured him with a sanctimonious lecture about data protection which could be roughly summarised as, "computer says no".

Gregory left a message with details of how he could be contacted, and hoped it would reach the intended recipient, then ran a social media search to see if he was able to contact Romola by some other means. He sent an e-mail, left her a message on her Instagram account and various others, but, since he could find no home address listed anywhere, nor any details of an event she might be attending in the city, that was all he could do for the present.

Far from satisfied, and feeling a failure of the worst kind, he did all that was left to do; he sought solace in one who cared.

"Any luck with the police?" Naomi asked him, after the second ring.

Gregory found a bench and sat down, huddled inside his coat, to tell her everything that had transpired that morning.

"You were right," she said, once he'd finished. "You *knew* it was Carl Deere, and you were right."

"For Carl's sake, as much as his victims, I wish to God I was wrong."

She understood the heartache it was possible to feel, even for the most troubled and dangerous minds.

"Have the police found Leonora, yet?"

Gregory shook his head, and passed a weary hand over his eyes. "No, but they will."

There was a heavy silence.

"It isn't your fault, Alex."

He blinked away sudden tears. "I know," he said, but was unconvinced. "I'm not responsible for the actions of others."

"Exactly," Naomi said, gently. "You did all you could. You've fought to have your concerns taken seriously for weeks, now, and that's what you were doing again at Scotland Yard this morning. If you hadn't tried to contact Leonora, it might have been much later that the police became aware, and you might never have seen the proof of what you suspected all along."

"I saw his face," Alex said, to reassure himself. "It was Carl, I *know* it was. He looked different, but it was him, just the same."

"He's altered the way he appears, just as we thought he might?"

Gregory tried to recall a picture of Carl in his mind. "He looks sharper than before," he said. "Tanned, and he's dyed his hair a darker brown. His eyes were already very dark, so there isn't much he could do about that, aside from using coloured lenses. He seemed more athletic, but I can't say for certain because I only caught a fleeting glimpse. If I hadn't been staring at his face through the glass, I might not have recognised him."

"Still, your description will help the police," Naomi said, focusing always on the positives, while they awaited confirmation of the worst. "They can put his picture out there, and warn the public."

Gregory took some small comfort from that. "Surely, the police can't deny the truth of the situation any longer," he said. "They have to reopen the investigation, with Carl Deere as their prime suspect."

"I can't think of any decent reason why they wouldn't."

Gregory tried to put aside the niggling doubt he felt towards the police hierarchy, and agreed with her. "I trust Hope to do her best."

"Me too," Naomi said. "She follows her gut."

Gregory smiled at that. "Let's hope it takes her down the right path."

Romola managed to hail a taxi, and huddled on the back seat as it took her home, rattling through the streets of London while her stomach tipped and lurched, and the image of a dead woman replayed in her mind. The cabbie made idle conversation but, when no response was forthcoming, gave up the effort and contented himself by driving as quickly and haphazardly as possible, eager to drop off his fare and find one who might be prepared to talk about politics or sympathise with him about the ever-changing street closures that were the scourge of his industry.

She paid him with shaking hands, cold as they were with shock.

"Mind as you go, love!"

She didn't 'alf look peaky, but then, every second person in London was on the drink or the drugs, and he had his own troubles.

Left alone on a quiet, suburban street in a part of West London known as 'Acton', Romola looked all around and, seeing nothing, hurried up a short pathway to the front door of her small, terraced house. The children were at school, and would be headed to clubs afterwards, so there was time enough to do what she needed to do.

She didn't *want* to do it, that much was clear.

She had no choice.

Put right the damage she had caused—or suffer the same fate as Leonora Stewart.

The front door swung open, and she dropped her keys twice before she was able to hook them on the peg where they normally resided. She allowed herself a few minutes to wallow in the terror of the morning; the grief of seeing one human shell wasted and spent, the fear of knowing it might have been her. She sank onto the hallway tiles and wept, for herself and for all her life could have been, until she had exhausted herself with the effort. Then, she dragged herself up again and went in search of a laptop.

She'd made her bargain, and now there was work to be done.

CHAPTER 23

When DCI Hope made her way back up to street level, leaving the murky scent of death and canal water behind her, the first thing she saw was Gregory, who stood as a tall, silent sentinel just behind the police line.

"I didn't ask you to come," she said. "Our policy on criminal profiling hasn't changed."

"I know," he said, and flicked a glance over her shoulder. "You found her, then."

The sadness bound together in those simple words was enough to break her, but she would not allow it.

"We're perfectly capable of working a crime scene," she told him. "You can go home, Alex. I've already told you that I'll let you know of any important developments."

At that moment, her sergeant joined them, his usual jovial expression replaced now with a vacant one that might have conveyed shock or grief, or both.

"The wagon's arrived to take her to the mortuary," he said. "They're waiting for you to give the final 'okay' for her to be moved, guv."

Hope began to speak, and then looked up at the quiet man beside her, who had asked nothing while asking everything.

"Carter, tell Scenes of Crimes to give us five minutes with her," she said.

He nodded, exchanged a smile with Gregory, and then moved off.

"Five minutes," she repeated. "That's all I can give you."

"That's all I need."

Gregory stood completely still, taking in the compact scene.

On another day, the pathway beside the canal would have been picturesque, with the mellow afternoon sunshine flooding through the branches of overhanging trees to brush the water, and the sound of birds and other small creatures rummaging in the hedgerows. It was a hidden world except to those lucky enough to enjoy it, but that quiet paradise had now been despoiled.

Small yellow markers were dotted here and there to indicate some item of forensic interest, while a tent rippled gently on the breeze beyond the pedestrian bridge, set back from the pathway and half concealed by long grass.

He took it all in, imagining Leonora as she had been in life, walking along the pathway towards the cut that would take her to her child's nursery. It was a small but significant blessing that she was taken before collecting her child, and not afterwards, but he was in no mood to celebrate.

"Unfortunately, the PCs who did the first walkaround missed her," Hope said, breaking the silence. "She wasn't visible from the pathway, but they should have been more thorough."

"Who found her, then?"

"Dog-walker," Hope replied. "There was still a police presence, so they didn't even need to call it in. They found one of the officers beside the station and we put a line up."

She was prattling now, for her own comfort.

"Were they responsible for the vomit over there?"

Hope shook her head. "They say not, but I plan to check again. People can be embarrassed to admit these things. It could have been Carl, or whoever was responsible, of course."

Gregory smiled. "Still hoping, Detective Hope?"

She didn't bother to argue, nor tell him that much of her hope had died away years ago, but stuck her gloved hands inside the pockets of her coat to warm them.

"It's unlikely to be Carl's vomit," Gregory said, moving carefully along the edge towards the place where Leonora still lay. "He hasn't been sick at any of his previous crime scenes, which is probably because he's not sickened by the work he's doing—he's excited...or, perhaps, a better word to use would be *exalted*."

"We haven't proven that he's responsible for those other murders," she said, and, before he could argue with her, she added, "That's what the brass will say. We'll test the vomit and see what we find."

"There are several sets of footprints," Gregory remarked. "You have the killer and his victim, the person who found them and the dog's, possibly a couple of police...are they all accounted for?"

"We'll isolate all the individual marks that we can," she said. "But, you know, it isn't unheard of for people to find bodies and be so terrified or shaken that they don't stick around. I've had petty criminals fail to report a body because they worry that we'll nick them for it."

He nodded, and fell silent again, this time closing his eyes to step into the footsteps of a killer. He knew that Carl followed Leonora from her chambers to the train, then from the train to here. He must have known this was her regular half-day, and that she preferred to take the canal route to the nursery. Regular habits were a gift to people minded to stalk or kill; it provided a ready-made schedule that could be used to their advantage.

"A perfect spot to kill," he murmured, taking in the quiet, the windows of the houses set far back from the river so it was almost impossible to see anything or anyone who might have been walking along the pathway at the end of their gardens.

He narrowed his eyes, squinting against the sun to see where the nearest cameras had been fitted.

"There's no CCTV between the access stairs down from the street level and here," he said.

Hope nodded, having already answered the same question for herself. "The first private camera is fitted above a garden gate four doors down. The others have heavy padlocks but no cameras."

"Who owns this one?" he asked, pointing to the old wooden gate, beneath which Leonora had been killed.

"An old antiques dealer," she said. "He's almost ninety and very infirm, but refuses to go into a home, according to his carer. He doesn't get out into the garden very much, and it's been left to go a bit wild. His family live abroad, in Dubai."

Nobody using the gate, nobody trimming the grass, Gregory thought.

"Carl had to kill her here," he said. "Any later, and he risked being caught on the cameras further down."

"We've requested the footage, anyway," she said. "But if he's aware of their placement, he'll have taken precautions."

Gregory drew himself in, and then stepped inside the uncomfortable heat of the forensics tent to look upon the remains of the woman he'd tried desperately to save. Death was never pretty, and this was no exception. It was in the nature of a clinician to face it more often than other people, and there were some under his care at Southmoor Hospital who fell ill and died through natural causes, while others ended their own lives, unable to live any longer with the knowledge of what they had inflicted upon others. It was a dichotomy he'd often pondered: namely, whether it was in the best interests of an abnormal mind to know the extent of that abnormality, and be sufficiently rehabilitated to develop remorse and regret. Compassion that might have been lacking in earlier life, once gained, could not be overthrown.

Ignorance, in some cases, was bliss.

Despite his experience, Gregory always reserved a special place in his heart for those whose lives were taken prematurely, and their bodies always bore the evidence of their fight to remain alive.

"It's likely he took her from behind, so there was no time for her to run," Hope said, stepping inside the tent beside him. "Look at the marks on her wrists."

Gregory had seen them, and drawn the same conclusion, but was more interested in the motivations of her killer than the means he'd employed.

"It's interesting that he moved her off the pathway, don't you think?"

Hope frowned. "Maybe he wanted to give himself time to get well away," she offered. "If the body was discovered too soon, we'd have caught him."

There was hope again, he thought.

"Carl had enough time to drown her in the canal, unseen," he pointed out. "That tells me he'd already done a thorough recce of the area, and was confident it would be sufficiently quiet down here to get the job done without interruption. Even then, it's high risk and out in the open, which tells us that he's become arrogant...it's an escalation from the previous murders, which were indoors. It would have been more consistent with his mindset for Carl to have left the body on the pathway for all to see."

"Did you see the scales?" Hope asked him, although they were impossible to miss. "He wanted her to look like 'justice'."

Gregory was only half listening, but spared her a nod. "Carl's never been accused of subtlety," he said, and drew a brief laugh from the detective at his side.

He moved closer, and crouched down beside Leonora's face.

"Something was in her mouth," he said, pointing a nitrile fingertip towards the edge of her lip. "There's a cut on her lip, here."

"The pathologist will do a thorough post-mortem," Hope said, but came beside him to see for herself. "I can't see anything?"

"It looks like a paper cut," he said, tracing the line against her open mouth. "It's torn the corner of her lip, here."

"She might have sustained that any time," Hope replied. "You can't draw any conclusions from that."

"There's no clotting," he said, patiently. "If it was torn earlier, while she was still alive, there would have been blood clotting. The skin is completely white."

"You've got eyes like a bloody hawk," she mumbled. "What do you think it means?"

"I'm not sure," he said, and resisted the urge to close Leonora's eyes, or brush the hair back from her forehead. She was gone, and it was only the matter that remained.

He stood up, abruptly, and pushed out of the tent. Hope followed him, and they walked back towards the stairwell and life beyond.

At the base, he peeled off his gloves and shoe coverings, dumped them in the forensics bin, and then said, "It could mean that someone was here before the police, and before the dog-walker," he said. "That someone might have been responsible for the vomit, too."

Hope signalled to the waiting technicians, who'd come to move Leonora into the care of the police pathologist. "I'll rush the testing," she said, and told herself she'd worry about finding the departmental resources later. "What about the others you think could be at risk?"

"I tried contacting Romola Harris, the journalist who trashed him the most, last time around," Gregory said. "No luck, so far. I'll try again, but move on to the next one, in the meantime."

"I'll have my hands full with this, but Carter will work his way through as many as he can."

"Thank you," he said.

"No," she replied. "Thank you."

"For what?"

"For not saying, 'I told you so', and for coming here even when you're not officially part of the team."

"You were right when you said you didn't need me to work the crime scene."

"No, but I needed a friend," she said. "You knew that, which is why you came."

"We both did."

She nodded, and stepped away to raise her hand to one of her officers.

"Be careful, Alex. Don't spend so long trying to protect other people that you forget to protect yourself."

Gregory watched her go, command in every line of her body, and knew that Leonora Stewart and her family were in capable hands.

CHAPTER 24

Gregory put through a telephone call to Hawking College and, having satisfied himself that Douglas was safe, well, and surrounded by a good number of the college faculty, he checked the time and made his way towards Piccadilly Circus shortly before five o'clock. By then, night had fallen, and the lights of the city centre blazed with adverts for everything from theatres and comedy stores, restaurants and sports brands to the latest domestic crime drama. The Circus was a confluence of large boulevards, like spokes of a wheel branching off along Regent Street to the north, Piccadilly to the west, Shaftesbury Avenue to the north-east and the smaller Coventry Street to the east, which would lead on to Leicester Square. Exiting the tube station, he walked a short distance along Piccadilly towards one of the city's largest bookshops, boasting an emporium of reading spread across several floors. Shoppers milled around tables touting 'New Reads' and 'Editor's Choice' and he bypassed them all, making his way directly to the second floor, where an event would shortly be held, featuring a brand-new author, Doctor Naomi Palmer.

Though it was not sold out, the crowd was a very healthy one, with more than eighty people having turned up to hear her speak on the subject of abnormal minds, peppered with experiences from her tenure as Director and Resident Psychiatrist at the Buchanan Institute in the Catskill Mountains. Gregory purchased a ticket from one of the booksellers standing guard, then took a seat near the back, unwilling to allow his presence to affect her in any way, given that she was not expecting him to be there.

"Choccie almond, dear?"

Gregory almost jumped out of his foldaway chair. "Sorry?"

The older lady seated beside him brandished a pink and white striped paper bag. "Chocolate almond? I always get a bit peckish during these things, don't you?"

Usually, he was the one on the podium, and he was never very hungry before an event. Now, his stomach gave an enormous growl.

"I think that's the answer, don't you? Thanks." Gregory accepted her generosity and munched his way through a few almonds while Naomi was introduced by the store manager.

We're so delighted to have Doctor Naomi Palmer visiting us here today, from the United States—

"Lovely, isn't she?"

Gregory nodded, watching Naomi smile modestly as her credentials were abridged for the waiting audience.

"If I was a nice-looking young man, like you, I'd think about asking her to dinner," the woman beside him whispered. "That's what my Derek did, and we've been married thirty-five years this Spring. Course, the younger generation are all into this Tinder Matching and Coffee Grinding, nowadays."

Gregory smiled and thought that, once everything was over, asking the lovely Doctor Palmer to dinner would be his top priority. Not that there was anything wrong with, 'Tinder Matching' and 'Coffee Grinding', but he'd rather not have to do either, given the choice.

He joined the crowd in applauding her entrance, and settled down to listen, soothed by the sound of her voice as she spoke of those less fortunate than themselves.

"Did you hear? There's been another one."

Bill Douglas paused in the act of gathering up his papers from the faculty meeting, wherein they had decided the outcome of several PhD hopefuls, and raised a bushy eyebrow at his fellow academic.

"What's that, Penny?"

"Another murder," she said, and wrapped a large cream pashmina around her neck as they prepared to brave the cold of the quadrangle outside. "This time, a woman was found on the canals near Warwick Avenue. Probably another sex crime; it usually is."

She gave an authoritative *harrumph*, though they both knew that male-on-male, non-sexual murders were by far the most common in society. Douglas didn't argue with her, but thought instantly of his friend, who had already told him of the morning's events.

"Whatever the motivation, a husband has lost his wife, a child its mother," he said quietly, and would have added that the country had lost one of its finest legal minds, if it wouldn't have been indiscreet to do so.

"Well, of course, naturally," she blustered. "I only meant…well, this country's going to the dogs, isn't it?"

Douglas removed his glasses, and took his time about polishing the lenses. "I think there's still a lot to be proud of," he said quietly. "Nothing is ever perfect, but the majority of people I've met are doing their best. The papers do try and convince us otherwise."

Penny snapped her fingers. "That's what I was going to tell you!" she exclaimed, and grabbed her mobile phone. "Look at this—you'll never believe it."

Douglas pinned a polite smile on his face, and waited for her to bring up the news.

Presently, she thrust the screen towards him.

"I'll bet you never thought you'd hear that name again, eh?"

Douglas looked down at the news page and felt his blood chill. There, emblazoned in black and white, was the headline:

INNOCENT MAN FINALLY BREAKS
SILENCE AFTER TERRIBLE ORDEAL

The piece was accompanied by an old picture of Carl Deere, which was still accessible in the public domain, and a long article written in the style of a face-to-face interview. Douglas read the article in silence, then re-read it to be sure he hadn't imagined its contents.

"Well," he said, and handed the screen back to her. "I must be getting along."

He reached for his satchel and began walking swiftly towards the door, his mind running over the content of the so-called 'exclusive', including claims that Carl had been very philanthropic in the past few years, including having donated large portions of his award from the Ministry of Justice to charitable causes—especially those organisations who worked tirelessly to overturn miscarriages of justice. The journalist covered his past arrest and wrongful conviction in nauseating detail, with a heavy bias against all those responsible, whilst at the same time painting Carl as some form of latter-day saint.

"It's nice to see that he's moved on with his life," Penny remarked, as they came to the outer door. "Look, we all know it was just one of those things, but perhaps it would be a good idea to take an extended break from any profiling work—what do you say?"

Douglas flipped up the collar of his wool coat, and gave her one of his patient smiles. "On the contrary, Penny. I'd say the police could use all the help they can get, never more so than now."

He bade her a good evening, then left.

Naomi reached out a hand, and smiled as she looked up to greet the next person in the queue to have their book signed, only to find herself looking into a pair of familiar green eyes.

"Hello, Doctor Palmer."

"Doctor Gregory," she said, and smiled more broadly. "How long have you been moonlighting here?"

He handed her a book, and she rolled her eyes.

"I'd give you a book anytime," she told him. "You don't need to buy one from the shop."

He shrugged. "I like to support them," he said. "And, in answer to your first question, I snuck in at the beginning of your talk—which was excellent, by the way."

"You're bound to say that."

"No, I'm not," he averred. "I wouldn't ever tell you anything that was untrue; especially not when it matters so much."

Naomi searched his face, and knew that was nothing less than the literal truth. "In that case, thank you," she said. "For the record, if I ever ask you a question like, 'Do I look fat in this dress?', you have my permission to tell any white lies you deem necessary to preserve my self-esteem."

"Same goes," he shot back, and made her laugh. "I—"

"Do you mind? There's a queue to get through, here." The bookseller gave him a stern look, which suggested it wasn't the first time they'd been called upon to deal with over-amorous readers, and he held up his hands.

"Sorry," he said. "If I could have the book made out to Professor Bill Douglas, with love and friendship, that would be great."

Naomi's pen stilled, then scribbled the words as well as a few more of her own choosing, before she snapped the book shut again.

"I'll meet you outside in half an hour," she said. "I guess we have a few things to talk about."

He nodded, and the light drained out of his eyes.

"I'll wait for you."

As he moved off, Naomi experienced an odd chill, as though somebody had just walked over her grave. Putting it down to heightened stress and paranoia, she shook it off and reached for another book, her smile already in place for the next person in line.

Ian O'Shea slid his key inside the door of his new London flat, flipped on the lights in the hallway and kicked off the shoes that had been pinching his feet all day. There hadn't been any time to make the place his own, so the walls were a bare, inoffensive shade of magnolia without any pictures to break up the space, and the furniture was spartan—the mattress for his new bed had been misdelivered, so he was putting up with a lumpy sofa-bed in the living room for the time being. Obviously, he'd invested in an enormous television, and there was both a kettle *and* a toaster in the galley kitchen, but, as far as homes went, he was happy to admit that his could use a bit of work.

Perhaps even a woman's touch—one in particular, if she was willing.

He padded through to the kitchen and rummaged in the fridge for a bottle of beer, which he took with him into the living room and chugged happily as he scrolled the match fixtures for the following day on the aforementioned enormous telly.

"First division," he grumbled, and stabbed at the remote until he settled on an old episode of *Frasier*.

His thoughts soon returned to Ava, and he found himself wondering whether she, too, would like that kind of sit-com. Would they be able to sit happily together, chatting over their day, while they laughed over Niles and Daphne? He had a sneaking suspicion they had an awful lot in common, if only she'd let him prove it to her, but his new boss was like a butterfly: bold and beautiful, but far from easy to hold without damaging a wing.

He checked the time on his watch, and reminded himself to wipe down the bathroom and kitchen surfaces before she arrived later. He might not live with a woman, but he knew what they liked, and cleanliness was up there with godliness.

Just then, there came a knock at the door, and Ian thought there was only one person it could be on the other side.

Pete.

Ian had been introduced to his immediate neighbour the previous day: an elderly widower who was hard of hearing but full of heart, and very eager to assuage his loneliness with the promise of a new, younger friend who liked football just as much as he did. For his part, Ian was glad of the offer, since his own father and mother had re-emigrated to Ireland a couple of years back, leaving him to follow or find his own path, and he missed them more than he cared to admit.

"Coming, Pete!" he bellowed, and heaved himself off the couch. "You're just in time for a beer—"

He opened the door, and shock registered on his face.

"You'd better come in."

CHAPTER 25

"Is anything wrong? You look as though you've had a hard day."

Jacob put his hand over Bill's, in silent support.

"I'm sorry, I'm not my usual self," the other replied. "Some difficult faculty meetings—"

He reached for his water glass, downing several mouthfuls to relieve a dry throat.

"I saw an article about Carl Deere, today," Jacob prompted, as gently as he could. "I wasn't sure whether to mention it, but, when I saw the look on your face, I wondered whether you'd also seen it, and been upset."

Bill looked across at the attractive younger man who awaited his reply. "It certainly brings back memories," he admitted. "As to whether it upset me...I'm used to the papers dragging my name up every time they hash over the story of Deere's arrest and trial. It's old news."

"That's good," Jacob said. "I have to say, I was surprised *The Daily Scoop* managed to secure an interview, especially since I recall they were rather nasty towards him, during the trial."

"I'd be interested to know how they found him in the first place," Douglas replied. "He hasn't had any kind of public presence since his release from prison, but perhaps they managed to track him down and make him an offer he couldn't refuse. I can't remember Carl ever having an allergy to money."

Jacob picked up a menu and studied the choices. "According to the article, Deere is a man of principle—all that charity work, and so on."

"You and I both know there's no such thing as true altruism," Bill replied. "If Carl has been generous with his money—which isn't confirmed, by the way—then, I ask myself, what does he have to gain by telling the newspaper about his exploits, except reflected glory? He wants to be seen as a do-gooder, or a *man of principle*, as you put it, but the real question is, why?" Douglas linked his fingers. "As for the rest," he continued, "if Carl has moved on with his life, then I'm very happy to hear it. Anger, revenge, bitterness… these are all highly corrosive emotions, and do no good to anybody in the end."

Jacob tapped the menu. "Penne arrabbiata," he said, and sat back, content with his decision. "I agree with you, but all of the emotions you mention can also be very motivating, can't they? Look at Alexandre Dumas."

"*Le Comte de Monte Cristo*?" Douglas said. "It's a classic, but, personally, I've always felt that book rather glamourised revenge."

"Really? I read it very differently."

"How so?"

Jacob popped an olive in his mouth and chewed. "Well, there was more than one side to Edmund Dantès," he said. "There was his main alter ego, the Count of Monte Cristo, who punished those who had caused him pain and hardship—rightfully so. On the other hand, let's not forget there was Lord Wilmore, his other alias, whom Dantès used to reward those who had been helpful, or to reciprocate kindness that had been shown to him. It demonstrates he's still a good man."

"It's interesting you should think that," Douglas said, with a smile. "I would think that, at best, it demonstrates he's conflicted. If adjectives such as 'good' or 'bad' are to be applied to people, I've always thought they should be derived from a person's behaviour. A person may think they have good intentions, or a good 'character' but if their actions have consistently negative consequences, and they outweigh those which have positive consequences, then the odds is stacked against the idea they're a 'good' person overall. The bad actions simply outweigh the good ones."

"Who is to judge whether something has positive or negative impact?" Jacob said. "Perhaps the positive impact of some actions can only be seen in the long-term."

"Well, let's consider Edmund Dantès again," Bill said. "Following his escape from prison, Dantès holds himself out to be the sole arbiter and judge of who is deserving and undeserving of his generosity, or the reverse, through the aliases you've mentioned. However, he has a *third* alias, if you recall; an Italian priest by the name of Abbe Busoni, which he uses to manipulate those whom he intends to punish in the end. His duplicity is interesting, don't you think, considering the day and age? Priests would have been trusted implicitly, so he's holding himself up as a representative of God, alongside everything else."

"God Complex—or a kind of revenge against the god he felt had forsaken him for so many years?" Jacob said, and gave the proposition serious thought. "Yes, that is very possible."

"Now, in Carl's case, he's no Count of Monte Cristo," Douglas said. "In fact, before his imprisonment, he was a rather lowly figure in a financial hierarchy, with a troubled background and no relationship history to speak of—nor many friends, if I recall."

"Plenty of people prefer their own company," Jacob put in. "As for 'lowly'..." He lifted a shoulder. "Perhaps he had nothing to prove."

"Oh, but he *did*," Douglas said, and thanked the waitress who came to take their order. "Deere always had issues with his father, for one thing, who was—by his own admission—cruel, tyrannical, abusive and exacting. Carl hated his father, but also sought his approval at every turn."

Jacob steepled his hands. "Well, his father's dead, now, isn't he? Perhaps that's released him from any feeling of obligation."

Douglas took another long gulp of water, and watched the play of light against the crystal. "Perhaps that obligation was the only thing keeping him sane."

Jacob was surprised. "The same thing that caused him trauma could also be...grounding?"

Bill nodded. "If I've said it once, I've said it a thousand times: they f— you up."

Jacob blinked, never having heard the professor swear before, and then laughed. "I must have missed that chapter in your last book."

"Look again," Bill advised him. "It's there, in not so many words."

"Speaking of Carl, what do you make of the latest murder in London?" Jacob asked. "I heard that his former prosecutor, Leonora Stewart, was found murdered earlier today. Wasn't the judge who convicted him also murdered, recently? Quite a coincidence."

Douglas grasped his fork and began winding spaghetti through the prongs. "I'm sorry for her family, and for all the people she might have helped." He paused, the fork halfway to his mouth. "I wonder whether, when Edmund Dantès was being the generous Lord Wilmore, he ever felt remorse about the vengeance he reaped while playing the Count of Monte Cristo?"

Jacob smiled. "We're delving into the realms of fiction," he said. "You've interviewed plenty of criminals in your time, professor. Why don't *you* tell *me* how likely it is that a real-life Monte Cristo would feel anything at all after deciding to take his revenge?"

"I think the people who kill others in the name of vengeance are looking for a reason they can be proud of, or that society might forgive," Douglas said. "The plain truth is that they like the rush, and they are compelled to seek it. They feel embarrassed by their own perversion, so they look for ways to justify it. At its heart, is self-deception."

"And have you always been honest with yourself, professor?"

Douglas sank back against his chair and raised his fork in acknowledgment. "No, I haven't always been honest with myself—but I'm the only person who's ever been hurt by that dishonesty. Can you say the same?"

Jacob inclined his head. "I'll let you be the judge of that, some day."

CHAPTER 26

By seven o'clock, Ava was fit to collapse.

The emotional toil of working Leonora Stewart's crime scene, followed by an afternoon mired in paperwork and meetings with the Chief Constable, had left her feeling exhausted and jittery, and a lack of food didn't help.

"You need a lift home, boss?"

Carter was tucking into a packet of beef jerky, and her stomach reacted.

"Ah, no thanks," she said, and wished she didn't sound so shifty whenever she thought of Ian O'Shea. "I'm going to a friend's house for dinner."

Carter's frown cleared, and he began chewing in earnest. "A *friend*, eh? Is this friend tall and blond, with an Irish accent?"

"Maybe."

Carter let out a guffaw, which was something she hadn't heard since watching the *Carry On* movies with her late grandfather.

"For God's sake, Carter, keep your trap shut—" she hissed.

"You gonna get some pizza and chill?"

"Hopefully."

He gave another one of his laughs, and she punched him fully in the arm. "If you've got nothing better to do than wind me up, you could at least share your beef jerky while you're at it."

Carter grinned, and offered the packet. "I can still give you a lift," he said. "I'm heading in that direction."

Ava was about to refuse, but was interrupted by a jaw-cracking yawn. "All right," she conceded. "That'd be great, thanks. I'll let him know I'm on my way."

She punched in Ian's number, and they waited while it rang out.

"Hmm," she said. "I hope he hasn't forgotten."

Carter shovelled the last of the beef into his mouth, then shook his head. "Nah," he said, between chews. "He's probably just on the throne and can't be disturbed."

Ava gave him a withering look. "There's no need to be *uncouth*," she said, but supposed it could be true. "Let's head over there and hope he's de-throned by the time we arrive."

Twenty minutes later, having been relieved of any confidence Ava might have felt in her sergeant's driving capabilities, they arrived in the borough of Islington.

"Well," she declared, as they pulled up outside a row of smart terraced houses. "I know who I'll be booking onto a refresher driving course, first thing Monday morning."

"We got here in record time, didn't we?" Carter was outraged.

"I rest my case," she muttered. "Give me a minute to find my legs again, and I'll be on my way."

He chuckled. "Which one is Ian's place?" he asked, peering through the windshield.

"Number 11," she said. "The flat on the first floor of that one, over there."

"Light's on," he said, and wriggled his eyebrows. "Loverboy must be home."

She smiled. "Would you mind waiting until I've gone inside?"

"'Course," Carter said, and thought that, despite her strength, his boss had a fear of the dark just like everybody else. "Have a great night, and I'll see you on Monday."

Ava thought of the overtime they'd have to put in tomorrow, but didn't have the heart to crush his dreams of a lazy weekend.

"Thanks—you too."

She hopped out of the car, slung a small overnight bag over her shoulder, then jogged across the pavement towards a black-painted door bearing the number "11" in brass lettering. The house had been converted into four flats, one on each level from the basement to the second floor, and the names of the residents had been written beside a series of corresponding buzzers on an old intercom panel—all apart from Ian's, as he hadn't yet found time to add his own name to the list.

She pressed the buzzer for the first floor flat and waited.

No answer.

Ava glanced back over her shoulder to where Carter remained parked by the kerb, engine running while he fiddled with the car radio.

She tried the buzzer again, and leaned into it.

Nothing.

"Bit unreliable, those things."

Ava turned to find a man walking towards her. He was somewhere in his eighties, dressed smartly in navy slacks and matching wool coat, while a small plastic bag of milk and bread hung from his arm. "Who've you come to see, dear?"

"Ian," she replied. "On the first floor."

The man cocked a hand to his ear. "Sorry, my hearing isn't what it used to be," he said, and gave her a charming smile.

"Ian O'Shea," she repeated, at a volume several decibels higher than usual. "He lives on the first floor."

"Well, you don't look like an axe murderer to me," he joked, and reached up to slot a key in the front door. "The intercom is probably on the blink, and we can't have a lovely young lady like yourself waiting out in the cold, can we?"

Ava was surprised to find tears nip the back of her eyes. Perhaps it was the kindness of strangers, or the idea that somebody thought her a 'lovely young lady'.

"Thank you," she said. "Here, let me help you—"

The door was stiff and heavy, with an automatic closing system, so she held it open while the old gentleman preceded her, then gave Carter a quick wave goodbye and, hearing his answering 'toot', stepped inside the communal hallway.

"I'm headed upstairs," the man said, having introduced himself as Pete Atkinson. "I'm on the second floor, above Ian's."

Ava worried about all the stairs he needed to climb, but needn't have bothered; he might have been profoundly deaf, but Pete was still as sprightly as a mountain goat—or, at least, a goat who'd climbed the mountain a few times, and could still just about manage it.

"This is your stop," he puffed, and retrieved the bag of groceries she'd carried upstairs for him. "Have a lovely evening, the pair of you, and tell Ian I'll pop around to do my victory dance when Arsenal bring it home tomorrow."

"I'll tell him," she smiled.

In a gesture from a bygone age, he tipped a finger to the tweed flat cap he wore atop his balding head, then moved off to continue his journey upward. Ava was still smiling when she raised a fist to knock on Ian's door, but it quickly slipped from her lips.

The wood framing the doorway had splintered, which was consistent with someone having forced the lock. With a hammering heart, she pushed it wide open and stood on the threshold, staring into the empty hallway beyond.

"Ian?" she called out, loud enough for Pete to hear from the landing above. "*Ian!*"

Not a sound came from within.

"It's Ava!"

When there was no answering call, she stepped inside Ian's hallway, which consisted of a long corridor with a coat peg and a console table. She caught a motion in the mirror above it and froze, before realising it was her own reflection. Looking away sharply, she continued along the hallway to the living room, breath caught in her chest as she braced herself for whatever awaited her behind that closed doorway.

Then, the breath simply drained from her body.

Ian was at home, as Carter had said. He was seated on his sofa-bed, still dressed in work clothes, tie half undone at the neck and a small hole visible in one of the black socks covering his feet. His head had fallen back against the cushions so that he might have been sleeping, dark eyelashes fanning the cheeks of his face, which was no longer tanned and vital, but ashen grey.

His throat protruded, a muscular column now slashed bare. Rivers of blood had drained from his body, staining his shirt and trousers, dripping onto the sofa where it congealed in small puddles.

Ava took in the scene, her mind capturing the devastation in a series of still images she would later revisit as nightmares, and then turned, very slowly, to leave the room and call her sergeant.

CHAPTER 27

Alex and Naomi stood on the platform at King's Cross, awaiting their train back to Cambridge, when his phone began to ring. Like one of Pavlov's dogs, he was immediately fearful, having learned that phone calls that came after working hours were usually from people with bad news to impart.

"Doctor Gregory? This is DS Carter."

Alex signalled to Naomi, and they began walking towards a quiet spot away from the main crowd.

"Has there been a development in the Stewart murder?"

"No, there's been another one."

Gregory's heart slammed against his chest in one hard motion, and he thought of his friend.

"Professor Douglas?"

"No, it's not him," Carter said quickly. "It's one of ours, Ian O'Shea. He's a new DI, back from a few years up in Birmingham, but he was at the Met to begin with. I think he was around more or less the same time Carl Deere was brought to trial—"

"I remember the name," Gregory said. "Ian was part of the team who brought Carl in."

It wasn't news to Carter, but he made a sound of surprise, because he wasn't supposed to know it.

"Do you need me to come over?" Gregory continued.

"That's partly why I'm calling," Carter said. "With my sergeant's hat on, I need to remind you to be vigilant going forwards, because, for Carl to kill twice in the space of twelve hours—"

"You're certain it was him?"

"Hard to know who else would have had sufficient motive, but we'll explore all the avenues," Carter replied. "It would be good to have your take on things."

"And, without your sergeant's hat on?"

"What? Oh, right," Carter said, and Gregory heard a long sigh at the end of the line. "She won't be happy I've told you this, but I'll take whatever comes, because this is important. Ava—DCI

Hope, that is—had, ah, something going on with Ian—"

"They were dating, you mean?"

"They were starting to," Carter said. "He was a nice guy, and they hooked up the other night. I think she really liked him, then...*this* has happened. She won't want anybody to know she's conflicted, because her private life is private, but...look, she's struggling, I can see it. I thought, maybe, if you talked to her, worked some of your voodoo magic of the mind, it might help?"

Gregory had to smile. When they found out he was a psychiatrist, most people imagined he could read their minds and see their most private thoughts. Though he could infer much from what they told him, as well as the many things they didn't, he'd never been forced to use witchcraft yet.

"You're a good friend," he said, because he understood why Carter was really calling. It was not to further the investigation, which might be a side-product of Gregory's involvement, but rather to help his friend. "Where is she now?"

"Inside O'Shea's flat, with the forensic team. We'll probably be here a while," Carter said, and rattled off the address.

"I have Doctor Palmer with me, and I don't want her to travel to Cambridge alone—"

"Bring her along," Carter said. "Maybe she can help me out because, I don't mind telling you, Doc, I'm starting to get the heebie-jeebies about all this."

"Carl isn't interested in you," Gregory assured him, and it was true. "You haven't wronged him, so you're not on his list."

"Not that I know of," Carter grumbled. "See you in twenty minutes."

At first glance, Ava seemed to be her usual self.

She moved around the crime scene with calm authority, issuing quiet orders and generally hovering over the forensic team to ensure nothing was missed.

"I want the pipework fully dismantled and analysed for DNA, just in case our perp washed his hands," she was saying, as Gregory appeared on the threshold. "I don't care how much extra work it is; O'Shea was one of ours, and deserves everything we have to give."

Her voice was strained, he thought, but admirably steady.

"DCI Hope."

She jumped a little in her polypropylene suit. "Well," she said, with forced cheer. "I bet you thought your work was done for the day. This city never sleeps, and nor do its murderers."

Her eyes were very bright, and never once strayed to the body.

Not once.

"I'm sorry this has happened," he said, remaining where he was so that she could choose whether or not to talk with him. "Carter called."

She nodded. "Of course he did, and I suppose he told you everything."

"Yes," he replied. "Your sergeant cares about you, and wants to help."

"If he wants to help, then he can do some legwork for a bloody change!"

The outburst drew the eyes of several others in the room, and she hugged her body, hating it, and hating herself.

"Why don't we get some fresh air?" Gregory suggested.

"We have a twenty-four-hour window, at most, while the evidence is fresh," she snapped. "I can't take any time out for 'deep and meaningfuls' now, Alex. Why not try your luck with Carter? He's obviously a fan of your head-doctoring."

Gregory didn't react to the baiting, because it was something he'd heard a hundred times before, from people whose anguish was far more acute than hers.

"Do you have a working theory?"

He changed direction, to focus her mind on processes and procedures. If she wanted to bury herself in work, he would play along, but it was a delaying tactic and the fall-out would come eventually, as it always did.

"Well, the lock was broken on the front door, so we have to assume Carl—sorry, I should say, 'the perp'—gained entry to the flat by forcing their way inside. This must have happened before Ian arrived home, and maybe he entered the flat just as I did, not knowing whether a burglar or some other intruder had come and gone already."

"It seems unusual that he would have seated himself on the sofa," Gregory remarked, and moved closer to study Ian's body, and the direction of his injuries.

"It's possible he didn't see them, at first," Ava said, while she tried to visualise the sequence of events. "Ian might have thought he was alone, and decided to sit down for a minute before calling it in. He'd been at work all day, so he must have been tired."

She swallowed, not wanting to think of their encounter in the break room, or his smile, or the touch of his hands. It did no good to remember, nor lament all that might have been.

You're a hard woman—

Ian's words haunted her.

"Then, judging from the direction of the attack"—she raised a hand to indicate a right-handed slashing motion—"it seems they came at him from behind."

Gregory looked at the deep cuts against the man's throat, which had torn through his trachea and carotid artery.

"Yes, I agree that would have been the approach," he said, and looked around the room, his eyes cataloguing everything. "What's the message?"

Ava was confused. "The message?"

"Yes, the message," he repeated. "You believe this was done by Carl Deere, is that right?"

She nodded.

"In which case, he likes to leave a message, as we've seen with his other victims. Usually, one conveying judgment or justice, as he sees it. Was there anything left on or beside the body?"

Ava forced herself to look back, and then away again. "No, but he was left in the same cruciform position as Leonora Stewart," she pointed out. "Perhaps Carl felt rushed, or didn't have the usual amount of time to stage things as he'd have liked?"

Gregory said nothing, but continued to stare at Ian's body in a manner that was unnerving.

"Tell me about the victim," he said, after a minute ticked by. "Was he the type to make enemies?"

"I hardly knew him," she said, but her body still remembered his. "He was fun, gregarious… charming, I suppose. He'd only been around the department for a few days and, as far as I know, everyone liked him. If he had enemies, they would likely be past collars, just like Carl Deere."

Gregory folded his arms, and considered. "If you're right, and your investigation doesn't throw up any other obvious suspects, that should give us even greater cause for concern," he said.

"What do you mean?"

"I mean that, if Carl Deere is responsible for killing Ian, then he has access to strict confidential records," Gregory replied.

Hope rubbed a gloved hand to her forehead, which was growing hot beneath the suit she wore. "I'm—I'm sorry, I'm not following you. If Ian was part of the team who brought Carl in, then there's an obvious motive. Home addresses are easy enough to find, aren't they?"

Gregory realised she didn't know the true nature of Ian O'Shea's involvement in Carl Deere's entrapment and arrest, so made it his business to enlighten her.

"Ian was part of the original team," he said. "But his name was kept off the official records for his own safety, and to protect his role in future investigations."

"Because he was Ghost Squad?" she guessed, and thought that would explain Ian's reticence in telling her about his involvement in the investigation when she'd asked him.

"No, he was one of the men working on the entrapment team," Gregory said. "He went out with Carl a few times, tried to draw out his fantasies along with any confessions. It was a dangerous occupation, considering, at that time, it was widely believed Carl was a prolific killer of young, handsome men just like Ian. He was a highly dedicated officer."

Hope cast wide, grief-stricken eyes towards the sofa. "He—" She gulped back tears. "That was why he moved away to Birmingham."

Gregory nodded. "Ian specialised in undercover ops, but not against his own side. I know this because I was involved in the original investigation." *And because I was asked to psychologically debrief all those involved in the entrapment,* he might have added. "As I say, several names were removed from the official record for safety reasons. If Carl has been able to access those names by hacking the digital files, then we have to assume he has significant means and technological capability, as well as psychopathic tendencies."

Hope walked across the room to the window, where she looked out at the city lights.

"I don't care what the Chief Constable says," she muttered. "Deere needs to be stopped by any and all means necessary. I'll do everything I can to bring him in."

"I know you don't want to hear this, but there is a conflict, Ava. It might be worth stepping back from this one."

When she turned around, her face was granite hard. "I know my own limits," she said clearly.

"I'm sad, of course, but I'm still clear-sighted. Besides, I have Carter."

They both knew that wouldn't pass muster, should it ever come up with senior management, but then, desperate times called for desperate measures.

"I trust your judgment," he said.

Ava almost smiled. "Will you come back on the team, then, Alex?"

"I never really left."

CHAPTER 28

When his phone began to buzz against the tablecloth, Bill Douglas swallowed the last gulp of a very decent glass of red wine, and gave Jacob an apologetic smile.

"Alex? Just a moment." He excused himself from the table and stepped outside into the frosty evening, where he listened while Gregory told him about Ian O'Shea's murder, and of DCI Hope's personal connection to the victim. "Further escalation," was the first thing he said. "Two killed in a single day, both in London and both ultra-violent. Carl's confidence is showing, now that he's had a bit of practice."

"Yes. More worrying is the possibility he's accessed the police mainframe," Gregory said. "There isn't any other way he could have known about Ian O'Shea's involvement, because his name wasn't on the public record. The only name Carl would have known is the one Ian gave him during the entrapment operation, which was 'Aiden Royston', if I remember correctly. Any attempt to track down that person would have been fruitless, because he doesn't exist."

"All the same, perhaps it's worth checking whether any other men by that name have been visited by Mr Deere," Douglas said. "Even in a case of mistaken identity, Carl might have found himself in a situation where he needed to eliminate any potential witnesses."

"You're right," Gregory said, and made a note to speak to DCI Hope about it. "It doesn't change the fact that, somehow, he tracked Ian down. He must have hacked into the system, or paid someone to look it up for him, neither of which is a good development for the Major Crimes division."

"Carl would have known what Ian looked like," Bill mused. "Although he didn't know Ian's real name, it's possible he might have stumbled across O'Shea sometime during his reconnaissance work. Maybe he saw Ian with DCI Hope, who he's probably been keeping an eye on, given her connection with us."

"Possible, but unlikely," Gregory said, after a moment's thought. "O'Shea only returned to the city in the past few days. He's been in Birmingham until now. It would be fast work."

Douglas made a rumbling sound of agreement. "However he found out, it's a concern," he said. "If it was Carl who killed Ian O'Shea, after that business with Leonora Stewart earlier today, then he's redoubled his efforts and it's obvious he's no longer as concerned about the degree of risk involved, so much as getting through the numbers. It's the most dangerous space for any killer, and it's a dangerous place for us, too."

Panic threatened again, but Gregory shoved it to the back of his mind. "It'll make him stupid," he said. "More prone to errors, if he hasn't made plenty already. Things have been moving so fast, the police teams can barely keep up with their own investigations and they don't have the resources. I've agreed to come back on board, to consult with Hope's team."

"Are you sure that's a good idea?" Douglas asked. "It'll enrage Carl even further, because he'll view it as a replay of the worst time in his life: the same profiler who was involved in the original operation, whom he considers partially culpable for his wrongful prosecution, is back for a second bite of the cherry?"

"I can't sit around waiting for him to find me," Gregory argued. *He'd lose his own mind, and be no help to anybody.*

Douglas knew when the argument was already lost. "Do you need me, Alex?"

"You can help me by staying *safe*," his friend replied. "It's going to be late before we get back to Cambridge; in fact, it might make sense for me to stay at my place here in London with Naomi, just for tonight. But—"

"Don't worry about me," Douglas interjected, and turned to look at Jacob through the glass window. "I have a friend with me, so I won't be alone."

"A friend?" Gregory said, with interest. "Which one?"

"Oh, just from the university," came the breezy reply. "You don't know him."

"Would I like him?"

"You'd find him very interesting," Douglas said. "I'll see you both tomorrow. Oh, and did you see the news?"

"About the murders?"

"No, about Carl." Douglas told him about the recent puff-piece about Carl Deere, and Gregory swore roundly.

"Who the hell wrote it?"

"Funny you should mention it, her name did ring a bell from somewhere. It was written by a woman called Romola Harris, from *The Daily Scoop.*"

"Son of a—"

"Now, now, her writing might not be quite up to snuff, but there's no need for—"

"*No*, Bill. Don't you see? It's the same journalist I've identified as being under threat of attack, because she was responsible for writing some of the most scathing coverage of Carl, back when things first kicked off. She's spun out plenty of follow-ups, since then, and none of it has been complimentary, even after his acquittal. Her reach alone would have been enough to have him run out of most respectable villages."

The penny dropped. "You think he got to her?"

"It's the only explanation for why someone like Romola Harris would suddenly write such a glowing report about a person she had no respect for, previously," Gregory said. "The timing is also very interesting, considering Carl's been on a killing spree. He knows the police would do anything to steer clear of any involvement, after what happened last time. He also knows his records and DNA profile have been destroyed, so it's extremely difficult to make a positive ID at any of the crime scenes. Finally, he knows that, if he presents himself as a philanthropist on top of being an injured party, he curries public favour and makes it even less likely the higher echelons of the Met would want to sanction an investigation based on nothing so far but supposition."

"You saw him on the train!"

"I'm also the man who nearly lost my career and reputation," Gregory said. "It would be easy for him to suggest I have a private vendetta against him. We need *proof*, Bill, but there isn't any—not without getting our hands on the man himself."

"Stranger things have happened."

"They can't happen soon enough."

"Go on, and be with Naomi," Bill suggested. "Remind yourself of all the good things, after a day filled with so much of the bad."

Gregory looked across to the squad car, where Naomi dozed on the back seat.

"Anybody ever tell you, you're a good listener?"

"Once or twice."

CHAPTER 29

Gregory's apartment overlooked the River Thames, from its position on the upper floor of an old Victorian warehouse conversion. He'd chosen that part of town for its vibrant community and plethora of nearby bars and restaurants which, for many years, had served as a proxy for things like 'friendships' and 'community' when the loneliness of an empty flat had become too much, even for him.

"Nice spot," Naomi remarked, as they entered the airy loft. "Oh, and look! You can see the river from here!"

She made a beeline for the floor-to-ceiling windows along the back wall of his living room.

"I didn't know profiling paid so well," she laughed. "Maybe I should offer my services to DS

Carter so I can make a down payment on one of these places."

Gregory wrapped his arms around her waist. "It's an empty place, just for one person," he said softly. "I used to tell myself I liked a simple, orderly life without unnecessary clutter, which included the company of other people. Now, I'm starting to re-think that mindset."

She turned to face him, still circled loosely in his arms, and gave him a crooked smile. "It can be hard, when you've been a misanthropic git for so long," she said, and gave him a pat on the cheek. "But don't worry, I'll help you. Tomorrow, we'll start with the basics, like how to talk to strangers on public transport."

"Bloody hell," he muttered. "Do I have to?"

Naomi laughed. "I think you might turn out to be my finest case study."

Gregory tugged her closer against his body.

"I'm definitely a 'work in progress'," he said. "You might find it takes longer than you think to whip me into shape."

"How long, do you reckon?"

A lifetime, his mind whispered. Spend a lifetime with me, and help me to become a better man.

At another time, the strength of his own feelings might have frightened him, but, as he allowed the thought to circle and then settle somewhere in the region of his heart, Gregory found there was no fear; only anticipation, and *excitement*, which was something he rarely allowed himself to feel.

"Alex?"

"Sorry," he said, and brushed his lips against hers. "I was just thinking that you should take as long as you like."

Naomi smiled. "We have all the time in the world."

Much later, Alex and Naomi lay in the semi-darkness of his room listening to the patter of rain against the windowpanes outside. They were quiet for long minutes, and it was a peaceful, contented silence, before he was compelled to break it.

"I was speaking with Hope and Carter, earlier," he said. "They know as well as I do that Carl has the advantage over us. He's killing quickly, without hesitation or remorse."

"Don't they have any leads at all?"

Gregory shook his head. "Carl must have been planning this for a long time," he said. "It's obvious, from the degree of knowledge he's acquired about each victim, and the total absence of any physical or digital imprint. Aside from an old flat he never even resided in, taken under the name Euan Squires, we have no idea where Carl is, or even where he's been."

"You're worried," she said. "You don't think we can find him?"

He didn't answer directly. "I can almost feel him breathing down our necks, Naomi, and it makes me sick to my core."

"In case he comes for you—"

"No," Gregory said quietly. "In case he hurts you, or Bill. You asked me whether I think we can find him? The answer is, I don't know. But what I *do* know is that I won't be able to try, if I'm worried about you."

She was silent, the professional part of her brain wondering what it took to create a person without any real care for himself or his own wellbeing, before remembering the childhood he'd endured.

No further explanation was required.

"What about a safe house?" she suggested. "Couldn't we all go somewhere out of the city?'

"Carl has been able to find even the most confidential addresses," Gregory replied, thinking of Ian O'Shea, who now lay on a cold metal slab in the mortuary. "It wouldn't help Bill, or me, but it might help you."

Naomi twisted around to look at him. "I don't like where this is going—"

"You know I spoke with my detective friend in the north, DCI Ryan? He's the best there is, Naomi. He also happens to live hundreds of miles from here, in a beautiful rural home with his lovely wife and daughter. The North is his stronghold, he has an entire team at his disposal—an army, if needed. If you were to go and stay with him and his family, I know you'd be safe. There isn't anybody else in the world I'd trust as much to safeguard your life."

Naomi shook her head, and he kissed her gently.

"I would rather stay together, but it isn't the right thing to do," he said. "There is real danger here and I should never have allowed you to be anywhere near it. There's a time for bravery, and a time for retreat. I need you to retreat, so that I can be brave and find this man without worrying that I'll lose the most precious thing I've ever had."

The power of his words couldn't fail to have impact, and she blinked away tears. "What about you, and Bill?" she said.

"There isn't anywhere we can run to," he replied. "Carl has made his final judgment and will follow through with his punishment, no matter where we are or how long it takes to find us. We can't hide away somewhere in the misguided hope that the police will find him before it comes to that. They're nowhere near to finding him, and the list is getting shorter by the day."

"I don't want to leave you, Alex."

"I know," he said, and held her more tightly. "I don't want you to leave me, either, but this is only for a short while, until we bring him in."

"Is it what Hope and Carter have suggested?"

"They agree with me that it's a good idea to get you away from the action," he replied. "Hope needs to speak to Durham CID about Irwin's death, anyway, so she's offered to take you up there in person."

"Like a chaperone?"

"Like a trained firearms officer, with years of experience," he replied.

Naomi let out a quivering breath, and made the only sensible choice. "If it will help you, I'll do as you ask," she said. "What are you going to do while I'm gone?"

"I've gone back over Carl's file again and again," he said, and rolled away from her to turn on the side light, since they were both wide awake. "I can't see anything new, but perhaps the answers lie in the things that are old. For starters, he had a compulsive habit of creating acrostics, of all things; it was a comfort mechanism he used during every interview with the police, and with the psychiatrists who assessed him ahead of the trial. I'm beginning to think 'VINDICTA SERVIVIT FRIGUS' might have been used as an acrostic while he was in prison."

"Show me," she said.

Gregory slipped from the bed and walked towards a desk beside the window, where he retrieved a pen and paper before walking back again. Naomi's eyes followed his progress, appreciating the view.

"You're very unselfconscious," she said, once he was beside her again.

He raised an eyebrow. "Am I? Perhaps, in some areas," he agreed. "I've never been particularly worried about nudity."

"You don't need to be."

He smiled, and reached over to kiss her again. "Carry on talking like that, and we'll get no sleep at all."

"Sleep deprivation only really starts to impair bodily functions after the first forty-eight hours," she said. "We can risk it."

"I always take the advice of my doctor."

Naomi smiled, but tapped the paper he held in his hand. "Business first," she said.

Reluctantly, he agreed. "If I write out the phrase VINDICTA SERVIVIT FRIGUS vertically, to separate each of the letters, you can see there are twenty-two of them," he said, writing them out along the left side of the page.

"Mm hmm," she agreed. "If it's an acrostic, what do you think each of the letters stands for?"

"This is all pie in the sky, but…I was thinking it could be each of the names of his intended victims. This is the list I've drawn up, based on the people I think he would hate the most, as well as a few others who might be close to that."

Naomi looked at the collection of letters, then at the list of names, and frowned.

"There are too many 'V's'," she said. "There's only one person whose forename or surname contains the letter 'V' and that's one of the jurors you've listed, Pooja Varma. That still leaves two 'V's' unaccounted for, unless I'm missing something?"

"The 'I's' are also a problem," he agreed. "There aren't many people whose name begins or ends with 'I' that would be of interest to Carl; the only one I can think of is Andy Irwin, the prison officer, who's already dead, and another juror, Aryan Ismail."

"What about Ian O'Shea?"

"All the other names I've worked out are based on surnames, not forenames," he replied. "It might not matter to Carl but, as I said, he's an obsessive-compulsive character in some respects. It would be an anomaly."

"On the other hand, Ian is dead, and we can't base a contra-hypothesis off the back of linguistics alone," she said, with a certain dry humour.

"Fair point. That accounts for three 'I' names, but still leaves two unaccounted for, as well as two 'V' letters and a couple of 'T's as well."

"No potential victims beginning or ending with 'T'?" she queried.

"None that come to mind," he replied. "However, I did wonder whether Carl's been a bit creative, to fit the letters in the phrase to the names on his list."

"How so?"

"Look at this," he said, and began scribbling on the page. "If you put the two spare 'V's' together, that makes a 'W', where there wasn't one before."

"For Whittaker, the judge," Naomi realised.

"Exactly. If you put one of the 'T's' together with one of the 'I's', that makes an 'H' sitting on its side," he said, and sketched it out for her. "That could be 'H' for Keith Hatman, another juror, or Romola Harris, the journalist at *The Daily Scoop*."

"I would have thought both could make the list," Naomi pointed out.

"So did I, which is why I thought the other spare 'T' would go together with the spare 'I' to make another 'H'," Gregory replied.

"Maybe we're clutching at straws because we're getting desperate," she said, studying the page. "It seems a long shot that any of this is correct. Perhaps he just liked the original Latin phrase because he was feeling vengeful."

"You're probably right, but the coincidence is remarkable. Look here."

Gregory filled in the remaining names on the acrostic, and turned it around for her to see:

V – Whittaker (judge). Borrow the 'V' below.
I – Irwin (prison officer)
N – Nithercott (juror)
D – Douglas (profiler)
I – Harris (Romola – journalist). Borrow the 'T' below.
C – Campbell (Detective Superintendent)
T – Move to 'I' and turn on side to make an 'H' for 'Harris' (journalist)
A – Achari (juror)

S – Smith (juror)
E – Eggleston (juror)
R – Reed (juror)
V – used to make 'W' for Whittaker.
I – Ismail (juror)
V – Varma (juror)
I – Hatman (use the T below) (juror)
T – Move to 'I' and turn on side to make 'H' for 'Hatman'.

F – Fairchild (juror)
R – Reed (juror)

I –
G – Gregory (profiler)
U – Upton (juror)
S – Stewart (prosecuting barrister)

"I have to admit, it does fit," she murmured. "But you've only listed eleven jurors."

"That's because the twelfth is already dead," Gregory said, and surprised her again. "Carol Isleworth died of natural causes—ovarian cancer—eighteen months ago."

"I'm sorry to hear it," Naomi said. "Do you think that freed up a space on the list?"

"Perhaps," he replied. "I thought so, but then Ian died, so that would account for the 'I'."

"Maybe he wasn't expecting to find Ian, so that's why he doesn't quite fit so well as all the rest," she said, still peering at the names and their corresponding letters. "Something doesn't feel quite right, but I can't say what."

"Let's sleep on it," Gregory suggested. "Maybe the answer will come to us in the morning."

Naomi set the paper aside, though she remained troubled.

"I can't stand to see your name on there, or Bill's," she said. "It makes it more…real, somehow."

Gregory took her face in his hands.

"Don't think about that, now," he said, and kissed her deeply. "Think about this, instead."

Naomi let herself drift, safe in his arms, surrounded by the night, and thought that, even if it should be their last, she would be forever grateful.

CHAPTER 30

"You have a lovely home."

Bill Douglas watched Jacob prowl around his living room, studying the overstuffed bookcases on either side of the fireplace, smiling at some of the framed images of the professor with his friends and colleagues that graced the mantelpiece.

"Thank you," he replied. "Would you like a nightcap? Some wine?"

They'd imbibed a healthy amount at the restaurant and then at the little bar around the corner from Hawking College, but the night was still young.

"If you are," Jacob replied. "Red, please."

"Of course. Make yourself comfortable and I'll be back in a moment."

It took more than a moment to find what he needed, but finally Douglas re-joined his guest with a drink in each hand.

"Here's to you," he said, and they clinked glasses. "Cheers."

"Here's to *us*," Jacob corrected, and knocked back a few fingers of Montepulciano. "I'm sorry I won't have the opportunity to meet your friends, this evening. You've told me so many good things about Doctor Gregory, in particular."

Bill took a seat on the sofa, and Jacob settled beside him. Not touching, but close enough that he could see the wild drumbeat in the other man's neck.

"Yes, Alex is a wonderful friend," Bill said, and took a sip of wine. "He's one of the most selfless people I've ever known, but he would be very embarrassed if I ever told him that."

Jacob swilled the liquid in his own glass, then set it down on the coffee table.

"Have you two ever…?"

Bill smiled, thinking of the number of times he'd been asked that question since choosing to come out to select members of his social circle. Alex was an attractive man, younger than himself but not too young, and their closeness raised questions to those with an enquiring mind, he supposed. He decided to take it as a compliment that others would suspect they were a couple, and wondered how easy life would have been had their wants and needs been aligned in the same direction.

A question that would never be answered.

"No," he replied, with a smile. "Our relationship is one of friendship and, perhaps, a kind of brotherly kinship. There's an age gap between us but, sometimes, he seems to be the older soul, although that varies depending on the circumstances."

"Mycroft Holmes to his brother Sherlock?" Jacob suggested.

"I didn't know you were a fan of Conan Doyle! I have his collected works on the shelf over there."

"Some of my favourite stories, as a child," Jacob said. "Are they what first sparked your interest in profiling?"

"There are certainly elements of the Sherlock stories that are very modern, despite their age," Bill replied. "I'm sure they're responsible for my initial interest in forensic psychiatry and profiling, even if I was unaware of it. And you? Were you a great reader, as a child?"

Thoughts of his childhood prompted Jacob to retrieve his glass. "Reading for pleasure wasn't encouraged," he replied eventually. "School books or textbooks were fine, but not works of fiction in general."

"That's a pity," Douglas sympathised, and topped off Jacob's wine. "I take it academia was encouraged?"

Jacob nodded and, when nothing more was forthcoming, Bill decided to confide a little about his own upbringing.

"I grew up with an authoritarian father in a traditional family environment, in a working-class town," he said, without any inflection. "Both of my parents worked equally hard, in their own ways. Feelings weren't actively discouraged, but they were never spoken of, so it amounted to the same thing."

Jacob listened to him, enraptured.

"My mother was a loving woman, as far as she was able to be, and we were close until she passed away. My father was the disciplinarian, and held strong views about almost every topic. Discussion or debate wasn't encouraged, whereas loyalty and hard work were rewarded."

"Not the ideal environment for a young man discovering his sexuality," Jacob ventured.

"No indeed," he replied. "The most important thing for them was for me to follow a secure pathway, earn a decent, honest living and settle down with a nice woman who'd be just like my mother."

"But you're nothing like your father."

"We share some similarities," Douglas averred. "He taught me honesty and respect for others; it's just that, unknowingly, he also taught me to be secretive about those things that didn't align with his world view. It's quite a contradiction."

"How did he react, when you told him you wanted something different?"

"Well, the first hurdle was university," Douglas said. "I was the first in my family to go, and it was a source of enormous pride for him, as well as fear. Anything that strays from the usual pathway is a concern for many people. As for my going to Cambridge, that was unheard of."

Jacob nodded. "What about when you told him you wouldn't be marrying the neighbour's daughter?"

Douglas paused, and then voiced his greatest regret. "I never told my father."

Jacob leaned in. "I'm sorry you never felt able to."

"I wanted my father's approval and acceptance, and for many years I wasn't sure that I would have either of those things, unless I conformed to his ideals. I deceived myself for so many years to try to convince myself that it was my ideal, too, but it never was."

"If he hadn't put you in that position, you'd never have *needed* to lie to yourself," Jacob argued.

Douglas shook his head. "I don't have that kind of anger towards either of my parents, because we must all be accountable for ourselves. As children, we're at the mercy of the adults in our lives, and sometimes that experience can bring untold sadness," he said, and Jacob moved away.

"Leaving us with a lifetime of bad memories," he muttered, irritably. "Like a hit and run, they leave us to deal with the destruction."

"Was your father difficult, Jacob?"

He gave a harsh laugh, which ended on a yawn. "You could say that."

"Perhaps you could speak to him about whatever is troubling you," Douglas suggested. "I left it too late to speak to my own father, but it may not be too late for you."

Jacob shook his head, and leaned back against the sofa.

"He's dead," he muttered. "It's too late, Professor. Much too late for me."

"It's never too late for your soul to heal. It's never too late for that."

Jacob laughed softly, eyes closing while his body relaxed into sleep.

"The old man hated me. As for her...a cat's a better mother. She never protected me. Never."

His accent had slipped away, and no longer bore the continental lilt Bill had come to know. Up close, Jacob's face was tanned with a little help from the bottle, and the lighter brown roots of his hair were beginning to show.

"That must have been hard," Douglas said, in a soothing voice.

"No," Jacob whispered. "She'll be gone, soon."

"Is she unwell?"

Jacob didn't answer, having fallen into a heavy slumber. Bill watched him for a few minutes, thinking over all that had been said. Then, with deft movements, he reached across with a shaky hand to extract a couple of hairs from the man's head. He froze, expecting him to wake up, but instead Jacob curled into the cushions and slept on. After slipping the hair into a plastic sandwich bag, Bill reached for their wine glasses and tiptoed back into the kitchen, where he packaged one up for dispatch to the forensics unit at Major Crimes.

After it was done, he checked the time and found it was almost two o'clock in the morning.

Too late to call Hope or Gregory, he thought, especially after the day they'd put in.

Tomorrow morning would be soon enough.

In the living room, Jacob slept until morning, while Douglas remained wide awake and vigilant throughout the long hours of the night. At daybreak, he left a note beside the man he knew as Jacob, telling him he had an early tutorial, that he didn't want to disturb him, and he should just pull the front door closed behind him once he'd helped himself to coffee and whatever else he wanted from the kitchen.

He even added a kiss at the bottom, for authenticity.

Then, he left, walking quickly towards the safety of the College.

CHAPTER 31

Gregory awoke to the sound of Naomi's peaceful breathing beside him, their bodies having curved towards one another sometime during the night so that they were entwined, skin against skin. He didn't move, content as he was to enjoy a level of intimacy he'd never experienced before, nor particularly sought.

Should he be frightened?

Control was a key feature of his life, and always had been, whereas his present circumstances rendered him completely out of control, except in the most superficial ways. He could not control the feeling that enveloped him whenever Naomi was near, or even when they were separated by an ocean, just as he could not hope to control the actions of a man hell-bent on revenge.

"Good morning."

He looked down to find her eyes had opened, and were now shining a deep, dark brown as they studied the lines of his face.

"Hello," he replied, and kissed her. "I don't know how you manage it, but your breath is remarkably fresh in the mornings."

"I wish I could say the same."

He grinned, and caught her up against him in one swift motion. "If you're trying to seduce me, it's working."

Naomi giggled, feeling light and happy. "How about a coffee before I move to stage two of my seduction technique?"

"What's stage two?" he asked, and began nuzzling her neck.

"Coffee first," she said, batting him away. "I thought you'd be exhausted!"

"I have remarkable powers of recovery."

"So I see."

"Still want that coffee?"

She thought about it for all of three seconds. "Caffeine can wait."

Reality could not wait forever, and, eventually, Alex and Naomi went about the business of facing it.

"I spoke to Ryan," he said, as he poured them both a coffee from the machine in his kitchen. "He's delighted to help. He or his sergeant will meet you and Ava in Newcastle this afternoon."

DCI Hope would be driving Naomi northbound, for safety, and would also speak to Durham CID while she was in the area.

"Your friend sounds kind."

Alex nodded. "He also happens to look like a film star, so try and remember the rest of us are only human," he said.

"I'm very happy with what I have," she said. "Besides, you're not half bad yourself, Doctor Gregory. I'm sure you've made a few patients hot under the collar, during your tenure."

"So long as I don't inspire them to murder anybody, I'm happy."

Naomi smiled, and took the mug he offered. "I like this," she said, after a moment. "I like spending our mornings together."

"And the evenings?" he asked.

"Those too."

Gregory splashed milk into his coffee, then moved around to sit on one of the counter stools beside her. Morning light spilled through the windows into a space that had once felt cavernous, but now seemed cosy and vibrant. There could be only one reason for that.

"I know we met over a year ago, but we haven't spent much time together," he began, trying to find the right words. "Despite that, I feel at home with you, Naomi. I've never felt more comfortable with anyone, or more comfortable in my own skin. That's because of you."

"The feeling is mutual," she said softly, and put a hand to his cheek. "I feel so happy when we're together."

He swallowed, standing on the cliff-edge once again, unable to prevent the fall. "I understand if you might think this is too soon, but, once you're back from Northumberland and all of this stuff with Carl is behind us, I wondered if you might want to stay here with me for a while."

She smiled slowly. "I'd like that, Alex."

His heart beat wildly in his chest, and he let out a long breath. "Okay then," he said, and drank his coffee.

"Okay," she agreed.

The moment was interrupted by the ringing of Gregory's phone.

"That's probably Hope," he said. "She'll be on her way to pick you up."

But he was wrong.

"Bill? Is everything okay?"

"I'm fine," he said. "There's been a potential development."

Gregory listened as his friend told him about his new friend, Jacob.

"DCI Hope's due here any moment to collect Naomi," he said. "Stay where you are, safe in the college, and lock your door if need be. I'll ask her to have a squad car sent over to collect you—"

"I had another proposal in mind."

Gregory began to argue, before remembering there was nobody better placed than he to suggest an appropriate course of action when it came to managing minds.

"If I'm right, Jacob will snoop around my house a bit, then head off to his next assignation. He didn't attempt anything, last night, and I hope he puts his tiredness down to a busy day in London as opposed to any chemical help he might have had from me in his wine glass," Douglas said. "For now, he thinks I'm oblivious, and is clearly enjoying the anticipation of getting to know me better."

"That could change at any time."

"Yes," Douglas agreed, and didn't need to elaborate. "We don't have long."

"Better get those samples to the lab, so a positive identification can be made," Gregory said. "It will change everything, if we can prove to the Chief Constable that Carl Deere is our man."

"All we can prove would be that the man calling himself 'Jacob' shares the same DNA as that found at the crime scenes," Douglas replied. "We still need to prove his real identity, and create the conditions for the police to bring him in with minimal danger to the general public."

"Or to you," Gregory said.

Douglas said nothing of that.

"Did he give you a home address?" Gregory asked. "Or any other personal information?"

"No, he was very careful not to. I retrieved his file from the Bursar's Office and checked the address and other credentials given on his application," he replied. "None of it is verified."

Gregory told himself not to count any chickens.

"We need to tread very carefully," he said. "Scare him off, and we won't see him again until he decides to come back and finish the job; we'd be living in a constant state of fear for the rest of our lives, never knowing his whereabouts."

"Agreed. At the moment, he's drawn to me," Douglas said. "I don't delude myself that it's for my charming personality, but rather because I represent a father figure. That's what he's attracted to. He enjoys the feeling while it lasts, before the hatred of his own father seeps in and curdles whatever positive emotions he might have felt. Add in the generous portion of anger he already harbours towards me, personally, and you have a tinder box just waiting to ignite."

"When did you first suspect it was Carl?" Gregory asked, after a pause.

"I think I knew for sure yesterday evening, when he mentioned Leonora Stewart," his friend replied. "Her name hadn't been made public anywhere in the press, so there was no other way he could possibly have known her identity."

Douglas thought back to that startling moment of recognition and moved to the door of his office, to check the lock again.

"I hope I gave nothing away," he said. "As for Carl, or rather, *Jacob*, he was completely at ease; excited, even. One would never have known that he'd killed two people that day, in cold blood."

"Do you know where he'll be today? Any idea at all?

"No," Douglas said. "I didn't stick around to find out, just in case he guessed what I'd done to him. I do have concerns for his mother, though. We need to find out where she's located and have her transferred somewhere safe, as soon as possible."

Gregory had already looked into it. "She's in a palliative care home in Ruislip," he said.

Douglas thought for a moment. "He said his mother would be 'gone soon'. I think that could be read in two ways, so it's better to be safe than sorry."

Gregory had not allocated a letter for Carl's mother on the acrostic, but, as Naomi had pointed out, it was just a collection of words and could not be relied upon as proof of anything.

"As for 'Jacob', I've asked him to meet me at the College, after work," Douglas continued. "I don't know if he'll come, or whether he'll know it's a trap. Hopefully, he thinks I'm still a doddering old fool who'd have his head turned by any young, attractive man."

"If anything goes wrong, anything at *all*, there won't be any coming back from this," Gregory said quietly. "He hasn't shown any mercy to his previous victims, so there's no reason to think he would make any exceptions in the future."

"We'll have to be ready for him, then."

"I'll let Hope know," Gregory said. "Carter is staying in London to head up the investigation, so we can work with him while she's away."

"How's Naomi doing?"

Gregory looked into the eyes of the woman he loved, and smiled. "Looking forward to meeting Ryan," he joked, and she gave him a shove.

"It's for the best," Douglas agreed. "But there's another person who might be in danger today, while Carl remains at large."

"Romola Harris?" Gregory guessed. "Yes, I plan to go and see her, as soon as Ava and Naomi are on their way. She might have written a flattering article about him, but I doubt it's enough to satisfy Carl."

Douglas was about to ring off when he thought of something else. "I could kick myself, you know."

"Why's that?"

"I should have guessed Jacob wasn't who he said he was," came the reply. "His essays were always mediocre."

Gregory had to laugh. "You're a hard taskmaster," he said. "He probably did his best, considering how busy he's been."

"It's all about time management," Douglas quipped, but Gregory thought of Ian O'Shea, and of all the others before him, and felt fear clutch at his heart once again.

"Bill? Be careful, please."

"You too, kiddo."

CHAPTER 32

Carl awoke from a heavy, drug-induced sleep on Bill Douglas' sofa, and rubbed a hand to his aching temple. Beside him, there was a piece of folded paper, and he reached for it and the glass of water Douglas had kindly left for him on the coffee table.

Jacob,
Had an early session, so left you to sleep.
Help yourself to a shower, coffee, anything else you need, and pull the door shut behind you.
If you're not busy later, I was thinking I could give you a tour of the College after dark? I'll be in my office from five o'clock.
B x

He read the words with a laugh, then re-read them, and then laughed again.

For a man heralded as being a leading expert on psychiatry and behavioural analysis, he was pretty clueless when it came to an attractive face and a bit of professional flattery. Levering himself upward, he tapped a finger on a framed picture of Bill with Alex Gregory, and the skin stretched across his teeth in a tigerish smile.

I could have had him, he told himself.

Like a lamb to the slaughter.

He amused himself by taking Bill up on his offer of the facilities, and enjoyed the comfortable bathroom and fluffy towels, which were seldom to be found in the hotchpotch of motels and airport hotels he'd been using instead of a fixed address. There were garage lock-ups, of course, and other deposit boxes around the country, but nowhere that could remotely be called 'home'.

It was something he'd never had, and never would.

He towelled himself dry with violent movements, enjoying the abrasion, the masochism of small hurts, and then dressed himself in the clothing he'd worn the previous day. He looked himself over with a critical eye, and realised it was time to touch up his hair, and the shade of tan on his skin, before paying a visit to the next special person who owed him an apology.

Before leaving, he wandered through the master bedroom, looking inside cupboards and drawers, feeling his anger rise with every passing minute.

Bill Douglas had prospered, accumulating keepsakes and mementos, while he'd been left to rot.

He'd pay for that.

Carl crossed the landing and came face-to-face with his former self.

He stood in the centre of the room Gregory had been using and stared at the photograph, which showed a thin, pasty-skinned man with dark eyes. He flexed the muscles in his arms, to remind himself of how things had changed, and stepped further into the room, eyes running over the names and faces, the arrows and scribbled notes connecting the murders.

"Very good," he approved.

Images of the victims were tacked to the wall, and he was reminded of how they'd looked as they died. The thought hardened his body and, this time, he didn't bother to make any excuses to himself. He lay back on the bed and gave in to the feeling, imagining how Gregory would look when the lights finally dimmed for him, too.

After an emotional farewell, Ava found herself in a car heading north, with DCI Hope at the wheel.

"Are you okay?" the latter asked.

Naomi nodded. "I'm worried, but that's natural. I don't want my presence to hold anybody back."

"I'm sure Alex doesn't see it that way," Hope was generous enough to say. "He wants you kept safe, and I have to agree it's the best option."

"I'm sorry to take you away from your work here in London."

Hope performed a nifty manoeuvre around a stationary taxi in the vicinity of King's Cross, and then shook her head.

"What? Miss all this?" she said, gesturing to the gridlock on the roads. "Never. As for the open investigations, Carter has it in hand. He can manage for twenty-four hours, and…" Her voice broke, as she thought of Ian. "It's—it's probably a good thing for me to get some space, for a short while."

"I was so sorry to hear about Ian," Naomi said, kindly. "That must have come as a huge shock."

Ava said nothing, and punched the accelerator as they reached Euston Road. "Nothing shocks me, anymore."

Naomi glanced across at the other woman, and saw a hard profile, the jaw set into lines of acceptance.

All the same—

"If you ever need to talk," she began.

"Thanks, I'll keep it in mind," Ava cut her off, not ready to receive kindness. "Once we're out of the city centre, we'll pick up the M25, then on to the M1 north. Should be in Newcastle in four or five hours, if we're lucky."

Naomi nodded, and then had a thought.

"I'm sorry, I should have mentioned it before. I don't have any things with me—no clothing, toiletries, or anything like that. We stayed at Alex's flat, last night, but my things are all in Cambridge."

Ava muttered something beneath her breath, but supposed it wasn't Naomi's fault. "We could make a detour via Cambridge, but it'll add time on to the journey," she said.

"Yes, but what if Carl is still there?"

"We don't know that Carl was there at all," Hope said, a bit irritably. "We only have Bill's guesswork. But, in any case, I'm armed. I'll do a sweep of the house before we go inside, to be sure it's clear."

"I could always buy some things, to tide me over?"

Hope considered it, as they reached the north circular ring road.

"It might be safer," she conceded. "But, if your computer is there, too, how will you work?"

Naomi nodded, miserably.

"We'll have to stop off," Hope decided. "Most likely, Carl is long gone."

Carl let himself out of Douglas' town house and had almost made it as far as the train station before realising he'd left his satchel. It was a small thing, no more than a prop, really, but it contained some useful implements he liked to keep on his person in case of emergency.

Hangovers, he thought. Can't hack 'em, these days.

He turned and walked back in the direction he'd come, and, as he walked, he replayed the events of the previous evening.

Had he really drunk too much?

Not really.

It was only at Douglas' house that he'd begun to feel sleepy, not before.

Had the good professor deceived him after all?

Then he thought of the pathetic little note, with its kisses at the end.

No, Bill Douglas believed what he wanted to believe, and that included the incredible notion that a younger, more virile man such as himself would ever give him more than a passing glance.

He passed a shop window, caught his own reflection, and winked.

Naomi remained locked inside the car while DCI Hope performed a sweep of Douglas' house, armed with her police-issue firearm. It was a tense few minutes for both women, until Ava reappeared in the doorway, the gun re-holstered inside her jacket.

She held the car door open for Naomi.

"All clear," she pronounced. "But let's get in and out as quickly as possible, so we can get back on the road. Just grab what you need, and we can send things on, if necessary."

Naomi nodded and they dashed inside the empty house. As they reached the bottom of the stairs, she remembered something else.

"I don't know if Alex mentioned anything to you about an acrostic?"

Hope nodded, from her position in the downstairs hallway, which afforded a clear view of the front and back doorways. "He mentioned it the other day. Something about the victims' surnames or forenames tallying with the phrase Carl wrote obsessively in his cell?"

"Yes," Naomi said. "He says Carl used to create acrostics and haikus, other little things like that, as a kind of comfort mechanism. He thinks it's possible Carl did something similar when formulating his 'kill list'."

"It's always possible," Hope agreed. "Let's talk about it in the car."

"I thought so, at first," Naomi said, the words rushing out. "But something doesn't add up, Ava. It troubled me last night and, when I looked at it again this morning, I think I know what's been bothering me about it."

"What?"

"The 'I's," she replied. "There aren't enough letter 'I's' to cover the existing victims, the ones

Carl is very likely to kill in future, as well as Ian O'Shea. He's also the only victim whose first name connects to the acrostic, rather than his surname."

Hope frowned. "There are lots of 'I's in VINDICTA SERVIVIT FRIGUS," she said. "I count five."

"Yes, but maybe Alex didn't have time to tell you, some of those have to be used to create the letter 'H' for everything to fit—"

Hope was losing patience. "Look, we don't have time for this, right now. Why not show me later?"

Naomi thought of the murder board upstairs. "I could show you quickly, now," she said.

Hope weighed up the competing demands, checked the doors again, and then signalled that Naomi should lead the way. "Two minutes," she said. "That's all I can allow."

Naomi hurried upstairs and into the spare room, pausing to scent the air, which held the lingering smell of an aftershave Gregory did not use.

Setting that aside, she moved to the back wall, and retrieved the black pen Gregory kept on top of the chest of drawers. "Look, this is how it fits," she said, and quickly set out the acrostic as Alex had done the night before. "You can see, these letters go with the 'T's to make 'H'."

Hope said nothing, so she continued.

"This one for Romola Harris, this one for Hartman…the other 'I's are accounted for. Ian O'Shea doesn't belong on this list, I'm convinced of it," Naomi said. "Then, there's the lock."

"The lock?" Hope said, dully.

"Yes, the lock on his front door," Naomi said. "Why would it be broken? Everything points to Ian having been murdered by someone he already knows, not by Carl Deere. It seems completely improbable that Deere would have been able to find out Ian's address, or his connection to the past, in such a short space of time after he'd returned to London."

"I'm sorry," Ava said, from her position at Naomi's back. "I'm very sorry to have to do this."

Naomi turned in time to see the butt of Hope's firearm as it swept down towards her skull, before the world went dark.

CHAPTER 33

Carl made his way around to the back of Douglas' house and vaulted over the garden wall, which he'd identified some time ago as being the easiest access point and the least visible to any casual onlookers. The row of gardens backed on to an alleyway where residents sometimes parked their cars or kept their bins, and he used one of them to find purchase before slipping quietly onto the dewy grass. He kept to the perimeter wall and made his way towards the kitchen door which, to his consternation, was locked.

"Should have left it open," he muttered.

Luckily, he'd also identified a small window in the utility room as another vulnerable spot, with an old latch that was easily overridden from the outside using a knife—or anything long and thin. He fiddled with the catch until it lifted and then, sucking in his stomach, let himself inside the house with barely a whisper.

As he did, he heard a heavy thud from one of the bedrooms upstairs.

Had Douglas come home early?

It was ahead of schedule, but he was happy to bring forward their time together, if need be.

Silently, he moved into the hallway and paused, listening with interest to the sound of more thuds, followed by the sharp sound of a woman in pain.

Curiosity compelled him onwards, his footsteps treading carefully to avoid any steps that creaked.

Through an open doorway on the landing, he saw a woman he recognised instantly as one of the detectives from the Major Crimes Unit, DCI Ava Hope. She had her back to him, and was smashing her own head into the wall, hard enough to draw blood.

Curiouser and curiouser, he thought, and took a step closer.

His eyes followed Hope's feverish movements as she amended the marks Naomi had made on the wall, adding Ian O' Shea's name to the acrostic Gregory had almost perfected. He wondered who the unfortunate 'Ian' was, then saw her scribble something else in large black letters, graffiti style.

YOU'RE NEXT

LOVE, CARL

His hands curled into fists, and he began to shake as he watched another corrupt police officer try to frame him for a murder he hadn't committed, for reasons best known to themselves. Teeth bared, blood pounding, his eyes fell upon a firearm lying on the floor beside the inert body of a woman who was, he presumed, already dead.

He stepped inside and picked it up.

Sensing him, Hope spun around and made a gagging sound in her throat, falling back against the wall while she cast around for another weapon.

He raised the gun, and shook it from side to side, in a parody of a finger.

"Tut, tut, tut," he said. "You've been a naughty girl, haven't you, Detective?"

He gestured to the name she'd added to the list of his supposed victims, then scratched his temple.

"I'm sure I would have remembered killing this 'Ian O' Shea'," he said. "I like to look people in the eye when I take their lives. Call it an act of respect, if you like. I'm an angel of justice, nothing more, and I like them to understand that when I explain the reasons they're going to die—"

"I can make a deal with you," she whispered.

"Sorry, but I don't deal," Carl replied, pleasantly. "Especially not with women who tell lies. That's a cardinal sin, you know."

"I can explain—"

The words fell away as the bullet connected with her head, where it entered the left side of her brain and came out the other side to lodge itself in the plasterwork with a neat splash of red.

He watched her slide to the floor in a delicate heap and, after a close inspection, was surprised to find she was still breathing.

In fact, they both were.

What to do?

Should he finish them off?

Neither woman was on his list, but then, the police officer had been no better than the others, so there was a degree to which she deserved to die as much as the rest.

What about the other one?

Natural justice, he thought.

He would leave it to a Higher Power to decide.

Just then, he heard the sound of banging against the front door downstairs, and realised the gunshot had attracted the attention of Douglas' neighbour.

Time to go.

"Good luck," he said, and blew them both a kiss.

With a little help from DS Carter, Gregory was finally able to track down Romola Harris' home address, and the two men arrived outside her house shortly before ten o'clock.

They rang the buzzer, but to no avail.

"Maybe she's gone into the office," Carter said.

"I already rang their front desk," Gregory said. "She called in sick again."

He stepped off the pathway into the small front garden and peered through a small gap in the shuttered bay window. Through it, he saw lights burning and a television set to mute.

"She's home," he said, and tapped against the glass. "Romola! It's Doctor Alex Gregory! I was hoping to speak with you."

"We can't force it," Carter said.

Gregory would not be beaten, and tried again, this time by shouting through the letterbox. "Romola! I'm here to help," he said. "I know you were at Warwick Avenue, yesterday!"

"You do?" Carter said, in a hushed tone.

"Who else do you think threw up in the grass beside Leonora's body?"

Carter made a sound of surprise. "Makes sense," he said. "Deere wants to get the jump on us, and keep himself looking whiter than white, so he frightens Romola into retracting her earlier articles in the form of one big puff piece. He sends her to the crime scene so she'll see Leonora Stewart's body and feel real terror, so he can be sure there'll be no misunderstandings."

"It's one way of guaranteeing a good write-up," Gregory said, and tried again. "Romola! We know about Carl Deere! Let us talk to you, and we can help!"

He heard a sound on the other side of the door and had the feeling she was studying them both through the peephole.

"We're not here to hurt you or arrest you," he said, looking directly at her. "We know you're frightened, and we know why. Let us help you, Romola, and maybe you can help us, too."

After a moment, they heard the sound of a door being unlocked, then it cracked open to reveal the frightened eyes of a woman in her forties who clearly hadn't slept.

"Romola?"

She nodded. "Who are you?" she asked them.

"DS Carter, from the Metropolitan Police, and this is Doctor Gregory, a criminal profiler and psychiatrist," Ben replied. "You're not in trouble, Ms Harris, but we need your help."

She thought of the woman's body and clutched the door more tightly. "I—I don't have anything to tell you—"

"I believe you do," Gregory said, in calm tones. "Why don't we all sit down over a cup of tea, and take it from there?"

"He'll kill me," she whispered, and tears ran down a face that was already ragged. "I can't risk it. Can't you see that?"

"I see that," Carter said. "We can protect you. We've already secured a safe house for you and your family, if you agree to help us with our investigation."

Gregory was mildly surprised by the speed at which Carter was able to secure a safe house; in fact, without Hope by his side, the man seemed vastly more competent than he was given credit for.

"Listen to me, Romola," he said, in the same quiet tone as before. "You can't make a pact with the devil, because he'll always come to collect. Carl doesn't consider you 'even', now, no matter what he might have told you."

She began to cry again, but held the door open for them to come inside. "Quickly," she sobbed. "He might be watching."

They followed her inside and, after one last thorough check, Romola shut the door behind them.

"I don't know much," she said, as they made their way into her kitchen. "I have no idea where he is, or anything like that. All I know is that he contacted me the other day for the first time, telling me I had a chance to put things right after I'd maligned his character."

She sank onto a chair beside a small wooden table. "Help yourself to tea, or whatever."

"We're fine, thank you," Carter said, surprising Gregory again. "You said he gave you notes? Were they paper or e-mailed?"

"Both," she replied, and pointed to her bag on the counter. "There's a paper note that was hand-delivered to the office inside my bag, if you'd like to read it."

Gregory retrieved it and began scanning the words. "And e-mails?"

She nodded. "Just one e-mail, telling me to meet him at a certain time, at the exact place where—where—" She laid her head in her hands. "That poor woman," she whispered.

"So you thought you'd be meeting Carl?" Carter said.

"Yes," she said, wretchedly. "I thought he was going to give me an exclusive interview, so I could write something that reflected his innocence. Instead, he wanted me to see Leonora Stewart, and what he'd done to her. There—there was another note—"

"In her mouth?" Gregory put in, and she nodded.

"Yes, how did you know?"

He shook his head, because it didn't matter. "Do you have it?"

It's in the pocket of my coat, which is hanging in the hallway," she said, and vowed never to wear it again.

Carter stepped back into the hallway to get it, and then read its contents before handing it to Gregory.

"There's a chance he hasn't finished using your connections to the paper," he said. "Carl might contact you again, seeking another article to paint him in a positive light. On the other hand, he might think that you aren't of any further use to him, and follow through on his threat."

It was brutal, Gregory thought, but the truth often was. "You have two choices, as far as I can tell. Either you sit here, paralysed by fear, and wait for Carl to kill you. Alternatively, you can take evasive action, and make up for having knowingly interfered with a crime scene—"

"I didn't mean to!"

"Regardless," he said. "You can help us now, and help yourself at the same time."

"That's right," Carter said, pulling up a chair beside her. "If you consent to sharing your e-mail login details and password, we can monitor the account remotely for any incoming communications from Carl, on the off-chance he sends you further instructions. In the meantime, we'll have a team come and collect you within the hour, and have the children taken out of school. All of you will go to a safe house, which Carl will know nothing about."

"How can you be sure?"

"Like I said, you have choices," he replied. "Either way carries risk, but one seems less risky than the other."

Romola looked between the pair of them, then at a smiling picture of herself with her children on a family holiday the previous summer. She thought of all she stood to lose, if she waited for the inevitable and did nothing, just as she'd done nothing all those years ago.

"I'll help," she said, and felt braver than she had in longer than she could remember. "Please, just find him, before he finds me."

Gregory put his hand over hers, in a gesture of support. "Thank you," he said.

Just then, the phone in his pocket began to vibrate, and he left Carter to work out the details while he stepped aside to take the call, which was from Ryan.

Something shifted, in the pit of his stomach.

"Ryan? Is everything okay?"

When lives were at stake, his friend wasn't one to adopt a gentle bedside manner. "I haven't heard from Hope," he said. "I expected to receive a call at ten o'clock; that was the agreed protocol. She told me she'd be making a single stop, and that she'd call me from the service station to let me know all is well. Should I be worried, Alex, or is it like DCI Hope to be lax when it comes to protocols?"

No, Gregory thought, with a sinking heart. It wasn't like her, at all. "I'll see if Carter's heard anything," he said. "I'll call you back."

He signalled to Ben, who left Romola to join him on the other side of the kitchen.

"Ryan hasn't heard from Hope," Gregory said, in an undertone. "The plan was for her to call at ten o'clock, or as near to it as possible."

"She's probably running late," Carter said, and checked the time on his watch, which told him it was now almost eleven. He tried, and failed, to keep the worry from his voice. "Ah—yeah, let me give her a call."

After a few tries, Carter shook his head. "No answer," he said. "Let me—oh, just a minute—"

He paused to take another call that was incoming, and Gregory stood there, oblivious to their surroundings, all his attention fixed now on the person at the other end of the line.

"Tell me," he said, as soon as Carter came off the call. "Tell me what's happened."

Ignoring him, Ben Carter turned to Romola Harris and excused them both, before taking Gregory's arm in a firm grip.

"Wh—what's happening?"

Carter said nothing until they were out of earshot. "I have some bad news," he said quietly.

Gregory heard his own thundering heart echo in his ears but held himself upright, detaching himself from the words that were unspoken but somehow inevitable.

"Naomi," he breathed.

"Yes," Carter said. "Ava, too."

"They're dead?" he whispered.

"I honestly don't know. They're at Addenbrooke's Hospital in Cambridge," Carter replied. "They need to be stabilised before either of them can be transferred to a specialist trauma centre here in London."

A hundred questions circled, chiefly—

Why were they in Cambridge, when they knew the danger?

None of it mattered, now. All that mattered was the woman lying somewhere between life and death, her future balanced on the edge of a knife.

"I need to go," was all he said.

"Alex, wait, I'll come with you—"

"I can't wait."

With that, he was gone.

CHAPTER 34

The journey to Cambridge seemed interminable, but when Gregory finally burst through the automatic doors at Addenbrooke's, he was greeted by a familiar face.

"Bill."

Douglas embraced him in a hard hug, then drew away. "Carter rang to tell me what happened...I got here as quickly as I could."

"Where's Naomi? Ava?"

"They're both in the ICU," Douglas said, in a voice heavy with unshed tears. "They needed surgery to stem the bleeding...they each have severe brain trauma, Alex."

Gregory scrubbed his hands over his face, distraught. "I can't lose her, Bill. Not when I've only just found her."

Douglas took him in hand. "Stay positive," he said. "Naomi's come through the worst, and so has Ava. They're in medical comas, to allow their bodies to heal. It's a waiting game now."

"Tell me what happened."

Douglas blew out a long breath, sadness mingling with frustration. "For some reason, they came back to the house—"

"I told them not to," Gregory muttered. "Ava knew about our suspicions around Jacob, and that he'd been at your house last night. She must have known there was a risk he'd still be there."

Douglas nodded, unable to argue with the logic. "I don't know what to tell you. Whatever the reason, they came back, and he must have been in the house waiting for them, as you say. I can only imagine they were overpowered in a struggle with Carl, who managed to take Hope's handgun and use it to bludgeon Naomi, then to shoot Ava at point blank range. It's a miracle either of them is still alive."

Gregory closed his eyes, and when he opened them again, they were empty. "How long were they unconscious? How long before they received treatment?"

Douglas didn't bother with any platitudes for he understood that to do so would be the greatest insult to a fellow clinician.

"Too long," he said, quietly. "Especially Naomi."

Gregory nodded, and swiped away the tears that fell from his eyes with an angry hand. Survival was one thing, but brain damage leaving a woman like Naomi in a permanent vegetative state was no kind of life at all.

"If she dies, I'll kill him myself."

"You don't mean that—" Douglas reached out to him, ready to offer whatever comfort he could, but Gregory stalked away. Anger was his solace, all that was left when his heart felt hollow. It was the anger of a young boy who had never known love, and of the man who'd learned never to seek it, but had found it all the same, only to have it snatched away.

"It's my fault," he said. "Naomi would never have been in danger, if it weren't for me. This is my fault."

"She knew the risks, just as Ava did," Douglas reminded him. "You took measures to protect her—"

"Not enough," Gregory spat. "Not *enough!*" Beyond reach, he ran his hands through his hair, ready to tear it from his head if only it would help. "Why didn't he kill them?"

Douglas rubbed his watering eyes, then replaced his glasses. "What's that?"

"Why didn't Carl kill them both?" Gregory asked. "He doesn't leave any of his victims alive, that isn't his MO. So why did he make an exception?"

"I can't say," Douglas replied. "Maybe he was interrupted by the neighbour who heard the first gunshot."

Further questions were forestalled by the arrival of DS Carter, who rushed into the foyer. "Any news?" he asked.

"They won't tell us anything more," Douglas replied. "We're not next of kin."

"Ava's mother is on her way," Carter said. "She'll be here within the next half an hour, traffic permitting. What about Naomi?"

Gregory thought of Naomi's family, and cleared his throat. "Her adoptive parents live in Manhattan," he said. "They can't be here until tomorrow evening, at the earliest."

Carter looked past them to the front desk. "Let me see what I can do."

As he went off to harass the medics, Douglas spoke gently to his friend. "Sit down, before you fall down."

Gregory shook his head and paced away, the sounds of a busy hospital buzzing like flies in his ears. Then, to Douglas' surprise, he began to laugh.

"Alex, for goodness' sake, what's there to laugh about?"

"I didn't know for sure, until now," he replied, with self-loathing.

"Didn't know *what*?"

Gregory looked across at his friend and, to Douglas, it seemed that the man's whole heart was reflected in his eyes.

"That I love her," he said softly. "I'm so bloody clever, aren't I? So *clever*, I didn't recognise the most basic of human emotions."

Douglas put an arm around him. "There's a first time for everything," he said. "You can tell her how you feel, when she wakes up."

Carter's quiet voice interrupted whatever reply Gregory might have given. "We can see them now, just for a few minutes."

Ava and Naomi lay side by side in the Intensive Care Unit, their beds separated by a curtain. The silence was punctuated by the rhythmic sound of various monitors surrounding their beds, and the repetitive beeping was both a comfort and a curse.

"I'll give you some time alone with Naomi," Douglas said, and stepped around the curtain to join Carter in visiting her neighbour.

Gregory forced himself to look at the woman whose warm body had lain beside his only hours before.

So pale, his mind whispered.

Her skin was an unnatural shade, almost translucent white, and dark tendrils of hair escaped the enormous bandage covering her head and framing a face that was, remarkably, free of cuts or bruises. A ventilation tube fed her body oxygen and breathed for her in a regular motion, while other wires and catheters swarmed her slim body, like something from a science fiction movie, not real flesh and bone.

One of the monitors let out a loud, unexpected alarm, and he gripped the end of Naomi's bed for support. A moment later, one of the nurses hurried in and checked the levels on each of the screens.

"Just a little fluctuation," she said, and made a note on the chart. "It can happen, and it doesn't always mean anything sinister. Are you Doctor Palmer's other half?"

He paused, then nodded. "Yes," he replied.

"I'm so sorry about what's happened," she said, and thought that a strong wind might knock him over. "Why don't you have a seat in the visitor's chair, over there? You could talk to her."

Gregory followed her advice, as force of habit, and sank down onto an ugly high-backed chair. "I don't know what to say," he whispered.

"It's a shock," she sympathised, then came around the bed to fiddle with the tubes to make sure everything was as it should be. "The main thing is that Naomi hears your voice. She might not be responsive, but there's nothing wrong with her hearing, so it can't hurt to talk to her, can it?"

Gregory thought of how lonely Naomi must feel, trapped inside the shadows of her own mind, which was a place he knew far too well. If his voice helped, even in some way, then he would use it.

He gave his thanks to the nurse, who smiled and left him to it.

"Naomi? It's me, Alex."

Her face didn't flicker, and the ventilator continued to pump up and down.

"I—I'm sorry I wasn't there to protect you," he continued, battling fresh tears. "I'm so sorry."

With the gentlest of touches, he brushed his hand over hers.

"I don't know why Carl attacked you both; it doesn't make any sense to me, because you weren't on his list…you were never on his list," he mumbled. "But I'm going to find out. I don't care how long it takes me, I'll have the answers by the time you wake up again—"

He paused, bearing down against fresh waves of grief.

"—and I need you to wake up, Naomi, because I *love* you. I love you very much. Can you believe it? I've never said those words to another living soul, but I'm saying them to you. I would like the privilege of being able to look into your eyes, the next time I say them."

He leaned across to kiss the skin on her wrist, which lay limp against the bedclothes.

"Come back to me," he whispered. "Please."

CHAPTER 35

Gregory found Carter and Douglas in the Family and Friends area of the hospital, huddled in discussion.

"What are the next steps?" he demanded of Carter. "I've brought you an eyewitness statement and Bill has delivered samples that will allow you to identify and match those from the crime scenes. Now, I want to know what the hell you're going to do to bring Carl Deere in, once and for all—or do you expect us to deliver him on a plate?"

"Alex, I know you're upset, and you have every right to be—" Douglas said.

Gregory turned on his friend with blazing eyes. "*Upset*, Bill? That's an understatement, don't you think? What are you going to tell me next? That I should 'take some time'? There's been plenty of time, and Carl has used it to kill innocent people while Major Crimes chose to protect their miserable, sorry arses, just like before."

"I'm sorry about what happened before," Carter said, with all sincerity. "I've never agreed with the decisions taken by senior officers at the time. I understand your anger, and I feel it myself. I want to help you however I can."

Carter thought of the Chief Constable and the Superintendent, and of how they would react when they found out what he was about to sanction.

He'd deal with that, when the time came.

"Our next steps depend on whether you can be certain that Jacob DaSolo is really Carl Deere," he said, turning to Douglas. "We can't turn a DNA test around in less than six hours, and you say he's planning to meet you this evening?"

Douglas nodded.

"Without any solid proof, we'll be doing the same thing we did with Carl the first time around—entrapment. If we're wrong about Jacob, it's safe to say, all of our careers will be over."

"I couldn't give a flying—" Gregory began.

"I'm not wrong," Douglas overrode him, with quiet authority. "The evidence, if you can call it that, may be circumstantial, but everything I've managed to glean from 'Jacob' tallies with what we already know about Carl." He began to tick them off his fingers. "Authoritarian father," he said. "Not unusual, in general, but he carries a significant level of hatred which he tries and fails to hide. He told me his father is already dead, which we know to be true of Carl's father, too."

Carter nodded. "Anything else?"

"Talk of murder, even second hand in the context of press reporting, made him animated and excited," Douglas said. "He was turned on by it which, again, tallies with what we already know of Carl's predilections for sadism, or someone with an unnatural interest in crime or violence."

He tapped his third finger. "Then, of course, there are the physical oddities," he said. "Dyed hair, deliberate tanning, speaking with a false accent—"

"Plenty of people create personas," Carter said. "Actors, for a start."

"Yes, but not in a classroom environment. When paired with the false credentials he supplied to the University, and the care he took never to let slip any personal details or give an address…it adds weight. Let's not forget that he knew about Leonora before anybody else did. There's only one possible reason for that."

"Did you recognise him?" Gregory asked. "Setting aside everything you've just told us, when you first met this 'Jacob', did you recognise him as Carl or think he reminded you of anyone familiar?"

"I wasn't sure, at first, because he looks dramatically different," Douglas explained. "He's much more athletic; in fact, his entire body composition has changed from the skinny young man we met, a few years ago. With the trappings of darker hair, glasses, tanned skin, a different accent and, I suspect, a different nose, it was hard to place him. I recognised him eventually, not because of how he looks, but because of how he *thinks*. A lot of his discussion, whether he was aware of it or not, centred around ideas of justice, right and wrong, and, of course, kept returning to the case of Carl Deere—he always had a touch of vanity."

"Why didn't you mention this sooner?"

Douglas gave a self-conscious shrug. "Until I could be more certain of my suspicions, I wanted to keep him as far away from you and Naomi as possible," he admitted. "I didn't want to endanger either of you, or waste scarce resources on a wild goose chase."

Gregory had never known anyone as selfless as Bill Douglas, and this fresh evidence of his urge to protect those he cared for was something they would talk about later, when Naomi was no longer critically ill, and when Hope was back on her feet fighting crime. He wanted to thank his friend for the kind of selflessness that was so rarely to be found in the world, but to do so then would have been his undoing.

Instead, he turned back to Carter with fresh resolve.

"If you authorise a recall of the digital records holding Carl's DNA profile, you can check the samples against it and pin the bastard down."

"We don't even know if the DNA record still exists, if it's been deleted from the mainframe," he said. "To find out would take time and money, never mind the official authorisation, which is unlikely to be given after that piece Romola wrote about Carl. It's been picked up by all the outlets, and the press is full of talk about miscarriages of justice and police corruption. There's no appetite whatsoever from the brass to draw attention to themselves."

"But you know it's the right thing to do," Gregory said, and played the only trump card he had. "Ava would know it, too. Please, Ben, trust us one last time."

Carter looked between them, then took out some loose change from his pocket. At their questioning look, he nodded towards the vending machine in the corner of the room.

"If I'm going to defy a direct order from my superiors, this calls for a Twix."

"Make it a double," Douglas muttered.

Later, when Carter took himself away to smooth over troubled waters back at The Yard, Gregory and Douglas opted to walk back from the hospital into the centre of Cambridge. A light drizzle covered the city in a shroud of mist, and it reflected their sombre mood as they prepared to face the demon that awaited them.

"How are you doing?" Douglas asked, once they'd covered the first quarter of a mile in silence.

Gregory tipped his face upward and tried to see beyond the clouds. "If I thought praying would help, I'd do it," he said, dropping his gaze to the pavement again. "Unfortunately, my mind won't allow the deception."

Douglas decided it was not the moment for a theological debate. "I keep asking myself whether I did the right thing in bringing Jacob back to the house, last night," he said. "I thought it would be the only way to make him comfortable enough for me to take a sample, but it brought the spider into our nest. There was no other way and, since you were both out of the house, I thought it would be safe."

"Not for you," Gregory remarked. "You were willing to risk your own safety, Bill. Why?"

Douglas' footsteps slowed, and then came to a halt.

"I don't have much in the way of family," he said quietly. "In fact, you're my only family, Alex. You're my friend and, I dare say, my protégé, but you're more than that. I'm proud of you, as I imagine I would be if I'd ever had a son, and I love you as I would have loved him. I won't have you, and the woman you care for, living under constant threat."

"Bill—"

"That's not to say I don't value my own life, or think I haven't got more to offer this world, because I do. But, when it comes down to it, I've lived a good life. I've had so many blessings, and you've been one of the greatest, Alex."

Gregory said nothing, but wrapped his arms around him in a tight embrace.

"I would have given anything for a father like you," he said, gruffly. "My own was undeserving of the name."

They remained standing there for another minute, before drawing apart.

"That's something you have in common with Carl," Douglas said. "Remember what we've always said; beneath the destruction and damage, there's a broken mind, a sickness that requires treatment. This man is not 'normal' like you or me, and now, he never will be. The horrors Carl inflicts are symptomatic of a bigger problem."

Gregory looked deep into the depths of his own psyche to find whatever scraps of pity were left there, which wasn't much. "He must be stopped," he said.

"He knows it," Douglas said quietly. "I think he wants us to stop him."

"What makes you say that? He's escalating—"

"Because, if Carl wanted me dead, I wouldn't be standing here, talking to you now. I believe, against his own better judgment, he made a connection with me that he didn't expect. He enjoyed talking, and feeling heard; he enjoyed the game, of course, but perhaps—just *perhaps*—he also enjoyed the company."

"Who wouldn't?"

"Well, quite."

They smiled, and began walking again.

"Do you think Carl knows that you know who he is—that Jacob is a fake, I mean?" Gregory asked.

"No, not yet," Douglas replied. "At least, not consciously. But subconsciously? Yes, I think he's well aware. He's choosing to feign ignorance so he can prolong the subterfuge, and thereby the connection, rather than snuffing it out, as he's done with all the others."

"He's so unpredictable," Gregory said. "He could snap out of it at any time."

"Yes," Douglas said. "With a man like Carl, it isn't a question of using brute force to bring him in, but rather his own psychology. Ironically, if the police had thrown resources at the problem and splashed his name everywhere, my feeling is that Carl would have gone to ground again and waited until a more convenient time to enact his plan. On that logic, his relative freedom provides enough rope to hang himself. He's become over-confident."

"Do you think you'll be able to get a confession from him?" Gregory said.

"I have to try," Douglas said. "You and I both know that, even with a positive match to the DNA samples taken from the crime scenes, any good barrister would point out that the match was only made by violating the rights of an innocent man. They'd argue inadmissibility, and have a field day convincing a jury that the police were up to their old tricks again, persecuting an ordinary guy just trying to live his life. They'd claim the evidence was planted." Douglas shook his head. "We *need* that confession, Alex. That's all there is to it."

"What makes you think he'll crack?" Gregory said. "Carl hasn't been moved by anything his other victims have said, or shown any sign of weakening resolve in his mission. I know there isn't anyone better than you, when it comes to matters of the mind—but still, it's a tall order."

"There's a chance, because he wants his father's approval," Douglas said. "A part of my attraction for him is the father figure role that I perform, unwittingly or not. I can certainly ham that up, and take his mind all the way back to childhood. It's the loss of control we need, Alex, to elicit the truth."

"But, if he loses control, there's every chance he'll kill."

"He can try, but that's where it pays to have a little help from one's friends."

Gregory thought of all the usual reasons why a person might be driven to violence, and recalled the first recorded incidents from a teenage Carl, whose juvenile record stated that he'd flipped from a mild-mannered young man into a sadistic one because he'd felt rejected by the object of his desire. This, after a childhood in which he'd been rejected by both parents. It wasn't an excuse, Gregory thought, but, having seen the woman he loved brought close to death, the prospect of their happy future hanging in the balance alongside it, he understood just how powerful love could be—and a lack of it.

"He must be lonely," he said. "It changes nothing of what he's done, or what he's capable of, but…I think Carl must be one of the loneliest creatures."

"Like Gollum," Douglas said. "Yes, there's a definite analogy there. Carl is consumed, enraged, held apart from society and, by many standards, no longer fully 'human'. He's lost sight of what it means to have empathy, if he ever knew it at all."

Presently, they found themselves beneath the shroud of mist, their footsteps echoing around the narrow streets as they hurried towards home.

From the shadows, the creature watched.

CHAPTER 36

"We're all set."

Carter joined both men in one of the smaller rooms next to Douglas' office at Hawking College, half an hour before Jacob was expected to arrive. In the corner of the room, a digital operative borrowed from Thames Valley Police fiddled with a wire stuck to Douglas' chest that would capture any forthcoming conversation, while another two officers wearing full protective gear stood against a wall, talking amongst themselves.

"How did you manage to convince the Chief to give the 'go ahead'?" Gregory asked.

"It wasn't looking promising, I can tell you that. But when I checked Romola's e-mail account, it turns out Carl sent her another e-mail around lunchtime today, just as you said he would."

"What did it say?"

Carter cast an awkward glance in Douglas' direction, but the man seemed to be engrossed in his observation of the quadrangle outside.

"You can say it," Douglas said, without turning around. "I assume Carl plans to kill me."

Carter didn't deny it. "Carl suggested that Romola meet him here at Hawking College, tomorrow morning," he said. "He gave her a time and an address, and said she'd find something of great interest."

"Carl would have no way of knowing about your assignation with Jacob," Gregory said. "It's practically a smoking gun."

"He would argue that he was sending her to see Professor Douglas, who was intimately involved in his initial arrest and trial, and would be an interesting person to talk to for any future articles," he said. "Nothing more than that; nothing concrete for a jury to convict him beyond reasonable doubt, but, knowing what we know of Leonora Stewart's murder, I think it's safe to assume he plans to leave a body for Romola to find tomorrow morning."

It was said with such bluntness, it stole Gregory's breath away. "I don't like this," he ground out. "If Carl overpowers Bill, there's no way we could get there in time to stop him from sticking a knife in his chest, or whatever else he has planned. It's too dangerous."

"I'm wearing protective gear, Alex," his friend reminded him.

"It wouldn't prevent a bullet going through your head, as Ava would tell you herself, if she could." It was a low blow, but the gravity of the situation called for it. "It's not too late to get out of here," he said. "We could leave, and go to a safe house—"

"We've been down this road," Douglas replied. "You and I agreed, we don't want to live a life in constant fear, which would be inevitable if we choose to do nothing."

"Not necessarily, if Carl is picked up and arrested this evening, then—"

Gregory trailed off, because he knew they couldn't hold the man known as 'Jacob' for more than seventy-two hours without charging him, and there wasn't sufficient evidence to do that yet. The moment he was released, he would come for them, or simply disappear.

Douglas watched the changing emotions pass over his friend's face. "Acceptance is always the hardest stage to reach," he said, and turned back to the window, where he saw a man of average height and athletic build walking with a distinct spring in his step as he made his way towards the building where they now stood.

"Showtime," he said, and made his way back to the office next door.

"It's open!"

Carl let himself into Douglas' study and found the professor hunched over his large wooden desk, marking essays.

"Hi Jacob," he said, looking up with a smile. "Take a seat, help yourself to coffee, and I'll be with you in a minute."

"I couldn't believe it when you told me what happened at the house, this morning," Carl said, keeping his voice as light as he could. "I must have just missed the action when I let myself out."

"A lucky escape," Douglas said.

"You said your friends interrupted a burglar and things got out of hand?"

"It's the current theory," Douglas lied.

"Shocking," Carl said, and set two coffees on a low table beside the sofa on the other side of the room. "I'm just glad you weren't caught up in it."

Douglas heard the anticipation, and was afraid.

"I'm sorry I fell asleep last night," Carl said. "It isn't like me...we didn't have the opportunity to get to know one another better."

The flirtation was all part of the act, Douglas knew. "We can start now," he said, and made his way across the room to join him, every step taking him closer to danger. "You were telling me about your family last night, Jacob."

"Ah, yes. Mummy and Daddy, dearest."

"I'm sorry you had a poor relationship with them."

"Are you?" Carl wanted to believe it, and his face softened, just for a moment.

Then, he remembered.

This was the man who had hunted him, snared him, then consigned him to Hell. He was no better than his father, and not to be trusted.

"Well, that's in the past," he said. "How are your friends doing?"

"Truthfully? I don't know whether they'll survive the night," Douglas said, and watched him closely. "If their attacker had done the decent thing and called for medical help, their chances might have been greater."

Carl realised Douglas obviously had no idea there was a fox in the chicken coop, and the fox's name was *Ava Hope*.

"It probably didn't enter their mind."

Douglas nodded, feeling sick to his core. "From an academic perspective, what do you think it takes for a personality to become so desensitized, so lacking in empathy, that they would be capable of inflicting that level of violence and then able walk away without a second glance?"

"I wouldn't know."

"Hypothetically," Douglas persisted. "After all, that's why you took the Master's course, isn't it? To understand the human psyche? Let's take a case study…Thomas Andersson, for instance."

Carl kept a smile fixed on his face. "The Soho Killer? I understand he had a childhood history of violence—"

"Violence begets violence, you think?"

Carl frowned. "Yes…at least, in some circumstances. Not all."

"Of course not," Douglas said. "Some people endure terrible beginnings and manage to emerge unscathed, or, at least, not as affected by the experience. Some display the beginnings of sadistic behaviour but retain a basic understanding of 'right' and 'wrong'."

Carl experienced a flash memory of how he used to be, and knew he could never go back. It was far too late for that.

"I'm most interested, academically, in thinking about what causes that kind of person to tip over the edge...to lose control and kill, or seriously injure. It's been my life's study."

"That's the problem with this profession, isn't it?" Carl sneered. "It's all extrapolation and stereotypes, based on limited experience of a few extreme cases."

"I agree," Douglas said, surprising him once again. "It can lead to misdiagnoses, in the wrong hands."

Carl searched his face, looking for a trap but finding none.

"Perhaps there's no loss of control," he argued. "Think of the military; in wartime, or in defence of a nation, killing another person isn't classified as 'murder'. What's the difference, if a person wants to defend a social ideal, such as the idea of 'justice'? If the structures society has built to deliver justice to wronged people fail, then is that person justified in enforcing them himself?"

"You tell me," Douglas offered, leaning back in his chair. "Do you think vigilante justice is ever justified?"

Carl made a small sound of irritation. "The word 'vigilante' is often used as a pejorative term," he said. "But did you know it comes from the Latin *vigilans*?"

"No, I didn't know that. Tell me more."

"It means 'watcher'," Carl said, getting into his stride. "It's a protective role, a heroic one—"

"Like Batman, you mean?"

"Exactly!" Carl cried, pleased with himself, and with Bill. "Batman acted in the public interest, as do many vigilantes."

"Never in their own interest?"

Carl shrugged, and wiped a trembling hand over his brow, which was beginning to sweat. "Well, of course, the impetus to begin helping society might start with some personal experience," he admitted.

"And wouldn't you say that the vigilante would be enforcing his or her own ideas of what constitutes 'right' and 'wrong', taking on the role of judge, jury, and, in some cases, executioner?"

"Better than some of the corrupt people who've been licensed by the State," Carl said, and watched the room start to spin.

"You would condone it, then?"

Carl managed a nod. "Y—yes, in some cases."

His body began to tremble more violently, and he hugged his arms around his waist, which cramped painfully.

"Are you cold?" Douglas asked, though the room was warm enough. "Would you like to go somewhere else, or borrow my coat?"

Carl shook his head.

"By your measure, someone like Carl Deere would be entitled to enforce his own idea of justice," Douglas said. "He was wronged by the State, wasn't he?"

"And by you and your friend," Carl muttered, between gritted teeth.

"How did we wrong you, Carl?"

He hardly noticed the change of name and looked up with unfocused eyes to face his accuser. "You know what you did," he said.

"I want to hear it, in your own words."

Carl laughed, and it was the keening sound of an animal in torment. "You armed the police," he said. "Your words, your *profile*, gave them the ammunition they needed. I hadn't killed anyone, Bill. I hadn't taken a life, then."

"But you have now?"

Carl began to cry, his body shaking uncontrollably. "You reduced me to this," he said. "Your actions, and the actions of the police, that barrister, the jury...*all* of them helped to bring me here. You forced my hand."

"I've never forced anybody's hand."

"I did what nobody else was strong enough to do," Carl said, and his vision dimmed again. "I did what was *right*, to balance the scales, so that nobody else would have to live through the same experience I did. I'll leave this world a better place."

"Would Leonora Stewart's daughter agree with you?" Douglas said, softly. "She has no mother, now; and, in any case, Stewart was acting as an agent of the State. If not her, someone else would have had to present the case for the prosecution. The end did not justify the means, Carl."

"She—she should have thought about that, before she took the case."

Douglas shook his head. "And why Naomi or Ava? Neither of them was involved in your trial or conviction," he said. "Why hurt them?"

Carl doubled over in pain.

"Oh, *Bill*," he managed. "Can't you see? It's all in the 'I's."

Within seconds, the police team burst through the door with Gregory in tow.

"He's unwell," Douglas told them. "I don't know what's causing it, but he hasn't ingested anything except coffee since he's been here."

Gregory, who was the most proficient medic amongst them, set aside every natural instinct and stepped forward to perform his duty. "Nothing blocking his airways," he pronounced, and felt for a pulse, which was weak and erratic. The man's colour was very poor, and he was struggling to breathe. "I think he's taken an overdose—Carter? We need an ambulance!"

Douglas moved forward and took Carl's contorted face in gentle hands.

"Carl? Listen to me. What have you done? What have you taken?"

The other man smiled beautifully, his dark eyes softening to something childlike.

"I couldn't—couldn't finish the job," he whispered. "Couldn't do it to you, Professor."

"Why kill yourself?" Douglas said. "I thought you saw this as a mission?"

"It is," Carl said, and began to retch as the lining of his stomach rejected the pills he'd taken half an hour before.

The answer came to Gregory in a flash of understanding.

"The 'I's," he said. "Carl's mother's maiden name is 'Innes.' Deere is his father's name, and 'DaSolo' means 'me' or 'I', or sometimes 'alone' in Italian. Carl counted himself as one of the 'I's on his list."

Carl shook uncontrollably, his pallor worsening while the whites of his eyes began to turn yellow.

"Bravo," he managed to say.

They heard Carter's urgent voice as he spoke with the ambulance service, who would arrive too late. In a last gesture of kindness, and in the hope of eliciting any last words from the man who was fading fast before their eyes, Douglas slipped an arm beneath Carl's convulsing shoulders and held him as a father to a child.

"Carl," he said, in a tone he might have used with one of his patients, back when he was a practising clinician. "I understand why you did what you did, although I can never condone it. Do you have anything you'd like to tell us before you leave?"

Carl's eyes rolled back in his head, and then, with a supreme effort, refocused one last time to fix on Gregory.

"It's in the 'I's," he whispered, in a voice they strained to hear. *"Look at the 'I's."*

CHAPTER 37

Gregory watched a couple of technicians from the Coroner's Office carry Carl Deere's body across the quad towards a waiting vehicle, which would transport him to the nearest mortuary for post-mortem examination. It was no great mystery as to how he'd taken his own life; his death bore the hallmarks of a massive overdose, probably of something as prosaic as painkiller tablets. In some lucky cases, a life could be saved if the toxin could be forcibly pumped from a person's body before it had time to enter the bloodstream, but, in Carl's case, he'd obviously timed his overdose to ensure there would be no possibility of recovery.

"Why didn't he finish his list before he died?" Douglas wondered aloud. "He was so determined in his mission...what changed his mind?"

"You did, Bill."

"I barely had a chance to do anything."

"You spoke together for many hours over this past week," Gregory said. "He got to know you, which was a mistake, but one he enjoyed making. He couldn't continue to think of you as the enemy once he'd come to know you, albeit only briefly. You forced him to confront his whole mission, and, by proxy, himself."

Douglas thought of what Carl could have been, of the life he could have led, and mourned the boy he'd once been.

"To kill with impunity, as he did, relied on a solid ideological foundation," Gregory continued. "I would guess that, simply by being yourself, the kind man that you are, his foundational understanding of you, and of all the people he'd murdered or intended to murder, was shaken. His victims were no longer cardboard cut-outs, or names on an acrostic, but three-dimensional people with families. It was impossible for him to continue as before."

"You can't save them all," Douglas said, mostly to himself.

"You saved those he might have killed," Gregory reminded him. "You prevented further loss of life."

Douglas nodded, and swiped a heavy hand over his tear-stained face. "Such a waste," he said. "A terrible waste, on every front."

Gregory thought of Carl's final words. "Why did he repeat the phrase, 'It's all in the 'I's?"

Douglas was weary. "I don't know, Alex. He was confused, most likely, his mind addled by the drugs. I wouldn't read too much into that."

"You're probably right. He wanted us to understand that he was part of his own mission, and always had been."

"It explains why he was so fearless," Douglas agreed. "He never planned on being caught, or, at least, not alive. He wanted us to understand the significance of his plan. What else could it be?"

Gregory shook his head, unable to shake the feeling that they were missing something important.

"I don't know. Nothing, I suppose."

"Come on," Bill said, and tucked an arm around his friend. "Let's go and get some rest. You'll need it, if you're going to be a proper support to Naomi."

Naomi.

When he thought of her, his heart broke all over again.

"What if she never wakes up, Bill?"

"I never deal in absolutes," his friend replied. "Neuroplasticity in the brain can be remarkable, so there's every reason to remain positive."

"Do you really believe that?"

"I wouldn't say it if I didn't."

"At least the immediate danger has passed," Gregory said. "Nobody can hurt her, now."

"Ava, too," Douglas remarked. "Thank goodness nobody will be coming for her now— and, in a funny sort of way, they have each other for company."

"Yes, that's something."

Within the concrete walkways that spanned the enormous roundabout at Elephant and Castle, a man hurried towards the epicentre where the relic of an old shopping centre remained. His footsteps echoed around the broken concrete, then clattered against cracked tiling as he reached the underground mall, where vacant salespeople stood behind cheap stalls that sold phone parts and, he suspected, phones that had fallen off the back of the nearest lorry. Tina Turner played from ancient speakers, her voice mottled and broken, like much of what remained in that part of the city.

He made his way towards one of the plastic benches, where another man dressed in loungewear and high-top trainers was already seated, playing on his phone. He did not take the seat beside him, but rather the one at his back, so they were not facing.

"Took your time," the man said, without looking up. "Thought somethin' had happened."

"No," Carter said, keeping a sharp eye on the occasional pedestrian who passed by. "There was a development."

He relayed the news of Carl Deere's suicide and, before it, the attack on DCI Hope and Doctor Naomi Palmer.

"Hope was attacked? Are you sure?"

Carter made a noise in the affirmative. "I was surprised, too," he said. "It doesn't change our suspicions."

"About Ian O'Shea's death?" the man said, and thought over the facts as they knew them. "You said there was no way Carl Deere could have known about Ian's involvement in Deere's original entrapment without hacking into police systems, or bribing someone in the office to give him Ian's name and home address."

"Yep."

"Well, I had Digital Forensics look into both of those possibilities, and it just doesn't wash."

Carter shifted in his seat, and opened a bag of cheese and onion crisps, which he ate slowly as they talked.

"There's no evidence of a hack," the man continued. "As for someone on the inside having accessed the system, there's no digital record of anyone having accessed Ian's file in the past four years, which pre-dates Carl Deere's conviction. That only leaves a handful of individuals in the Met who might've known Ian's address and personal involvement first-hand, none of whom have any ongoing connection with Deere that we can see."

Carter sighed, though it was only what he'd expected to hear.

"Hope didn't know anything about Ian's involvement in Deere's entrapment," he said. "He told her he wasn't involved, adhering to confidentiality protocols, exactly as he was supposed to. By chance, she saw his name on Gregory's list of Deere's potential victims and, not knowing his role was an undercover one, presumed he had some other reason to lie to her...such as him being a member of Ghost Squad."

"How ironic," his contact said. "She offed the poor bloke based on a suspicion, whereas she's had the real thing sitting under her nose for the past two years."

Carter continued to eat his crisps. "She seemed devastated when she found out he was just a dedicated officer with a good reason to withhold details of his involvement," he added. "Touching, in its own way."

"Not getting soft, are you?"

Carter laughed. "Hardly," he said. "But the present situation does complicate things."

"Does it?" the other man said. "I don't see why our investigation can't continue as before."

"She's inactive," Carter said.

"So? Go back over what we already know, until she wakes up," the other man suggested. "Surely, there'll be something at O'Shea's apartment."

"She already told me, and whoever else, they had something going on. There's a legitimate reason for her DNA to be all over the place, without her being a suspect."

The other man tucked his phone back into the front pouch of his sweatshirt.

"You know, sometimes, this gig starts to get under your skin," he said. "Maybe there's nothing to find. She might be clean."

Carter laughed again. "Yeah, and I think I just saw a pig fly over Elephant and Castle."

"You're sure, then?"

Carter thought about the long hours he'd spent in the company of DCI Hope. "Yeah, I'm sure. I just don't know how to prove it."

"She's dangerous, Ben. Remember that."

"Only if she wakes up."

The next morning, Alex stood in the doorway of the Intensive Care Unit.

He held two bouquets of flowers in his hands: one of amaranths for DCI Hope, and one of bold yellow sunflowers for Naomi, because she'd told him they were her favourite. Ava's mother, an elegant lady by the name of Irene, was seated in the visitor's chair beside her bed, asleep, and he set the flowers down on the end of the bed, so that she would not be disturbed. Then, he took the visitor's chair beside Naomi, and injected a note of cheer into his voice as he spoke quietly to her statuesque face.

"Good morning," he said, and reached across to kiss her hand. "I've got some good news, if you could call it that. Carl Deere took his own life, so you won't ever have to worry about him again, darling. Nobody has to worry about him, not anymore."

There was no response, not even a spike in Naomi's heart rate to suggest that she'd heard him.

"He took us by surprise," Alex continued. "All this time, we've assumed Carl would try to complete his mission and then disappear somewhere, as he did before. At least now the families of the victims will know who was responsible."

He waited, but there was no fluctuation.

"Carl was the missing 'I'," he continued, as if she'd answered him. "We must have made a mistake, somewhere, or perhaps you were right all along. The acrostic is meaningless, and I should never have wasted any time on it."

Gregory raised gentle fingers and ran them over the soft skin of her cheek.

"I still don't know why he did this to you," he said. "But it doesn't matter. All that matters is that you get well again, so you can tell us what really happened, and we can get on with our lives."

He took a moment to compose himself before continuing.

"Things have moved so fast, I don't have any real idea of what you'd want," he said softly. "But I suppose I can tell you a few of my private dreams, and you can let me know if you agree with them when you wake up."

The heart monitor beeped, and he told himself it was Naomi inviting him to continue, so he did. He spoke of travelling the world, of laughter and lazy days on foreign sands; he waxed lyrical about all the ways he wanted to make her happy, to support her writing career if she needed it, to build a life together, if she wanted it. As he was about to address the topic of marriage and children, one day, there came a small cry of delight from the neighbouring bedside chair.

"Ava? *Ava*! Oh, thank God…thank God…"

DCI Hope blinked against the bright lights of the room, and saw a woman in her mid-fifties leaning over her, crying happy tears. Beyond her, a tall, dark-haired man watched the tableau with soulful green eyes.

A nurse hurried into the room and checked her vitals.

"Here, Ava," the nurse said, and carefully propped her up against some pillows. "Let me get you some water, you must be thirsty."

She looked at the nurse in confusion.

"Who's Ava?"

The others in the room looked amongst themselves, then back at her.

"Don't you remember?" Gregory asked her.

She looked at him blankly, her eyes clouded by pain. "I don't remember anything".

AUTHOR'S NOTE

Owing to a prolonged illness during 2022 and 2023, there was an extended delay in the publication of *Panic*. Therefore, at the outset, I would like to express my sincere gratitude to all of my readers for their patience in awaiting its release. Similar thanks go to all of my publishing team, and, in particular, Laura at W.F. Howes, who has been unstintingly kind, alongside the lovely narrator of these books, Richard Armitage, whose own novel I had the pleasure of reading lately. Thank you very much for your forbearance!

Storytelling is my passion, and I love revisiting Dr Gregory, whose character seems to develop in every novel. Unlike some of the other characters I've written, his journey to finding happiness is not an easy one, but his commitment to helping others never wavers, which is a pleasure to write and, I hope, a pleasure to read. Likewise, his 'partner in crime', Professor Douglas, calls to mind all those self-effacing, truly kind people I've had the pleasure to meet over the years, whose pleasure derives largely from helping others. His personal struggle with identity is an approximation of some of the personal testimonies I've been entrusted with, over the years, although it goes without saying that every individual experience is just that: an individual one.

One other small point to mention is the shopping centre at Elephant and Castle. This was demolished a couple of years ago, but I have portrayed it on the fictional pages here, nonetheless; call it nostalgia, if you like.

I wish you a very happy read, and look forward to presenting you with the next instalment, entitled *Amnesia*.

Until next time…

LJ ROSS
MARCH 2024

ABOUT THE AUTHOR

LJ Ross is an international bestselling author, best known for creating atmospheric mystery and thriller novels, including the DCI Ryan series of Northumbrian murder mysteries which have sold over ten million copies worldwide.

Her debut, *Holy Island*, was released in January 2015 and reached number one in the UK and Australian charts. Since then, she has released more than twenty further novels, all of which have been top three global bestsellers and almost all of which have been UK #1 bestsellers. Louise has garnered an army of loyal readers through her storytelling and, thanks to them, many of her books reached the coveted #1 spot whilst only available to pre-order ahead of release.

Louise was born in Northumberland, England. She studied undergraduate and postgraduate Law at King's College, University of London and then abroad in Paris and Florence. She spent much of her working life in London, where she was a lawyer for a number of years until taking the decision to change career and pursue her dream to write. Now, she writes full time and lives with family in Northumberland.

If you enjoyed *Panic*, please consider leaving a review online.

If you would like to be kept up to date with new releases from LJ Ross, please complete an e-mail contact form on her Facebook page or website, www.ljrossauthor.com

Scan the QR code below to find out more about LJ Ross and her books

LOVE READING?

JOIN THE CLUB...

Join the LJ Ross Book Club to connect with a thriving community of fellow book lovers! To receive a free monthly newsletter with exclusive author interviews and giveaways, sign up at www.ljrossauthor.com or follow the LJ Ross Book Club on social media:

#LJBookClubTweet

@LJRossAuthor

@ljrossauthor